SKYBORN

ALSO BY LOU ANDERS

Frostborn

Nightborn

THRONES & BONES

SKYBORN

❖ BOOK 3 ❖

LOU ANDERS

illustrations by JUSTIN GERARD

CROWN BOOKS
FOR YOUNG READERS

NEW YORK

Text copyright © 2016 by Lou Anders
Jacket art and interior illustrations copyright © 2016 by Justin Gerard
Maps by Robert Lazaretti copyright © 2016 by Lou Anders
Rules of Queen's Champion Board Game copyright © 2016 by Lou Anders

Visit us on the Web! randomhousekids.com

Educators and librarians, for a variety of teaching tools, visit us at RHTeachersLibrarians.com

Library of Congress Cataloging-in-Publication Data
Names: Anders, Lou, author. | Gerard, Justin, illustrator.
Title: Skyborn / Lou Anders ; illustrations by Justin Gerard.
Description: New York : Crown Books for Young Readers, [2016] | Series: Thrones and bones ; book 3 | Summary: Thianna and Karn's quest to retrieve the Horn of Osius takes them to Thica, where the two heroes try to overthrow the queens by beating them at their own game.
Identifiers: LCCN 2015035093 | ISBN 978-0-385-39040-8 (hardback) | ISBN 978-0-385-39041-5 (glb) | ISBN 978-0-385-39042-2 (epub)
Subjects: | CYAC: Adventure and adventurers—Fiction. | Animals, Mythical—Fiction. | Board games—Fiction. | Fantasy. | BISAC: JUVENILE FICTION / Science Fiction. | JUVENILE FICTION / Legends, Myths, Fables / Norse. | JUVENILE FICTION / Action & Adventure / General.
Classification: LCC PZ7.A518855 Sk 2016 | DDC [Fic]—dc23

Printed in the United States of America
10 9 8 7 6 5 4 3 2 1
First Edition

To my oldest friend,
Louis Nicholas Christian Glenos,
who led me to Greece
and forced me to ride a moped
across the hills of Atlantis

Uskirian Empire

Somber Sea

Pymonia

Dendronos

Naparta

Eronos

Fortress of Atros

Dodotara

Ithonea

Sparkle Sea

Pythiran Ruins

Zapyrna

Starissa

Mount Thronos

Caldera

Sanctuary of Empyria

Mereon

Labyrinthia

Creos

Harmos

Lassathonia

N

W   E

S

THICA

0   100   500   1,000

MILES

CALDERA

1 AMPHITHEATER
2 TOWER OF DAMNAMENEUS
3 TEMPLE OF NOE
4 TWIN PALACES
5 HATCHERY

6 TEMPLE OF SESTIA
7 BARRACKS
8 WYVERN ROOSTS
9 SKY DOCKS
10 HIPPALEKTRYON STABLES

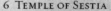

0   500   2000   3000

FEET

 CONTENTS

CHAPTER ONE: The One Truth 1

CHAPTER TWO: From a Bad Crow 18

CHAPTER THREE: The Court of Land and Sky 36

CHAPTER FOUR: Friends in High Places 52

CHAPTER FIVE: It's All Fun and Games 67

CHAPTER SIX: Weight of Responsibility 89

CHAPTER SEVEN: Slip and Slide 110

CHAPTER EIGHT: Cock's Crow 127

CHAPTER NINE: The Hammerfist 136

CHAPTER TEN: Cat's Conundrum 152

CHAPTER ELEVEN: Tangled Webs 160

CHAPTER TWELVE: Either with Your Shield or on It 176

CHAPTER THIRTEEN: Head Games 186

CHAPTER FOURTEEN: Three's a Crowd 196

CHAPTER FIFTEEN: Strong Blasts Carry Far 220

CHAPTER SIXTEEN: Family Squabbles 225

CHAPTER SEVENTEEN: Running of the Bulls 235

CHAPTER EIGHTEEN: Casting the Dice 253

CHAPTER NINETEEN: The Best-Laid Plans 264

CHAPTER TWENTY: Queen's Champion 279

CHAPTER TWENTY-ONE: The Battle for Caldera 292

CHAPTER TWENTY-TWO: Heading for Disaster 308

CHAPTER TWENTY-THREE: From a Thorn, a Rose 326

Glossary 339

The Rules of Queen's Champion 351

Thican Timeline 355

King Herakles Hammerfist's
     Best Spanakopita Ever Recipe 363

Acknowledgments 365

SKYBORN

CHAPTER ONE

The One Truth

The javelin flew with lethal speed. A long, thin messenger of death in an otherwise blue sky. It was fast, but Sirena struck even faster. The young girl's blade sliced the wooden shaft in half. The two pieces clattered on the polished marble squares of the courtyard. Then everything was still except for the noise of waves crashing on rocks far below, the beating of hearts, and the rushing of blood.

"Well done," her opponent said.

Sirena narrowed her brown eyes.

"Of course it was," she replied. "Compliments are a waste of breath. You tell me nothing I don't already know."

Her opponent nodded grimly and drew her sword. She was close to Sirena in size and age. Both wore bronze breastplates molded to the contours of their torsos above tunics hung with strips of black leather. Both carried shields, while their heads were protected by bronze helmets with proud black plumes.

"Is your mind as sharp as your weapon?" Sirena's opponent charged as she spoke, sandals pounding on the smooth stone of the courtyard. "What is the One Truth?" the soldier asked.

Sirena shifted her own stance to meet the assault.

"War is the mother of all," she replied, catching the blade on her own. With a twist of the wrist, Sirena opened the soldier's guard, driving her shield hard into the armored breastplate.

Stunned by the blow, the soldier fell to the ground. Sirena pointed the tip of her sword at the girl's throat.

"I yield," her opponent said.

Sirena hesitated before withdrawing her blade.

"You *yield*," she said. The word was like dung in her mouth. She would never speak it herself.

Sirena didn't spare the fallen girl another glance. She adjusted her grip on her pelta, the distinctive crescent-shaped half shield of Calderan soldiers. The hot sun beat down on her as she squared her small but muscled shoulders. She gazed for a moment at the bright stone columns of the Twin Palaces where they gleamed in the noonday sun, but she didn't look to the stands where her audience of one watched. Then Sirena advanced to the next challenge.

"What is Damnameneus's theorem?" A harder question from a tougher warrior. This opponent was taller than Sirena and older than her own twelve years. She would not be so easily bested.

"The square of the hypotenuse," replied Sirena as she swung her blade at the patch of bare neck between the woman's helmet and armored torso, "matches the total of the squares of the other two sides."

"Correct," the woman said, stepping out of Sirena's reach and bringing her own sword around in a sweeping arc.

Sirena dropped to the ground and rolled under the woman's attack. Then she came to one knee and drove her sword between the black leather straps of the soldier's tunic and into her thigh.

"I know it's correct," Sirena said. "I don't need you to tell me that. I only require that you fall."

Admirably the woman did not cry out as her leg collapsed. Better yet she did not waste words spinning flattery or admitting defeat. She lay still, appraising Sirena with hard eyes.

Good, Sirena thought. She is a proper soldier. I shall remember this one when I am a queen. She should be promoted. But not too high.

"Describe Metarchus's thoughts on justice?" the third opponent asked.

Sirena turned just in time to avoid a searing bolt of flame. She leapt aside, landing in a crouch.

"Nothing is straighter than that which is straight. Nothing is juster than that which is just."

Sirena stayed low, racing under the long fire lance and tackling the soldier around the legs. They went down together, but only Sirena stood up. She could not deny that she was proud of her performance. Philosophy, mathematics, combat—she had mastered them all. But the day was not yet won. Almost.

The cliffside courtyard was laid out in a grid of eight-by-eight squares, with opponents waiting on alternating rows. It was a giant game board for deadly play. Sirena had advanced past the midpoint now and had only one challenge remaining.

"Who said, 'There is nothing eternal except for change'?" the last soldier asked.

"Lanera the Playwright, in her first tragedy," Sirena replied. She disarmed the woman in two moves, stabbed her through the shoulder with a third.

"But she was a fool." Sirena looked to the stands now, to her single observer. She called across the intervening space, "Caldera is eternal. Thica is eternal. We make it so."

The sound of clapping rang out over the hilltop.

"Bravo!" Queen Melantha shouted. "Bravo!"

Sirena sheathed her sword, then removed her helmet and shook out her long black hair. She moved to join her aunt, the Land Queen of Caldera.

"Your mind and your body are in top form," Melantha

said. "You will make a fine champion this day. And a finer queen when the time comes. Your mother would have been proud."

Sirena nodded, her cheeks reddening from something other than the hot sun. She might refuse compliments from an inferior, but the praise of her aunt she would accept.

"We will crown you champion properly tonight, then," she said. "But let's take refreshment together now."

Sirena smiled. So much that she had always wanted was hers now. But her pleasure was to prove short-lived.

"Perhaps I will join you in that celebration," said a newcomer. "Though we'll raise our cups to something other than what you have in mind."

Queen Xalthea, the Sky Queen, stepped out from between marble columns. Together, Xalthea the Sky Queen and Melantha the Land Queen ruled the island-continent of Thica. One commanded the forces of the ground and the other the forces of the air.

"Good fortune to you, Xalthea," said Melantha. "If you had come just five minutes earlier, you wouldn't have missed my niece's performance."

"It hardly matters," said the Sky Queen dismissively. "Something far more important has occurred."

Sirena glared at the co-monarch. What could be more important than her life's goal? Ever since her own mother's death, her aunt had groomed her for this day and all the days to follow.

Ignoring the angry eyes of the young girl, Xalthea turned to the Land Queen.

"They've found it," she said.

Melantha didn't understand what the Sky Queen meant at first. But Sirena did. She knew exactly what "it" was. The knowledge descended on her like a boulder dropped from a tower.

"The Horn of Osius," she whispered.

"Yes," said Xalthea. "The Horn of Osius has been recovered. Our empire is secure." She turned to Sirena. "Or it will be. If you do your part correctly."

"My part?"

"You are the closest in blood," the Sky Queen said.

"I don't know anything about the horn," Sirena protested. "I'm a soldier. I'm the Queen's Champion. I'm going to be—"

"Not anymore," interrupted Xalthea. "My needs—our needs—are more important. You will leave your aunt's side and take your place by mine."

"No!" protested Sirena.

"No?" said Xalthea softly. Sirena froze. When the Sky Queen spoke so calmly she was at her most dangerous.

"Perhaps there is another way," interjected Melantha. But her voice was tentative, hesitant. She lacked the determination of the Sky Queen. She lacked the fire.

"You know there isn't," said Xalthea. "Or are you challenging me?"

Sirena looked at her aunt, daring to hope. The two

queens of Caldera rarely disagreed, but there was a precedent for resolving disputes when they arose. A deadly precedent.

Melantha dropped her eyes.

"No," she said. "No, of course not."

Sirena felt cold despite the midday sun. How could she stand by her aunt if her aunt would not stand by her?

"But—but—" she stammered. "But this is everything."

"Thica is everything," said Xalthea. "Caldera is everything."

Sirena's aunt laid a hand on her shoulder.

"Remember the words of Lanera the Playwright," said Melantha. "Take some comfort in her advice: 'A ship should not be secured by a single anchor; a life should not be tethered to a single hope.'"

"I already told you Lanera was a fool," said Sirena. She met the Land Queen's gaze. "Go to the crows."

Watching the hurt swell in her aunt's eyes, Sirena almost took back her words. But what was said was said. She allowed Xalthea to take her arm above the elbow and lead her away from everything she had always wanted to whatever her new life would be.

It was a treasonous thought, but she wished the horn had never been found. Wished it had stayed lost on the other side of the world. But how had this come about? She wanted to know who was responsible for undoing her happiness.

"Tell me," asked Sirena as she entered Xalthea's wing

7

of the Twin Palaces, "how was the horn recovered? Has Talaria finally been captured?"

"That traitor died long ago," said the Sky Queen. "But apparently she had a child. A girl of mixed race who blew the horn and alerted us to its presence. My soldiers have been after it for some months, and it's finally come back to us."

A girl. A child of Talaria.

"This girl," asked Sirena, "what's she called?"

Sirena wanted to know her name, this half-breed who had inadvertently ruined her life.

"Her name isn't important," replied Queen Xalthea. "Though you might find it amusing—Thican and barbarian names cobbled together." The queen chuckled. "I'm told she is called Thianna Frostborn."

"Sweet Ymir's feet," said Thianna Frostborn with a whistle as she slid from the wyvern's back.

"I don't know how sweet *his* feet are," Karn Korlundsson said from where he still sat atop the reptile. "But if yours are any indication of what frost giants' feet smell like, I think I'd choose a different word. Now move over and let me down."

Thianna chuckled as she stepped aside, then reached a large hand up to help her best friend dismount. They stood together on the hillside and looked at the lights of the coastal city before them, though, as a half giant, Thianna stood a head and a half taller than Karn.

"Thica is a big land to find one horn," Thianna observed. "I wish we'd had time to learn a bit more about what we're in for."

"You're not tackling it alone this time," Karn replied.

"Don't think I could?" Her eyes had that glint in them that they always got when she contemplated a challenge. "Don't worry," she said, breaking into a chuckle. "I've learned my lesson."

Thianna was referring to their recent adventures in which they had fought dark elves and other dangers in a race to find the lost Horn of Osius, a powerful weapon now in the hands of their enemies in Thica. She had set off alone on a quest to find the horn at the behest of the dragon Orm. Then Karn had been sent to rescue her. Now, together, they were going to get it back.

"No more adventuring without my trusty Norrønboy," she continued. Karn was from Norrøngard, the source of the nickname. It was better than Short Stuff, her other name for him.

"Good," he answered. "But it's not just me coming with you. Don't forget; we've got Desstra's help now too."

Thianna's dark eyes clouded.

"I don't know how much help she's going to be," the giantess grumbled.

"You don't mean that," said Karn. "She's already proven herself."

"To you maybe."

Karn winced. True, the dark elf had opposed them for most of their quest, even tricked and betrayed Karn to her superiors in the sinister organization known as the Underhand, but when she had switched sides at the end, she had sacrificed everything to save them.

Karn thought to say more, but then the shadow of a giant bat swooped low overhead. Desstra's mount, Flittermouse, glided to a nearby tree, where it grasped a branch and hung upside down. Karn watched as Desstra somersaulted from her saddle to land nimbly on the ground. He wondered how much of their conversation the elf's keen ears had picked up.

Despite Thianna's feelings, Desstra had proved very helpful getting here. Choosing a night when both the moon and her satellite were invisible, her giant bat had guided them in the dark to this coastal city. But now that they were in Thica, they couldn't risk traveling overland in the sky where the only fliers would be Thican soldiers wielding deadly fire lances. Not that the surly wyvern would carry them any closer to the home of its once-masters. And Flittermouse wasn't large enough to carry anything heavier than one small elf. They'd have to make their own way from here on out.

The elf ran a hand through the fur of her upside-down mount's cheek.

"I'm sorry to say goodbye to you again, boy," she told the bat. "I wish I could take you with me."

Flittermouse squeaked sadly, as though it understood. Probably it did.

Desstra stood on tiptoes to hug the animal around its neck.

"Don't go back to Deep Shadow," she whispered, speaking of the underground city of dark elves. "There's nothing for either of us there. I hope you find a new home where you fit in, one where they treat you nicely."

The bat's eyes said it hoped the same thing for her. Desstra sighed. Then she let go of her mount and approached Thianna and Karn.

"Sun's coming up soon," she said. "We'd better get inside the city before it does."

"Yeah, we already know that," said Thianna. "So not very helpful."

"Good thinking, though," said Karn, glaring at the giantess. Thianna shrugged. Beside her, the wyvern hissed.

"I guess this is goodbye to you too," Thianna said.

If you expect me to shed any tears at our parting, it spoke into her mind, *you're going to be sadly disappointed.*

"I know you're really crying inside," Thianna said with a chuckle. Then she surprised the reptile by hugging it around its long neck.

Get off! Get off! Get off! its thoughts screamed. It tugged its neck in a useless attempt to dislodge the frost giant, but when Thianna released it, the wyvern added, *For what it's worth, I hope you succeed at your mad scheme.*

"Sure you won't come?"

Bringing you here to the coast was risk enough. I'm leaving now, before the dawn arrives. Live well or die well, Thianna Frostborn.

Then, without another word, it flapped its wings and rose into the night. Flittermouse squeaked once, then the bat too flew away into the darkness.

"A tearful farewell?" asked Karn. Lacking Thianna's ability to communicate with reptiles, he had only heard the frost giant's half of the conversation.

"What do you think?" she replied. "Still, I guess that wyvern was as sentimental as they get." She chuckled. "I must be growing on it."

"Kind of like mold on cheese?" teased Karn.

Thianna punched his shoulder playfully, then guided by Desstra's night vision the three companions began making their way down the hill.

They knew from Karn's experience studying maps of the world that the city was called Ithonea. Choosing it as their point of entry into Thica had been a compromise between avoiding the most obvious, direct route while not wanting to detour too far out of their way. They slipped into the city just as it was waking up. There were no guards or gates to impede their progress. Non-Thican boats were kept at bay by the Death Ray of Damnameneus, a large parabolic mirror that harnessed the sun's rays to project a beam of light that set ships afire. Similar mirrors were erected around the entire Thican coast.

Thianna had visited a half-dozen cities since she'd left her mountaintop last year. Each was as different from the other as it was from a frost giant's village. Ithonea was no exception. It was a city of twisting, narrow streets that wound between white-painted houses roofed with large terra-cotta tiles. It stretched up a hillside, broken into districts by ancient walls and crumbling fortifications that still stood from the era of Gordion conquest. Paved steps that ascended narrow passageways were painted an aquamarine blue. At a glance they looked like tumbling fountains spilling over rocks. As Ithonea came to life, so did Thianna's enthusiasm.

"My mother's homeland," she pronounced in awe. "I never imagined that I'd see it, but here we are."

Although the half giant was taller than anyone else, the people around her all shared her dark olive complexion and dark hair. Even the nonhumans she saw amid the crowd looked more like her kin than the frost giants she had grown up with. This was indeed her mother's country, and she drank it all in. Beside her, her companions had donned cloaks and hoods to hide their pale skin and, in Karn's case, fair hair. Desstra also wore quartz lenses to protect her eyes from the sun.

Thianna's nostrils quivered at the smell of grilled lamb.

"Food!" she said enthusiastically. "Hey, what do they use for money here?"

"Drachmas," Karn replied. "I'd be surprised if they took our foreign coin." He fingered the silver ring on his left hand. The face was cast to look like the rings of a tree stump. It was the symbol of the secret society known as the Order of the Oak. "I wonder what this is worth."

"You're thinking of pawning it?" Thianna was surprised. "Didn't Greenroot say it would mark you as a friend of the Order, maybe open doors for you?"

"Surely not here," said Karn, but he left the ring on his finger.

They followed the market as it wound uphill. Thianna observed that the shops became more expensive the higher they rose. She also noticed that they had begun to draw stares from the Ithoneans, some of them unfriendly. Despite her height, however, most of the looks were directed downward, toward their legs.

She stopped walking when a little boy blocked her way, gaping at her with his mouth open. Thianna frowned at him, a rude retort taking shape on her tongue.

"Awesome!" he said, and his face lit with admiration.

"What?" said Thianna, taken aback.

The boy pointed.

"My legs?" she asked. "What is it about my legs?"

The child reached out tentatively to poke the fabric of her woolen breeches.

Suddenly the boy's mother was beside him, her face pinched with disapproval.

"Come away from her, Pogos," she said, ushering her son back from Thianna.

"We were just talking," said the giantess.

"I don't care if it's all the rage among you young people to dress like barbarians," said the child's mother. "Your parents would be ashamed."

"What are you on about?" replied the frost giant, her face flushing in anger.

"Your pants!" the woman spat. "Look at you, parading around like a savage in pants!"

With that she hurried her child away.

It was then that Thianna realized they were the only ones in the city sporting leg wear. Everyone else was dressed in robes or, as a concession to the heat, knee-length tunics bound at the waist. No one besides herself, Karn, and Desstra had anything on their legs. Thinking of Desstra, Thianna realized the girl had vanished.

"Where's the elf?" she asked Karn.

He looked around and shrugged. "I don't know."

"Maybe she had a change of heart after all," Thianna said.

"Or maybe she got you breakfast," said Desstra, surprising them by appearing in their midst. She passed Karn and Thianna wraps of grilled lamb in pita bread.

"How did you get these?" asked Karn.

"Drachmas," replied the elf, jingling a newly stolen coin purse affixed to her belt. Karn winced at her casual thievery, though he knew the need was great. And unlike other dark elves he had met, she wouldn't have harmed anyone for it.

"Thank you," he said, glaring at Thianna to do the same.

"We need to find the Thican Empire's local garrison," she replied, ignoring him.

"Already taken care of," said Desstra. "Yes, I'm that perfect," she added when Thianna raised an eyebrow. "There's an old keep midway up the hill." She indicated the way. "Just far enough away you'll be able to eat your breakfast before we get there."

Sure enough, by the time Thianna and Karn had finished eating and Thianna had purchased and wolfed down a second breakfast, Desstra had led them to the garrison. They saw several soldiers lounging about before the gate.

"This looks like the place," said the frost giant.

"Yes," said Karn, who recognized the distinctive bronze and black leather armor. "But are *all* Thican soldiers women?"

Sure enough, the soldiers out front were exclusively female. As had been all the Thican soldiers they had encountered on their adventures.

"I guess we'll find out," said Thianna. "Are we ready to do this?"

"If you're certain," said Karn.

"The only way out is through," she replied. "Let's go

make some new friends." Then she marched forward to the gate, her height and her strange companions drawing looks from the soldiers.

"Looks like we've got their attention," Karn observed.

"One way to be sure," his friend replied.

Thianna slid the arming sword from her sheath. Beside her, Karn drew his sword, Whitestorm, and Desstra readied a pair of slender darts. Now the soldiers became alert, readying swords, spears, and the deadly fire lances. They shouted for backup and rushed into defensive positions.

Thianna let them assemble, then walked straight up to their line of menacing weapons.

"I'm Thianna Frostborn," she said. "And these are my companions." She held her sword ready. Then she dropped it on the ground at her feet, where it clattered loudly on the paving stone.

"We yield," said Thianna.

"You what?" asked a confused soldier.

"Are you deaf?" replied the giantess. "We *yield*. So what are you waiting for? Capture us and take us to your leader, already. We surrender."

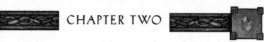 CHAPTER TWO

From a Bad Crow . . .

"Useless, stupid thing!"

Are you talking about me or the object in your hands?

Sirena looked from the horn in her grasp to the old wyvern chained to the marble columns in the corner of the room. Shadows played across the beast's leathery skin from the single torch set in a sconce on the wall.

"Take your pick," she replied. "It's true for both of you."

The wyvern made a coughing noise in its throat. The noise echoed off the stone walls. Sirena's cheeks burned as she realized it was laughing at her.

Angrily she pressed the mouthpiece to tight lips and blew a hard but soundless blast. It was gratifying to see the animal wince.

Careful, he said into her mind. *You don't know what you'll wake with that.*

"I don't care if your whole roost wakes up screaming."

I wasn't talking about them. Strong blasts carry far.

Sirena fell silent. The beast had a point. She knew now that it was just such a forceful, inelegant use of the horn that had alerted them to its presence last year. One day all the wyverns in their cliffside roost had shrieked at once. They had heard the soundless call of the Horn of Osius and knew that a lost thing had returned to the world.

You would have rather it stayed lost, wouldn't you?

"Stay out of my mind," Sirena said. But the wyvern was right. She hadn't known it then, but all her present troubles stemmed from the day Thianna blew the horn.

Such a small thing, such a powerful tool! All Calderan women were mildly telepathic. They could send simple directions to the minds of the wyverns—rise into the air, fly north, fly south, land—but not true communication. Real mind-to-mind contact that ran both ways was only possible for the women of Sirena's family. And only when they held the horn. Moreover, the horn allowed its wielder to impose her will on the creatures, to compel them to obedience. However, the wyverns were getting old, and the spell laid down by the horn at their birth was stretched very thin. Rebellions would arise. And the new generation would hatch soon. If Sirena couldn't master the horn by then, she wouldn't be the only one to topple off the mountain. The Calderan way of life would fall as well. To preserve that, there was little she wouldn't do.

Ah, but you were on the path for glory. How high you might have flown!

"Queen," Sirena said through tight lips. "I was being groomed to be Land Queen." Her eyes hardened. "And then that barbarian girl had to go and wreck it all."

If only the half giant Thianna hadn't unwittingly alerted Sirena's people that the horn had been found after thirteen years. True, this wasn't the same horn. In convoluted events that hadn't been made entirely clear to her, another Horn of Osius had been recovered in Gordasha. But Thianna had set these events in motion, turning Sirena's world upside down. Now the Sky Queen had a horn again. And the Sky Queen needed a horn blower more than the Land Queen needed a successor. Sirena had been brought to this cell yesterday, had spent all that day and all last night practicing to master the magical instrument. She felt as much a prisoner as the creature in front of her.

Such an interesting position you occupy, the wyvern continued. *Niece to both the Land Queen and to the Keras Keeper . . .*

Keras meant horn in the language of Thica. Keras Keeper was the traditional title for the one chosen to wield the horn. It was meant to be a position of honor.

When the horn was lost, the scales tipped one way, continued the wyvern. *When it was found—*

"Go to the crows, you old lizard," she swore.

Sirena blew another angry blast just to watch the animal wince.

"Enjoy that?" she asked.

I enjoy your frustration, it replied when it had recovered. *Though I warn you again about the danger of such forceful use of the horn.*

"It's less than you deserve. If you hadn't fled with Talaria all those years ago, neither of us would be in this dark room right now."

She looked at the creature before her. A year before her own birth, it had been found in the far north, riderless and without the horn. They had dragged it back to Thica, chained it to this wall for all the intervening time. Its wings were ragged now, with burn scars and torn holes in the right wing. Its back was bent from years of captivity. Other scars crisscrossed its leathery flesh, some of them more recent.

"Why did you keep your tongue so long?" Sirena asked. "Why wouldn't you ever tell them what happened?"

The crow does not take the eye out of another crow.

"What does that mean?"

My kind will be free of you one day soon. The magic of the horn wears off. And you are no closer to understanding it than you were yesterday. You cause pain, but you compel no obedience. The Great Hatching approaches.

As if Sirena needed the reminder. The Great Hatching was the time when all the wyvern eggs would crack open at once, an entire generation of reptiles born on

21

one day. The horn's enchanted music, silent to human ears, had to be played then. Its soundless note wove a song in the newborn wyverns' minds that would last for years. Done correctly at the moment of their emergence into the world, the song would stamp the bonds of servitude on their psyche for decades to come. But only if done correctly.

If you haven't mastered it by then—

"If I haven't mastered it by then, I'll come back here with a flame lance and burn your wings off."

You would have made a bold Land Queen. Pity such fierceness is wasted on a mere Keras Keeper, mocked the wyvern.

"What does an animal know?"

The wyvern swung its head to fix her with a penetrating eye.

You see me as an animal? A beast? Then you are a fool. Animals don't converse like we are doing.

"Some monsters talk."

Yes, yes they do. The wyvern looked past her shoulder to the door to the room.

Sirena turned.

"I hope I'm not interrupting." Leta's smile was cold and snide. Her step was uneven as she entered the room uninvited. Despite her limp, the soldier had been promoted to head of the Keras Guard when she had returned from Gordasha bearing the Horn of Osius.

"What are you doing here?"

"The Sky Queen wants an update on your progress."

"Tell Xalthea that mastery of the horn is difficult, but that I am working with it."

The wyvern made a wheezing noise in its throat. More laughter.

Leta glanced at it. The scars on her face pulled unflatteringly when she frowned.

"This is all your fault, disobedient creature. You and Talaria. And then her half-breed daughter." Leta scowled. "That family was always trouble."

From a bad crow, a bad egg. The wyvern chuckled in its throat again. Leta turned to Sirena.

"It is about eggs that I am here. The Hatching is in five days. If you haven't mastered the horn by then—"

"I don't need your reminder."

"Perhaps you do. More than just your position is at stake."

Sirena stared at the presumptuous soldier. How dare a mere guard threaten her? It infuriated her. As did the wyvern, laughing despite its captivity.

"Go to the crows," she said. "Both of you."

"Wake up, Thianna, you're going to want to see this."

The frost giant groaned and tried to roll over, causing their transport to sway perilously. She rubbed at her eyes and hauled herself upright.

"Watch it!" said Karn. "You're rocking our cage."

"As cages go, this is a nice one," Desstra observed. "Not that I'm thrilled to be here."

The three had been placed in what their captors called a phoreion, a sort of curtained litter that was suspended from ropes and carried by four wyverns. It was ornate and might have been suitable for transporting royalty if it weren't barred and locked.

The wyverns had flown for an entire day and throughout the night, carrying Thianna, Desstra, and Karn almost due west. Although all three of them were intrigued by the sights below—vast forest, ancient ruins, a formidable mountain range—eventually exhaustion had overtaken them and they had nodded off to sleep one by one.

At some point during their flight, the soldiers had passed them to another patrol. Perhaps they didn't want to risk an escape by landing. Or perhaps they had another reason to hurry. Whatever the cause, the captives had little to do but watch the land roll by beneath.

Thica, as it turned out, was huge. As they left the mountains, Thianna caught a glimpse of sweeping plains to the south and the sea to the east.

"We've crossed the whole continent," she exclaimed.

"No wonder they want the horn back," Karn said, ever the strategist. "You couldn't control so much territory without the wyverns. If they don't have mastery of the air, they don't have an empire." Then he added, "You know, I doubt that any Norrønur has ever traveled this far."

"No other Ymirian has, that's for sure," said Thianna. "That's something, isn't it?"

"Yes, isn't travel wonderful?" Desstra observed wryly. "Always something new to see, new places to visit, new foods to eat, interesting new people trying to kill or capture you."

"Hasn't been that long since you were the one trying to kill us, elf," said Thianna.

"At least it's capture this time," said Karn. "And we're on the same side."

"It's still early," said Thianna. "I'm sure someone will be trying to kill us by afternoon."

Thianna fell silent as they approached an enormous caldera, a bowl-shaped depression easily a hundred miles in diameter. It was formed by a volcano, which had flooded when one side collapsed and allowed the ocean water to flow in.

Slightly south of center there was an island, with a steep outcropping of rock that was sheer on one face but sloped on the other sides. A narrow bridge of land stretched from the shore of the caldera to the south side of the island. On the western coast an impressive dock was protected by two stone harbor moles, each with a colossal statue at the ends. A city stretched up the slope of the outcropping, from buildings set so densely they seemed to be piled one atop the other at the docks to magnificent palaces and temples at the island's summit.

The summit was obviously their destination.

Thianna felt an odd sensation, like wasps buzzing around her ears. She swatted with her hands, but the feeling wasn't in the air. It was in her mind. It didn't take her long to identify the cause.

Wyverns. The space over the city was full of wyverns. They circled the island, taking off and landing constantly from an overhang at the top of the precipice. There was no doubt that they were approaching the hub of the Thican Empire.

When Thianna had first encountered the Horn of Osius, it had awakened her ability to communicate telepathically with the reptiles. Being in a dragon's mind had enhanced that ability. She looked upward to one of the four wyverns carrying them.

Hello, she thought.

What?

The way its head whipped around was almost comical.

Is that you?

Yes. I'm saying hello.

No, I mean. Is that you? *The half-breed that found the horn. The one they call Frostborn.*

That's me.

Karn recognized the look of concentration on Thianna's face. He tapped Desstra and pointed first at the frost giant and then at the wyvern. Desstra nodded.

The cause and solution of our troubles. They say you destroyed one horn. Have you come to destroy another?

That's the plan.

If you don't mind my saying, you're doing a rousing job of it so far.

Ah, thought Thianna. I see you're just as warm and cuddly as other wyverns I've known.

The creature hissed at her.

I don't have to be warm. I'm not warm-blooded.

Fair point. What is this place? she asked.

The humans call it the city of Caldera.

Because it's in a caldera. That's kind of on the nose, don't you think?

You aren't the most imaginative species. Too busy sticking each other with pointed sticks to do much else.

Speak for yourself.

I am speaking for myself. How else would I speak?

Another fair point. So, who are these Calderans?

This time the wyvern snorted.

Who are the Calderans? it said. *Are you as ignorant as you are big? You are a Calderan.*

"Oh," said Thianna aloud.

"You mean we have to go up there?"

"Up there is exactly where we will go," his father replied.

Asterius gazed at the city before him. It looked crowded, confining, disorderly, and . . . well, awfully high.

"A proper city would lie flat on a plain," the boy pronounced, "not bound up the hillside from rock to rock like a goat."

Asterius punctuated his words by snorting with enough force to flip the ring in his nose. He glanced around. None of his father's retinue appeared to share his humor or his concern. He pawed the dirt with a hoof in annoyance.

"Things are not always like they are at home," his father replied patiently. "The Calderans live differently than we do, but they depend on the agriculture of our plains to survive."

"Then why don't they come to us instead of demanding we come to them?" Asterius asked.

The king gave a nervous chuckle, then reached a hand between Asterius's two horns to pat his son on the head.

"You are proud, I know," his father said, "And that is a good thing. But remember that it is those same virtues that make a minotaur great that can lead to his undoing. It is a fascinating conundrum."

Asterius shook his head to dislodge his father's palm. He didn't want an ethics lecture. And he didn't want to be treated like a child. He wanted a sword and a shield, like the bull men and kine women around him. He would be thirteen soon. It was time they treated him like a warrior.

He regurgitated his breakfast. Ruminating usually helped him calm down, but today chewing the soft cud did nothing for his agitation.

The minotaurs had traveled all the way from their city in the southern grasslands to be here. They were a small band of only ten—his father (who was the king of Labyrinthia), eight of the king's most trusted warrior-advisors (you didn't get to be the one without being the other), and his son (reluctantly). It was Asterius's first trip to the capital city of Thica. So far he wasn't impressed.

Things became grudgingly interesting, however, when they reached the land bridge that would carry them across the caldera's lake to the island-city. A party of Talosians had arrived just ahead of them. Asterius had never seen the bronze automatons before. He wondered what it would be like never having to eat or sleep. Did they even feel the sun and wind upon their faces? And could it be true that they had clockwork springs and gears instead of blood and bone? How could such creatures live?

More travelers joined them as they crossed the narrow strip of rock and entered the city proper through its south gate. Asterius repressed a shudder as the buildings rose up around them and the ground began to ascend. He tossed his horns and squared his shoulders. If none of his father's warrior-advisors showed fear, he wouldn't either.

He studied everything as they walked. The streets here weren't as wide as those at home, and they were less well maintained. It was easy to turn a hoof if you weren't careful. And while the heart of Labyrinthia was at its center, as was right and good, here it was clear that buildings and people gained in importance as you climbed the rock. He looked at the faces of the folk staring at them from the doorways and windows of dwellings and shops. They were mostly human and dwarven, though only the dwarves carried weapons.

"So these are the Calderans?" he asked his father. "I thought they would be more warlike."

"Oh no," replied the king. "Most of these are not Calderan."

Asterius swished his tail in confusion.

"But isn't this the city of Caldera? Who are all these people?"

"At least half the folk you see here are what you'd call helots," his father said. "They are a slave class, owned by the state. Calderan women aren't allowed to do any work other than soldiery. So their businesses and industries are overseen by their men and run by their slaves. But the helots are allowed to keep a part of their labor, and they can only be killed at certain times of the year."

Asterius snorted again.

"Oh, that's much better than a regular slave."

"Then there's the perioikoi," his father continued, ignoring his sarcasm. "Freedmen and freedwomen who serve their military as blacksmiths, caretakers, and auxiliary troops. These are mostly dactyls. Dwarves are always good with metalwork and smithing."

"So where are the actual Calderans?" Asterius asked. His father pointed up.

"The Calderans themselves are less than a quarter of the population," said the king. "And of that, only the women are allowed to hold any rank or position. It's a pyramid system, like the city itself, with a few people on top supported by the larger blocks below."

"That's crazy," said Asterius. "How can you have a city where almost nobody's a real citizen?"

"I admit it seems strange," said the king. "I suppose we could say that it's another fascinating conundrum."

Asterius snorted. "It's just strange," he said. "Wait until I tell my friends when we get home."

"Home, yes," said his father. King Asterion looked at his son like he had something more he wanted to say.

"What is it, Father?"

"Best not speculate where I don't know," replied the king. Asterius would have pressed him to say more, but then they reached the summit of the hill and his jaw had dropped too wide to speak.

The phoreion descended toward a circular landing platform. It was one of five, each at the end of a walkway that extended over the cliff face.

"What is that?" said Karn. Thianna followed his finger to what looked like a life-sized game board with spectator seating on opposite sides. It was laid out in marble slabs in a courtyard between two palaces, just visible in their line of sight.

"What do you know? Looks like you might find some fellow gamers here."

"Hopefully someone who can give me a real challenge for a change," he replied.

"I think I resent that," said the frost giant.

"I know I do," Desstra added.

Karn continued to stare at the oversize game board with rapt curiosity until, as they approached the ground, the surrounding buildings blocked his view. The wyverns set them down on one platform, then moved to adjacent ones so that attendants could see to the returning soldiers and their mounts. A soldier unlocked the phoreion.

"Get out," she said curtly.

"Manners," said Thianna.

"Now," ordered the soldier.

"But we were having so much fun," said the giantess, climbing onto the ground. As she stretched to her full height, she smiled to see the woman's eyes widen.

The view off the sides of the narrow walkway might have been daunting to any but an Ymirian. Thianna glanced casually at a steep slope that fell away for hundreds of feet to where waves broke on sharp rocks in the waters below. Another might have been intimidated, but she merely felt relieved to be stretching her legs after a day and a night of confinement. Karn walked beside her. He kept his face guarded, but she could tell he was studying all the angles of their new environment, looking for advantages and weaknesses. Karn could size up territory like the checkered squares of a Thrones and Bones game board. Desstra followed behind them, quiet and alert.

Whatever the elf's thoughts, they were hidden behind her quartz lenses.

An impressive number of soldiers, all with fire lances aimed their way, stood awaiting their arrival. One woman, her face covered in a full helmet, wore a black cape draped over her shoulders as an obvious sign of rank. She stepped forward. Thianna saw that she moved with a slight limp.

"We will have no trouble from you this time," she said in a commanding tone.

Thianna grinned.

"Looks like you've heard of us," she said.

"Heard of you?" The woman sounded surprised. "Don't you know who I am?"

Desstra spoke up. "No, why?" she said. "Have you forgotten?" Despite her misgivings concerning the elf, this drew a grin from the frost giant. Not so much the soldier. The woman frowned at the sarcasm. She glared at the elf, then she lifted off her helmet.

"Do you know me now?"

"Yes, unfortunately," said Thianna, fist clenching. "You're that woman who's going to regret getting on my bad side."

Beside her, Karn and Desstra tensed as well, but their weapons had been taken from them. Of course, they all recognized the scarred face of the soldier the instant her face was revealed—the cause of their current troubles. She had been the only one of Sydia's team to survive the adventure in Norrøngard. She had followed Thianna

33

first to Castlebriar and then Gordasha. Disguised as a wandering wizard, she had helped them in their quest. But when they had succeeded, she had snatched the horn away from them in their moment of triumph, forcing Thianna to trade it for Desstra's life.

"My name is Leta," the soldier explained. "As much history as we have together, it's right you should know that."

"Leta," said Thianna slowly, tasting the name of her enemy for the first time.

"You've been promoted since we saw you last," said Karn, jutting his chin at the ranks of soldiers behind her.

The woman smiled.

"I have you two to thank for that, you three, really. If you hadn't cared so much about the life of this little elf."

Desstra's ears dropped. She was ashamed to be reminded. And to have Thianna reminded. The frost giant still resented that she had been forced to give up the horn to save a former enemy.

"When I returned with the Horn of Osius," Leta continued, "I was celebrated. They made me the Head of the Guard for the Keras Keeper."

Thianna shrugged. "I could pretend to be impressed. But I don't know what a Keras Keeper is."

"The one who will blow the horn at the Great Hatching. The Keras Guard protects the Keras Keeper."

"Ah, a trumped-up bodyguard," said Thianna. "How nice for you."

"It is," Leta replied. "Though not, I think, for you three. The queens want to meet you."

"Queens?" asked Thianna. "Don't you mean queen?"

"I mean queens, plural," said Leta. "Come along, this way. At the very least, I think it will be instructive for you to see who you have been defying." She beckoned to several soldiers, who fell in around the three companions.

Karn, Thianna, and Desstra were marched from the landing platform. They saw that the two palaces up ahead were separate wings of a larger, three-building structure. The magnificent marble walls were covered in elaborate carvings and surrounded by tall columns supporting triangular roofs. Before one palace was the statue of a wyvern. Before the other, a strange creature that appeared to be half horse, half rooster. They were heading for the middle building adjoining the two.

"Welcome," said Leta, "to the Twin Palaces, and to the Court of Land and Sky."

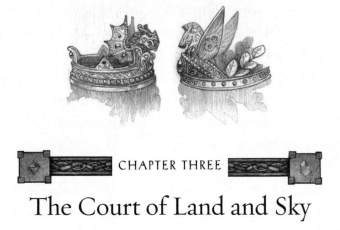

CHAPTER THREE

The Court of Land and Sky

"It's sort of like a Jarl's longhouse back home," Karn observed, looking around the Court of Land and Sky and comparing it to the wood and turf constructions of his own land. "A big open room, just like home—check." Indeed, the room was enormous, with marble columns holding up an arched roof. "Fire pits—check." Two large round pits blazed with flame. Their smoke curled upward to holes placed in the ceiling. "A throne at one end. Well, actually, two thrones—check, check." Two marble thrones stood upon a single dais at the far end of the room. Each was accessible from its own staircase that led up from the floor. Another pair of staircases wound down from balconies to either side. "It's a Jarl's longhouse. Just like home."

"Sure," replied Thianna, glancing around at the ornately carved statues and the bizarre assortment of beings crowded into the room. "Only, made of marble. Painted in gaudy colors. Full of strange creatures. Ruled by our enemies."

"Okay, maybe not so much like home after all," Karn said.

"I don't know," said Desstra. "Power-hungry leaders pushing everyone else around. Sounds like home to me."

The three watched as the various groups of people and creatures assembled inside the court. In addition to human beings, Thianna noticed strange, bronze-skinned folk and large, one-eyed creatures who resembled deformed giants. She saw the horned and hoofed people called satyrs, and even stranger things.

"Look," said Karn. He pointed at a group of beings who appeared like human women but had actual fire for hair.

Their escort paused. Leta turned to face them.

"We will wait here until the queen—excuse me, until the queens—call for us," she said. "But I am warning you, give us no trouble." She glared at Desstra. "Especially you, little elf."

"I just want you to know," Desstra replied, smiling sweetly, "that I am going to pay you back in full one day."

The Keras Guard's hand dropped to the pommel of her sword.

"Probably not today, though," Desstra added hastily.

Leta relaxed her hand and turned to face the front of the room.

"All hail," called a herald standing before the thrones. "Queen Xalthea and Queen Melantha approach."

"Two queens," said Karn.

"Is the extra in case one breaks?" asked Thianna.

"You would know this had your mother been loyal," Leta said over her shoulder. "Though I suppose you would not exist, then. Caldera is a diarchal matriarchy."

"That's just a fancy way of saying it has two queens," Desstra said.

"Then why didn't she just say that?" asked the giantess. "Do they give out points for using big words?"

"Xalthea is Queen of the Sky," Leta continued, ignoring them. "Melantha is Queen of the Land. Together, they rule all of Thica."

"And if they ever get into an argument?" ask Thianna. "Who wins?"

"Oh, we have a wonderful system for handling that. Maybe we'll show you sometime." The soldier glanced at Karn. "You in particular would appreciate it, I think."

Karn was about to ask why that was, but then two figures strode out onto the balconies flanking the thrones and all attention turned their way.

Thianna found it remarkable how the two women could look so similar and so different at the same time. They both moved with a regal bearing, they both had the dark hair and olive skin of the Thican people, they both commanded attention. But the woman on the left had a cruel air about her. Queen Xalthea reminded the frost giant a little bit of Sydia, her enemy who had ultimately perished with the first horn in the jaws of the dragon Orm, while the woman on the right seemed softer. If not kind, at least Queen Melantha did not appear overtly malicious.

"Your monarchs will now accept your tribute," the herald proclaimed.

A party of satyrs came forward. They presented the queens with bouquets of flowers wrought in gold. Neither monarch seemed very impressed, but the Land Queen thanked them. Next the strange metal people gave the two monarchs a clockwork mechanism they said was for calculating the tides. Karn thought that sounded useful and wished he could see it better. Thianna's attention, however, was jumping all over the court.

"My mother," she whispered. "Could she have stood in this very room?"

The trouble started when the group of flame-haired women—they were called empusa, and Thianna gathered from the looks they were drawing that they were bad news—tried to present a statue to the queens as a gift. It was a remarkably lifelike stone carving that depicted a man with a bull's head. He held a large, double-bladed ax in both hands, readying it as if about to strike.

"That's a minotaur," Karn explained. "I've heard stories about them."

"Minnow what?" asked Thianna.

"Minotaur."

"Halt this obscenity!" a voice roared.

"Who dares speak?" The herald scanned the assemblage for the source of the interruption.

"I, King Asterion, dare." A large figure pushed his way forward through the crowd, coming to stand before the thrones and beside the empusa. Thianna saw that it was a living version of the statue—a great, bull-headed man. He carried his own double-bladed ax. And from the way he stomped his hooves and snorted his wide nostrils, he was very angry.

"Correction," said Karn. "Now *that's* a minotaur."

"This is no statue," the king continued. "It's my cousin, Tappos. He disappeared into the cave of the gorgons two weeks ago and never came out. I told him foraging for mushrooms wasn't worth risking their gaze. But he wouldn't listen. He's an idiot, I'll grant you that, but he's not a statue."

"He is now," said the herald.

The minotaur blew an angry breath.

"Then let me take him back home to Labyrinthia. He should rest among fellow minotaurs in the grasslands, not be exhibited as a trophy on some godsforsaken mountaintop."

"Careful, Asterion," said the crueler of the two queens. "The gods may have been driven from their mountaintops, but the goddesses have not. Don't offend them, or me, by casting aspersions on our city."

"Apologies, Queen Xalthea," said the minotaur king, pawing the ground nervously. "It's a lovely city you have here, I'm sure, as such places go. If elevation is your thing and all. I only meant that Tappos is not a piece of art."

"Ah, but he is," the queen called Xalthea continued. "Quite a lovely one at that. I understand you beast folk may not have an appreciation for the finer points of higher culture, but let me assure you that Tappos is now a most exquisite piece of statuary."

"Nonetheless, I demand they return him to us," said Asterion.

"You demand?" Xalthea raised an eyebrow. Though her tone was soft, Thianna observed how everyone— even her fellow queen—suddenly became tense.

"Or . . . ," stammered Asterion, "accept him as *our* tribute, not *theirs*."

"Absolutely not!" yelled an empusa, and the fires on her head shot a full foot higher into the air. "We risked the gorgons' cave to claim it. It is our tribute and ours alone."

"He's not tribute, he's my cousin!" roared the minotaur, hefting his ax menacingly. He snorted in the empusa's face as the flames writhing around her head began to spread to her shoulders and run down her arms.

"Enough!" shouted the herald. At her words, soldiers

on the balconies hoisted fire lances into position. "Lower your ax and quench your flames or you will both roast on the spot."

Grumbling, King Asterion slowly lowered his weapon. The empusa's fire damped until it burned only on her head.

"We are pleased to accept this fine statue." Queen Melantha spoke for the first time. "However," she continued, "we will do so on behalf of both parties, as a joint gift."

"Joint?" Xalthea seems as surprised by her co-monarch's words as the minotaur and empusa.

"Yes, joint," said Melantha. "As Tappos was King Asterion's cousin, I'm sure the empusa would be happy to share the credit for gifting him to us." She looked at the empusa sternly. "I suggest that you are happy."

The empusa bowed, though her flames guttered and cracked when she cast a sideways look at the minotaur.

"And you, Asterion," said Xalthea. "Are you happy?"

"Happy enough," said the minotaur king. "He is, after all, my cousin. A conundrum."

"Then we are pleased with your tribute," Melantha continued.

"But now we have other matters," Xalthea finished. "You have all brought your children as instructed?"

There were rumblings throughout the assembly at this, but the queens ignored them.

"Send the young ones forward."

No one immediately moved to comply. While Xalthea

maintained her fake smile, soldiers moved through the crowd, encouraging the children to come to the front.

"We have a wonderful opportunity for you," the Sky Queen continued. "You're all to come and live in the palace."

The grumblings turned to shouts of alarm from the adults and cries of fear from the children.

"This is outrageous!" the minotaur king roared, losing his temper again. "We already pay you tribute enough. Now you want our children as hostages!"

Xalthea frowned.

"They are no such thing," she said. "At the palace, they will be honored guests. And they will receive all the benefits of courtly life. We will give them the same education we give our citizens. Surely no beast folk have ever had the like."

"A pretty cage is still a cage," Thianna whispered to Karn. The frost giant had plenty of experience with bullies, and she knew when she was facing one.

"You will all be honorary citizens of Caldera," Queen Melantha said, smiling encouragingly at the young ones. "In time you will appreciate this honor."

"Don't think we don't see through this," Asterion continued. "You worry you can't control the next generation of wyverns after the Great Hatching, so you take our children from us to compel our loyalty!"

"I won't go," a young minotaur suddenly roared. "Father, tell her you won't let them take me!"

The boy ran to his father, who put an arm around his shoulder protectively.

From the balcony, Thianna saw multiple fire lances trained on the pair. The crowd noticed too, and they stepped away from the minotaurs.

"Asterion, you may leave your child in our care now, or your honor guard can carry his ashes back to Labyrinthia in a funeral urn. A little one."

The king lowered his horns.

"I am sorry, son."

"No," the boy cried. "Fight them, Father. We can fight them together!"

"No, son." The minotaur king bowed his head in shame and anger.

"Why won't you fight them?" his son wailed.

A guard gripped the boy's arm, but he shook it off.

Asterion knelt before his child.

"Today is not the day," he said. "One day you will understand."

Thianna saw the young minotaur's face fall. His shoulders slumped as he was led away to join the rest of the hostage children.

"We will show you to your new quarters," Queen Melantha said to the children as they were herded out of the room. "I promise, it will not be unpleasant for you," she added, though the air was full of wailing voices.

"How could all their parents just give them up like that?" Thianna asked.

"I don't think they had any choice," Karn replied. "But it was a mistake."

"Ymir's frozen toes, it was a mistake," agreed Thianna.

"No, I mean a tactical one," said Karn. "Their control is slipping. Pushing their subjects like this is going to cause a rebellion. Sooner or later, somebody is going to oppose the queens' hold and take a shot at them."

Thianna looked at him, an angry glare in her eyes.

"They'll have to stand in line."

Asterius fought back tears as the soldiers led him from the room. Around him an unfamiliar assortment of people moved. Some were human—their bodies familiar but their small, hornless heads so strange. How did they think with such tiny craniums? How did they fight without any horns? How did the bronze contraption beside him think at all? At least the satyrs in the group had horns, even if they were embarrassingly tiny.

They passed through a doorway into a large space. Despite himself, Asterius gasped. To say the room was opulent was an understatement. Rich tapestries hung from the walls, and lushly upholstered chairs and couches were arrayed around the detailed mosaic of the floor. A central table was piled with food. Several of the younger children cried out excitedly at this and ran to sample the delicacies. Asterius noticed a tray offering an assortment of grasses and wheat. He started to join the others, but then his pride returned. He had just been ripped from his father's side. He wouldn't be won so easily. This didn't stop his stomach from rumbling as he watched the little ones gobble down the treats. He folded his arms and belched up the cud he had been chewing earlier to give his watering mouth something to do.

"I guess lifeless stone is no substitute for open grasslands," said someone beside him. "Or a thick forest."

Asterius started. He had mistaken the creature beside him for a decorative plant. But now that he looked, he saw that it was a sort of girl. She had bark for skin, and the minotaur couldn't tell if her leaflike clothing was something she wore or grew. Branches twining up from the green growth on her head at least resembled horns.

"Are you a drus?" he asked.

"I'm a dryad," she said, smiling shyly. "Drus is what we call the boys."

"I've never met tree folk before," said the minotaur.

"Well, Dendronos is far to the north," she said.

"And Labyrinthia far to the south."

"I guess we're both a long way from home," the dryad said. She smiled shyly again. "My name is Daphne."

Asterius thought she seemed very nice. But then he remembered that he was little more than a glorified prisoner in Caldera. It was his duty to be miserable and difficult. Making friends ran counter to that.

"Asterius, son of Asterion, prince of Labyrinthia," he

said, drawing himself up so that his horns were as tall as possible.

"Well, then, if you put it that way, I'll have you know that I'm Daphne, seedling of the Council of Elders, princess of the forest kingdom of Dendronos."

"Forests," he snorted. "No better than this silly mountaintop."

"It is better," Daphne said. "Anyway, I'm sure it's a lot more interesting than some flat, boring old plain."

"What would a plant know?"

Daphne stamped her foot and walked stiffly away from him. Asterius felt a tinge of regret watching the fluttering leaves of her retreating back. He knew no one in Caldera, and she had been nice to him. But he wasn't here to make friends. The first chance he got, he was going to escape.

"So this is the half giant."

Queen Xalthea leaned forward on her throne, peering down her nose at Thianna.

"Yes, my queen," Leta said. "Her father was a frost giant from the land of Ymiria."

"We have giants here too," Xalthea said. She wrinkled her nose as she spoke, as though she couldn't stand the taste of the word *giants* in her mouth. "Uncouth, loutish beasts that plague our hills."

"I'll show you who's uncouth," Thianna growled.

Beside her, Karn placed a hand on her shoulder. They were in enough danger without his friend losing her temper.

"Yes, that's pretty much how they behave here as well," the Sky Queen said. "Stomping and roaring and brandishing their clubs."

Thianna flushed in anger and embarrassment.

"But we must remember that she is also Talaria's daughter," said Queen Melantha in a somewhat gentler tone. The Land Queen addressed Thianna directly. "Your mother lived here for a time, child. She held a position of great honor."

"Until she cast it away," Xalthea said with a sneer. "To live with barbarians in a frozen wasteland."

"Still, Xalthea," said Melantha, "if this girl hadn't recovered the Horn of Osius we would not have it now. It is due to her intelligence and resourcefulness, more than that of our own soldiers"—here she threw a frown Leta's way—"that the horn has returned to where it belongs."

"Are you suggesting we owe her our gratitude?" said Xalthea. "When she has opposed us at every turn?"

"With only her mother's example, how else could she act? But let the young woman see our culture, our great civilization, and perhaps we can direct her resourcefulness to a more appropriate direction."

Xalthea addressed Thianna.

"My co-monarch believes that I should thank you." The Sky Queen's smile was as welcoming as a snake's.

48

"But I don't feel like it. No. You have cost us too much trouble in addition to the loss of a valuable officer."

"You've got a messed-up definition of *valuable* if you mean Sydia," said Karn.

"Males have no place speaking to our queens like that," said Leta. "Barbarian males, even less. You will hold your tongue or lose it."

"It's *you* who have no place talking to my friend like that," said Thianna.

"And this other one, the sickly-white little girl, is she your friend too?" asked Xalthea.

Thianna glanced at the elf. Desstra looked at her hopefully. The giantess turned to the queens.

"She's with me," Thianna said.

"Then you can all go to the prisons together."

Leta's soldiers moved to take hold of Thianna, but suddenly Desstra sprang. The nimble elf seized hold of a soldier's lance and used it to vault over the confused woman. Landing, she swung a leg to swipe the soldier off her feet.

Thianna took advantage of this distraction by grabbing two more soldiers by their necks and smashing their heads together. Their helmets rang out loudly as they collided. Stunned, the women dropped to the ground.

Karn quickly relieved the fallen guards of their swords. He tossed one to Thianna and kept another for himself. The crowd fell back around them. Amid the cries of alarm, he thought he heard several people cheer.

Certainly one exultant peal of laughter sounded like the roaring of a bull.

Then the guards were converging on them from all directions. In the fray Thianna managed to secure another sword. She fought two-handed, a blade in each fist. Karn found that a nonmagical blade was harder for him to wield than Whitestorm had been. He defended himself admirably, but he couldn't force an advantage. Elsewhere, Desstra struggled against several soldiers. She was outnumbered, but the elf was too fast for them to catch.

The two monarchs watched all of this impassively from their dais. "You see," said Melantha, "she is quite a capable young woman."

"Perhaps," said Xalthea. "A pity then she's a half-breed."

"The half-breed is making a fool of our soldiers," observed Melantha.

"The crowd gives her an advantage. She is just a child. If she fought in the open, she would be ash by now."

"The crowd seems to like her," Melantha pointed out.

Indeed, quite a few of the people in the audience were openly cheering the giantess as she fought against their oppressors. They might not have the nerve to rebel themselves, but they were happy to see someone else do it.

Thianna laughed as she battled two opponents. She thought she might actually get away. Then a shadow fell across her. She looked up just in time to see a heavy wall canopy falling over her head. With a cry of "Troll dung!"

she was carried to the ground by the weight of the tapestry. Blows rained down on her through the canvas as more soldiers kicked and beat her under the hanging.

"Okay, okay!" she yelled. "I quit."

When the canopy was pulled away, Thianna saw Karn and Desstra surrounded with flame lances trained on them. The audience had fallen back, giving their enemies a clear shot. The fight was over for now. But Thianna also saw something else: a young girl, about her age though obviously not her size, who glared at her with angry satisfaction on her face.

Thianna realized it was this girl who had torn the hanging from the wall and thrown it over her. She was the only one in the room smart enough to bring the frost giant down. As the soldiers marched her from the court, Thianna gave the girl a slow nod to let her know she'd marked her. They'd meet again, Thianna was sure, and the frost giant swore that next time she'd have the upper hand.

CHAPTER FOUR

Friends in High Places

"That was fun while it lasted," Thianna said. They were moving through corridors, presumably heading to wherever prisoners were kept. Desstra trailed a little ways behind them.

"You need to trust her," said Karn. He spoke deliberately in Norrønian so that their guards couldn't understand.

"We wouldn't be in this mess but for her," Thianna replied.

"Well, we're in it now," Karn snapped. "And we need to work as a team if we're going to get out of it."

Suddenly their guards stopped short.

Another group of soldiers stood in the corridor in

front of them. And someone was with them—Queen Melantha.

"Where are you taking these three?" the queen asked.

"To the prison cells," a perplexed guard replied.

"These are not common prisoners to be housed in common cells," the Land Queen said. "We must find better accommodations for them. For now, you will house them in the palace wing where the hostage princes and princesses are lodged."

"But our orders—"

"Come from one queen and now from another."

The guards bowed. Caught between rulers, they clearly didn't want to upset the one in front of them.

Queen Melantha approached Thianna.

"I cannot go against my fellow monarch, the Sky Queen," she said. "But I can mitigate the blow. You will be more comfortable while we decide what to do with you."

The queen turned abruptly and left with her guard.

"What was that about?" asked Karn.

"I don't know," Thianna said.

"A friend?"

"I don't think so. But maybe not an enemy."

Melantha mused over Talaria's child as she walked away. The girl was unusual, not only for her size. But there was a strength to her, and strength should not be wasted or disrespected. Not when it could be harnessed.

"That was foolish."

The Land Queen looked up. She wasn't used to being challenged. Then she saw who had spoken so boldly. Her niece leaned against a wall. Poor Sirena. She seemed so much smaller, so much younger, without armor, shield, and sword.

"You were eavesdropping on your queen?" Melantha said with a sad smile.

"I was surprised by encountering my aunt," the girl answered. "I didn't expect to run into you. I only wanted another glimpse of the barbarian."

"For what purpose?" the queen asked.

"To understand my enemy," said Sirena.

Melantha sighed. She felt sorry for her onetime protégé, snatched away from her by the Sky Queen when the horn was found. She felt herself a better mentor than Xalthea, if the Sky Queen would even see herself in that role. But if the barbarian girl could be tamed, perhaps things could be as they were.

"Thianna's mother was a Calderan," Melantha pointed out. "That makes her one of us."

"I don't think she sees it that way."

"No, I don't think so either," agreed the Land Queen. "But perhaps she can be made to understand our way of life."

Sirena snorted in derision.

"She has a stiff back, that one. I don't think beating on it will make it bend."

"True," agreed Melantha. "But there are other ways to be persuasive. The sword is only one weapon among many, Sirena."

"What do you mean?" asked her niece. Her hand instinctively dropped to her side, clutching at a blade that wasn't there.

"Tell me, who wouldn't lick her fingers when they have been dipped in honey?"

Most of the food in the room was airborne.

Chickpea soup spattered against walls. A grilled octopus caught a young satyr square in the face. The bronze automaton stood in a chair and whipped mussel shells at unprotected heads with mechanical precision.

"A food fight?" Thianna stared at the chaos being wrought by the hostage princes and princesses.

"You have to admit," said Karn, "this behavior isn't much worse than the royals we've met before."

A plate of feta cheese narrowly missed Thianna's shoulder and spattered against the wall. She frowned as she watched it stick momentarily to the polished marble, then drop off to hit the floor with a loud squelching noise.

"I'll handle this," said Desstra, stepping forward.

"No," Thianna replied. "Let me."

She walked right into the fracas. She didn't flinch when sausages and bread zipped back and forth around her. She simply strode right to the center of the room. She drew a deep breath. Karn saw and covered his ears so that Desstra would see and do the same. Thianna could be loud when she wanted to.

"Everybody freeze!" the frost giant roared.

All activity in the room ceased. The hostage royals stood gaping at the enormous girl in their midst. A lone loaf of bread, tossed before the brawl ended, sailed through the air at the giantess's head. Thianna caught it one-handed without looking, then took a big bite from the end.

"Mmm—that's better," she said through a mouthful. "Now, what's going on here?"

Several children spoke at once. "He started it" seemed to be the dominant explanation. They were all pointing at the minotaur.

"You?" said Thianna.

"I did not," said Asterius. "You hornless folk are all too thin-skinned."

"He did too start it," said a small figure emerging from under the table.

"Gnome?" Thianna asked.

"Dwarf!" said the boy. "My name is Jasius, and I'm a dactyl. Just 'cause my beard's late coming in doesn't mean I'm a gnome."

"Sorry, I—"

56

"Anyway, this one here—"

"Asterius, son of King Asterion," proclaimed the minotaur.

"Son of a something, I'm sure," said Jasius the dwarf. "Anyway, he said he was too good to eat with animals. Can you believe that?"

"So one of the satyrs threw a plate of cheese at him," volunteered a human girl.

"Things kind of went sour from there," said a boy. "It was fun, though."

"Yeah, fun," said Jasius. Thianna remembered that he'd been hiding under the table.

"But shouldn't you all try to get along?" said Karn. "I mean, you're all going to be living here together. You're all in the same boat."

"We are not in a boat," the automaton said. "We are in a palace."

"It's an expression."

"We have an expression about boats too," said a satyr. "Too many opinions sink them. Who said we need yours?"

"Right. Like you were doing so well before we got here," said Desstra.

"And what a waste of food," said Karn.

"They'll bring more," said a girl with flames for hair. "Our parents will only stand for this if we're treated well."

"So they hang fancy curtains on our prison walls," said the minotaur, tugging angrily at a tapestry. "Don't tell me you like it here!"

"Then why don't you do something about it?" said Thianna.

"Like what?" said Jasius.

"Break out," the giantess replied.

"We wouldn't stand a chance on our own," said a satyr.

"Then why not team up?" asked Karn.

"Team up?" the dwarf asked.

"Work together against the Calderans," said Desstra. "If all of your people combined forces, you'd have them outnumbered."

"Combined forces?" snorted the minotaur. "Not with these animals."

Thianna just had time to roll her eyes before the food started flying through the air again.

Sirena held the horn in her hands. She made no move to bring it to her lips. She didn't expect it to perform any differently from last time. So why repeat the same action over and over? Wasn't that the definition of stupidity?

The wyvern sat motionless against the wall and studied her. Even though it was the prisoner and she the Keras Keeper, she felt that it pitied her. There were only so many times you could make it wince with a loud blast and still feel satisfied. If she knew how to do anything more with the horn she wouldn't be in this mess.

On the day of the Great Hatching, if all she could

do was to set the infant reptiles shrieking in pain, she wouldn't have control. She'd have the opposite.

And without control of the wyverns, there would be no control of the skies. Caldera was just one among dozens of major city-states across the enormous island-continent of Thica. You couldn't rule such a territory unless you could fly. Without a clear ruler, the disparate peoples would fall into war just as quickly as that collection of bratty kids had started a food fight. Yes, she'd heard about that. Just another example of how desperately this land needed her people's guidance. Make no mistake, Sirena knew how much was at risk. But why did it all have to ride on her shoulders?

She raised the horn again and blew a somewhat softer blast.

The wyvern shook its head as if it were chasing away an insect. Sirena sighed.

"I don't suppose you have an irresistible urge to obey me?" she asked.

That's not the impulse that comes first to mind, no, it said.

"Not even a little?"

I suppose I could pretend if it makes you feel better. Should I sit up and do tricks? Oh, but wait, you have me chained down. I'm sorry, but I don't think I can help you.

"I didn't expect you to. No, I don't think anyone can help me. I'll have to figure it out for myself. If that big lug of a barbarian girl can do it, then . . ."

Sirena froze, an idea taking shape in her mind.

"If that big lug of a barbarian girl . . . ," she repeated. She recalled Queen Melantha's words about honey and fingers.

You're not serious? asked the wyvern. It was reading her thoughts again. But she couldn't complain. The idea was crazy, Sirena knew.

"It's not like I'm drowning in other options," she said.

The barbarian girl caused all your troubles.

"Well, now she can fix them."

The room was still a mess, with food splattered everywhere, but the atmosphere had largely calmed down. Young people sat by themselves or paced in frustration. A few even picked at the remains on the table.

All eyes turned as the door opened. A soldier marched in.

"Thianna Frostborn!" she called out.

The giantess rose up from where she had been sitting.

"What is it?" she asked.

"Someone wants a word with you," the woman replied.

"One of the queens," Thianna conjectured.

"But which one?" asked Karn.

"Guess I'll find out."

Thianna looked at the eggplant and tomato smearing her clothing.

"I'm not exactly dressed for an audience with the monarchs," she said to the soldier.

"You aren't going to one," the woman replied. "Your presence is requested by someone else."

"Who?" Thianna asked, but the soldier turned and walked back out into the hallway, leaving the door open for Thianna to follow.

"I guess I'll find that out too," said the giantess. "Hold the fort down here, will you, Norrønboy?" she said to Karn.

"Don't worry," replied Desstra archly. "We will."

Thianna followed the guard into the hallway. Behind her, the door shut and locked.

"Do you think she'll be all right?" Desstra asked. It pained Karn to see the look of concern on her face, given the cold shoulder his best friend threw to the elf.

"She's Thianna," he said. "If she gets into any trouble, I'm sure we'll hear the noise from here."

"The first thing we do, let's see about a bath."

Thianna found herself in a large, richly appointed room, and greeting her, the girl who had bested her in the Court of Land and Sky. It hadn't been but a few hours since this girl had pulled a tapestry down on Thianna's head, but now she was acting welcoming and friendly. Why this change in attitude? Guards stood outside the door, of course, but no one bothered them here. Thianna eyed the smaller girl with suspicion.

She was dark of hair and eye, her skin a rich olive complexion. Like all the Thicans. Like Thianna herself. Probably about Thianna's age too. About Karn's size, but there was a real toughness about her. She held herself like she knew how to fight. You could tell in the way she balanced on her heels. How she stood straight. Held her arms. But there was something else about the girl that was familiar. Thianna couldn't put her finger on what it was, but the feeling nagged at her. Like she knew the girl, or someone like her. Still, she wasn't trying to stick a sword in her.

"A bath?" Thianna said. "But I'm not sleepy."

The girl blinked at this. She couldn't know that Thianna still preferred to sleep on a block of ice, which she produced magically by freezing the water in a bathtub.

"You've come a long way," the girl explained. "I imagine that you've been on the road a great deal of time. The hot, dusty road." She spoke slowly, punctuating her words in the hopes the giantess would take the hint. "In the heat. With the dust. On the road."

"Actually we flew most of the way," Thianna said. She imitated the girl's tone. "In the sky. In the breeze. With the clouds."

"In the same clothes?"

Thianna frowned. She was starting to get the point.

"We changed clothes once," she said defensively.

"Only once?"

"It was just a few weeks ago in Gordasha. I had a bath then too. By accident." Thianna smiled as she remembered her entrance into the city, tumbling out of an aqueduct into a private pool. They had swapped their northern attire for clothing more appropriate to the city then, although they had kept their britches.

"A few weeks ago!" The girl rolled her eyes.

"Yes," said Thianna.

"Well, we do things differently here in the Twin Palaces. Come on, you'll feel better after a bath. Certainly you'll smell better. And you can change out of those"—she wrinkled her nose in distaste—"pants."

"What is it with my pants?" said Thianna. "Why is everyone so upset about pants?"

"Civilized people don't wear them. Only barbarians do."

"Well, what of that? I am a barbarian."

The girl thought about this.

"Aren't you a Calderan too? Your mother was a Calderan."

"My mother was a Thican."

"She was a Calderan first and foremost. The Calderans are the rulers of Thica."

Thianna frowned at this.

"Is that what you are, a Calderan?"

"Yes, my name is Sirena."

"Sirena?" The name reminded her of Sydia, but that comparison wasn't the reason she seemed familiar.

"After the sirens," Sirena continued. "Dangerous women who sing from the rocks around the islands of Sarn's Teeth and mesmerize sailors with their voice. My mother chose the name." She paused to laugh bitterly. "She had high hopes for me. Like yours, she passed away when I was very small."

Thianna resisted the urge to point out that Sirena was still small, at least compared to half giants.

"How do you know about my mother?" she asked instead.

"I know a lot about you," Sirena replied. "But you can tell me more. Come. Let me treat you like a fellow Calderan and we can talk. You'll enjoy it, I promise."

Thianna wasn't sure she would, but the feeling of familiarity nagged at her, so she allowed Sirena to lead her into another room. This one was dominated by a huge square-shaped pool set into the floor and tiled in marble mosaic. Two female servants poured hot water from jugs into it. Thianna eyed the pool, thinking that if she froze it, then it would make a more comfortable bed than the last few bathtubs she'd slept in. She might have room to stretch out for once.

The girl motioned at the tub.

"I'm not getting in that," said the giantess.

"Sestia, grant me patience," Sirena muttered.

"Who?"

"Goddess of war, combat, and . . . strategy," said Sirena.

Then she brightened as if something had just occurred to her. "Is it true you can do ice magic?" she asked.

Thianna nodded.

"Can you show me?" Sirena asked.

"Why?" Thianna asked warily.

"I've never seen anyone do magic."

Thianna couldn't help but smile. She understood the fascination. She'd always been intrigued by magic herself growing up, and she was proud of her rapidly growing skill.

"I guess there's no harm in that," said the frost giant. "I just need a little water." She walked to the tub and reached a hand down to cup some of the liquid. "I'll do something small. Maybe make a snowball," she explained. "Skapa kaldr skapa—" she began to chant.

Sirena approached her where she knelt, peering at the water in her palm as ice began to form.

"Amazing," she said. "It's really starting to freeze." She rested a hand on Thianna's arm. Then the girl suddenly slipped her foot across the giantess's and gave her a twist and a shove. As Thianna was already bent over, the wrestling move worked and sent her spinning off-balance. She fell face-first into the pool.

And came up sputtering and spurting.

Her face was angry, but Sirena burst into laughter.

"You tricked me!" the giantess said.

"You have to admit, it worked," Sirena replied. "And you really did need a bath."

Thianna fumed, but then she nodded grudgingly.

"At least let me cool it down," she said. "It doesn't have to be so blasted hot."

She held her palms above the water and chanted the frost charm. A sheet of ice formed across the surface of the pool, though it instantly began to melt.

"That's better," she said. Thianna sank down into the water, though she had to recline on her elbows to get it to the level of her neck.

"See?" said Sirena. "Civilization isn't all bad, now is it?"

Thianna considered this. It was sort of pleasant. And large enough she could fit all of herself in it. Usually that took a river.

"So this bathing thing," she said. "Calderans do it often?"

CHAPTER FIVE

It's All Fun and Games . . .

"Where is the rest of it?"

Thianna stood looking at herself in a mirror. The looking glass would be considered full-length for anyone else. The giantess had to tilt it back to see her head in it. They were in yet another room in the suite. Why did these people need so many rooms? This one seemed to be just for dressing in. She supposed that when you changed your clothes more than once a season, you had to have somewhere to store them all. Since her own clothes were now soaking wet, she was wearing something that Sirena's servants had furnished.

"That's all there is," said Sirena. "It's supposed to hang to your ankles."

"It barely comes to my knees," replied Thianna. The

robe was more like a tunic on the giantess. Fortunately, it was sleeveless, so her broad shoulders weren't confined. They had given her a leather belt to bind around her waist. And the largest pair of adult men's sandals that could be found.

"Now you look like a proper Calderan."

"You mean a proper Thican?"

Sirena shrugged.

"You look civilized. In form, at least, if not in size."

Thianna grunted at this. But Sirena motioned her to the door.

"Where are we going?" the giantess asked.

"There's something I want to show you," Sirena replied.

Thianna wasn't sure what she thought about this girl. She didn't trust Sirena, certainly not. But as no one was trying to put a sword in her, she was prepared to see where things went.

Karn studied the board game on the table. The playing field was laid out in an eight-by-eight grid, with no special markings or different-colored squares. Each team had eight playing pieces. There were six that were obviously pawns. One side's were shaped like little wyvern riders. The other side's pawns rode something else, a strange feathered animal that Karn couldn't quite recognize. Then there were two larger pieces per side, a tall Thican warrior with a shield and an even larger piece that wore a crown. He desperately wanted to know how the game was played.

Karn twisted his silver ring as he pondered. Then, satisfied that he'd memorized the layout, he started moving pieces experimentally. He wanted to see if he could work out any of the rules just by shifting things around.

"You are performing these operations incorrectly," said someone beside him. Karn turned and saw the bronze automaton glancing over his shoulder. Although it was made of metal, its face seemed capable of displaying a good deal of emotion. This close he could hear the noise of tiny gears spinning inside, whirling like some of the complicated clocks he remembered seeing in the markets of Castlebriar.

"Then show me," said Karn, stepping aside. "Though I think I was doing pretty good, considering I don't even know what the game is called."

"It is named Queen's Champion," said the automaton.

"Thanks," said Karn. "And what are you named?"

There was a soft click as the automaton raised an eyebrow.

"I am a Talosian," it said. "We are all called Talos."

"All of you?"

"Yes. After the first of us, who was forged by the god Cratus the Smith to be his best companion. I am Talos Ten Thousand Fifty-one."

"There are over ten thousand of you?" said Karn.

"There are never more than three hundred of us at a time," the automaton replied. "We only fashion another of our kind when one is destroyed. I was fashioned twelve years ago after Talos Nine Thousand Eight Hundred Seventy-four ceased function."

"Why do you look like a child?" ask Karn. "I mean, if you are . . . 'fashioned.'"

"Because I am a child. When I am older, I will be upgraded with a new and larger body."

"Wow. That's really . . ." Karn stopped before he said something offensive. The past few months of travel had broadened his mind considerably. "Interesting," he finished, and meant it. "My name is Karn Korlundsson," he said. "Be healthy."

"Health has no meaning to me," said Talos.

"It's just what we Norrønians say in greeting," said Karn.

"Then why not simply say hello? Or 'good fortune,' as Thicans do?"

"Because it's a nice thing to say. Never mind, you were telling me the rules."

Talos explained that the playing pieces all moved one square at a time in any direction, except on their first move, when they were allowed to step forward two spaces. When a piece landed adjacent to an opposing piece, it could challenge. This was done by rolling a six-sided die. The challenging player was allowed to add one to the results of their roll, and the highest number won. The losing piece was removed from the board and the winner advanced into their space.

"Why use dice?" asked Karn.

"To simulate the unpredictability of swordplay," Talos explained. "Combat is everything here, you will find."

"And yet no one challenges the two queens."

Talos paused at this but did not speak.

"What about these two pieces?" continued Karn, indicating the two nonsoldiers.

"The Queen and her Champion," said Talos. "The Champion piece is the strongest on the board."

"It would be."

"When in combat, it rolls two six-sided dice and takes the highest result to represent this strength. Also, if the Queen comes under attack, before dice are rolled, she may exercise her 'Prerogative' and substitute the Champion in her place."

"How do you win?"

"The game ends when the Queen is defeated or when all playing pieces other than the Queen are defeated and she stands alone."

"I think I got it," said Karn. "Shall we play?"

Talos seemed surprised by this.

"I have played many times and you have only just learned the rules," it said. "Despite the random element the dice bring, you are unlikely to win."

"Don't be so sure," said Karn. He could feel the muscles of his own face twitch as his gamer's enthusiasm kicked in. "I've played a game or two."

"You like the view?" Sirena asked.

"It's okay," said Thianna, then realized that the Calderan girl was probably expecting a more enthusiastic reaction. "You have to understand, when you grow up on a plateau in the Ymirian mountain range, you get a little spoiled when it comes to views. There's really nothing like it. But, hey, let me look at Caldera."

The giantess stared down from the tower. To her right, she could see the palace grounds laid out at the summit of the hill. In front of her, houses clustered along the first of two intercity walls. Beautiful fountains issued streams that ran swiftly down channels in the hillside. They flowed through the town to the base of the hill, where they spilled into the lake. Dwellings and other buildings tumbled down the slope all the way to the docks, while the roads from the hilltop to the bottom zigzagged precariously through all. And stretching out into the waters, two enormous seawalls protected the harbor, with colossal statues standing guard at the end of each breakwater.

"I wonder what's going on there," she said, indicating the lowest section of the city.

"Why would you want to know?" replied Sirena. "That's where the helots live."

"Helots?"

"You would call them slaves. Or maybe serfs. They are owned by the city."

"You're kidding?" Thianna knew slavery was still practiced across much of her world, even in Norrøngard. She didn't approve, though she wasn't surprised. Sirena went on to explain the three-tiered division of Calderan society.

"It's really not that bad," she said.

"Ask a helot and see what they say," said Thianna.

"Funny," said Sirena. "But why would you want to go down there when you can be up here? The docks are crowded, dirty, and dangerous."

"Let me tell you something I've learned the hard way. The real action is always down the hill."

Sirena nodded at this. "I imagine it was a very small place where you grew up. I mean, small for frost giants."

Thianna smiled. "My village was only a handful of people."

"It must have been awful," said Sirena. "Cold, treeless, barren." Her shoulders twitched as if shaking off an imagined chill.

"Not at all," said Thianna. "The mountains are magnificent. They stretch on forever. And it's not barren. We have giants, and trolls, and, well, they're not very nice. But the frost sprites are fun. There are a few snow goblins left. A couple of linnorms. And when the sun dips in the evening, the ice shines in so many colors." The giantess pictured the scene in her mind. She surprised herself by how much she missed it.

"I imagine that it is quite something to see." Thianna spun around. Queen Melantha stood in the doorway to the tower stairs. She nodded slightly at Sirena and then at Thianna. "May I join you?"

"I didn't think queens had to ask," said the giantess.

Melantha smiled slightly at this. She walked to the edge of the platform they stood on and leaned on a railing.

"We both wanted you to see the city from here, to understand Caldera. We want you to understand our city."

"Why?"

"It was your mother's city too."

Thianna felt a flurry in her chest at the mention of her mother. Talaria had really lived here, walked these streets. Maybe even stood on this balcony.

"So tell me about it," she said.

"Well, to start with," Sirena said, "we are in the Tower of Damnameneus. You know who that was?"

Thianna shook her head.

"He was a dactyl dwarf. A mathematician." Sirena glanced upward, where the enormous parabolic mirror rose above them. "Also an inventor. He built these as well."

"He designed them," corrected Queen Melantha. "The first were built thirteen thousand years ago, after the war with the Naga Rajya."

"Who?"

"A kingdom to the east. We invaded them, but our soldiers mutinied and we were forced to turn back. The mirrors were supposed to protect against a counter-invasion, and so they were only installed on the east coast. The Naga Rajya never came."

"But someone else did," said Sirena. "From the west."

"The Gordion Empire," Thianna guessed.

"You know of them, then?" Melantha said.

"Yeah, well, thanks to Karn and my adventures, I'm finally getting a handle on this whole 'history' thing."

"Yes," said the queen. "Thica was conquered then. We were just a part of the empire for centuries, made to adopt Gordion ways and culture."

"They forced their gods on us," said Sirena angrily. "Their armies. Their money. Their food."

"I like some of their food," said Thianna. Sirena snorted. "But Gordion was a long time ago," the frost giant added.

"Yes, it was," said the queen. "And when the empire fell, we collapsed into warring city-states."

"We were invaded by country after country." Sirena's tone was bitter. "Picking at us like vultures while we fought among ourselves. It hasn't been a hundred years since Caldera reunited the Thican Empire."

"We built the rest of the mirrors then," said Melantha. "They were stationed around the entire coast, as they always should have been."

"We won't be invaded again. We won't be weak," said Sirena.

"I've found there is more than one way to be strong," said the giantess.

"You can't be strong if you don't know who you are," said Sirena. "These clothes we are wearing"—she fingered the hem of Thianna's tunic—"this is how the ancient Thicans dressed. Do you understand? We're rebuilding our way of life here. Everything that Caldera does is to make us great again."

Thianna looked from the girl to the woman.

"And all the city-states are on board with this?" she asked. "They didn't seem any too happy about leaving their children here."

Melantha looked away. "Like parents, we must be firm. They would fall to war among themselves the instant we withdrew our hand."

"You don't know that."

The queen paused.

"One does not have to be certain to be prepared. Thianna, Sirena needs to understand how the horn works."

This was new. Sirena couldn't use the horn. Surprising. But it also explained why they were being so nice.

"Why doesn't she?"

"When Osius built the horn, he bound its power to his bloodline."

"His bloodline," repeated Thianna. "But if it only works for his descendants, why did the dark elves want it?"

"They might have learned to use it given sufficient time," said the queen. "But we don't have time. We need the horn in just five days. Sirena must master it before then."

"Why her?" said Thianna.

"Believe me, I've asked myself that a lot lately," said the girl. "It's not the way I wanted the dice to fall."

Queen Melantha laid a hand on Sirena's shoulder. "Sirena is my niece," the Land Queen explained. "I was grooming her to be my heir. But then you blew the Horn of Osius, and the wyverns heard its call all the way from Ymiria. We knew then it had returned, and so Xalthea pulled Sirena from me and made her Keras Keeper."

"My life was totally upended," said Sirena.

"I'm sorry," said Thianna, and meant it. "But I still don't quite understand why it has to be her."

"It doesn't now," said Melantha. "It could be you again, and Sirena could resume her place as my heir. The empire could stay together; peace could be maintained. And you could join Calderan society."

"Me?" said Thianna. "But that's not what I've been after. I'm here to destroy the horn."

"We know," said the queen. "But now we have shown you its importance. Your importance."

"But I still don't understand," said Thianna. "Why does it have to be Sirena if it isn't me? Why did Xalthea give her the job if she didn't want it?"

"Because Osius's power runs strongest through his bloodline," said Sirena.

"Yes, you've explained all that," said Thianna. "But why?" And then she understood. "Wait! Bloodline. You mean—she—me—we?"

The giantess looked at the girl who had seemed so familiar, who knew how to fight, who had such fierce determination.

"That's right," said the queen. "Sirena is your cousin."

"I win again," said Karn.

The satyr scowled.

Karn stepped back and laughed.

All of the hostages had crowded around the game. They'd had to move the table out into the center of the room after he'd beaten Talos three games in a row. After that, Karn had taken on a succession of princes and princesses, none of whom had proved any real challenge for the strategy game expert.

"How many wins is that now?" he said to Desstra.

"Seven," she said. "But don't stop. I'm loading up on drachmas." She jingled her coin purse, which bulged significantly more than it had before.

"You're *betting* on me?" Karn said in disbelief.

"It beats betting against you," the elf replied. "I learned that lesson in Gordasha."

"I'm surprised you're still getting takers," Karn said. "After all, I haven't lost yet."

"They're all royal," said Desstra. "Little darlings of

their city-states. They all think they're the best at every-thing and everyone else is inferior. I tell you, I couldn't pickpocket their money faster."

"I'd rather you didn't do that," said Karn.

"We will need these drachmas when we get out of here," she replied.

"Okay," said Karn. "I got you." He tapped the board. "Who's next?"

"I am." It was the minotaur boy, Asterius. He pawed the ground with a hoof, just like a bull would.

"Not too proud to play with animals?" asked Karn. He was feeling pleased with himself and couldn't resist.

"No shame in stomping you into the dirt," Asterius replied. Karn saw the familiar glint in the bull boy's eye. The minotaur might prove a worthy competitor. Excite-ment stirred in the Norrønur's belly in anticipation. Then something else occurred to him. The minotaur had started the food fight. He was the most disruptive person of the group. But maybe Karn could use the minotaur to pull all these squabbling royals together.

"Why don't we make it interesting?" Karn asked.

Asterius shrugged and pulled a golden drachma from his pocket.

"Not that," said Karn. "I think Desstra has taken enough coin already."

"Speak for yourself," said the elf.

"Shhh," Karn said. "We're betting for something bigger."

This quieted the room.

"What, then?" said the minotaur.

"If I win, then when I bust out of here you have to help me."

"I told you, I'm not going to fight alongside an animal. Anyway, you won't win."

"Then what are you afraid of?"

Asterius snorted at the word *afraid*.

"I fear nothing," he said. "But what about you?"

"Yes?" said Karn.

"If I win, then we have another contest. A minotaur contest."

"What's that?"

"Head-butting," said Asterius.

Karn looked at the thick skull on the minotaur and the two sizable horns growing out of it.

"Karn . . . ," said Desstra, a warning note in her voice.

"You're on," said Karn. He spat in his hand and held it out to seal the deal. Asterius stared at the outstretched palm for a moment, but then he grasped the intent. He spat in his own hand and offered it to Karn.

"I don't like this," said Desstra. "You couldn't take being hit by that head."

Karn looked again at the minotaur's huge skull.

"Then I'll just have to win, won't I?"

The elf shrugged.

"Place your bets, everyone," she said to the group. "Looks like we have a real fight on our hands. Who wants to bet on the minotaur?" Several hands went up at once. Desstra gave Karn a sympathetic look. "Doesn't seem like they think you have a chance this time," she said.

"I will bet." The automaton stepped forward. A coin slid out of a slot in its palm and was caught between two of its fingers. "I will bet on Karn Korlundsson."

"My mother and your mother were sisters," explained Sirena as they walked back to the Twin Palaces. "And Queen Melantha's brother was my father."

"So you're a niece to both the Land Queen and my mother. What happened to your parents?"

"My mother died in battle."

"I'm sorry," said Thianna.

"Why should you be sorry?" asked Sirena. She seemed genuinely surprised at Thianna's sympathy. "When a Calderan goes to fight, we tell her she must return 'either with your shield or on it.' She died fighting for her country. There is no higher honor." Thianna detected a note of pride in the girl's voice. And perhaps a touch of envy. "I'm the one you should feel sorry for. They took my sword and shield when I became Keras Keeper. I will never be allowed to die for Caldera."

Thianna considered this. It wasn't the way she thought about things.

"What about your father?" she asked.

Sirena shrugged. "What about him? Men aren't

allowed to bear arms or rule. He oversaw Mother's businesses, lived apart from us. He still does, I suppose."

"You don't know?"

"It doesn't matter. I was being groomed to succeed Melantha, but as your mother was Keras Keeper, when the horn was found I was forced to take her place. My quarters, that bathtub you enjoyed—that is the home of the Keras Keeper."

"Those were my mother's rooms?" Thianna stopped walking in shock. Of course, it shouldn't have surprised her. But her mother had lived there, in the palace. Had bathed in that very tub. Thianna only had dim memories of her mother. Talaria had died when she was very young. Her mother had lived here, amid royalty, yet Talaria had never seemed anything but perfectly happy in their modest home in a cavern of ice and stone.

"They could be your rooms," said Sirena.

"Right, imagine me in a palace," said the giantess.

"I admit," said Sirena, "it would take some getting used to. On everybody's part. I'm sure Xalthea would be thrilled."

They both laughed at this. Sirena laid a hand on the larger girl's arm.

"I'm serious, Thianna. You can take another bath in your mother's tub tomorrow. And I can teach you what you need to know to fit in here."

"I don't know. This is a lot." Thianna shook her head to clear it. "It's not why I came here."

"I know," said Sirena. "There's just one more thing."

Thianna raised an eyebrow.

"Something else I want you to see," said Sirena. "It might help your decision."

She led Thianna to a doorway, where two soldiers stood outside. The women stepped aside so that she could enter. As she passed, Thianna caught one of them looking at her askance, but the woman looked away. Like Queen Xalthea, Thianna suspected the soldier frowned on her mixed heritage.

They stepped into the room.

A wyvern was chained to the far wall. The creature looked pathetic. Its skin hung loosely on its frame. Its scales were dull, its eyes glassy. There were scars across its left wing. The patagium was ragged and had several nasty holes.

"What's happened to it?" Thianna turned to Sirena in horror.

"It's being punished," the girl replied.

"Punished? For what?"

The wyvern jolted suddenly. Sirena jumped, but the giantess didn't flinch. It swung its head as far toward them as it could, staring intently at Thianna.

Talaria?

"What? What did you say?"

Of course not. How could you be? And so much bigger too!

"You knew my mother?"

Sirena stared openmouthed at Thianna.

"You can speak to it?" she said, amazed. "But you're not touching the horn."

Thianna realized that Sirena couldn't hear the wyvern's thoughts right now. The soldiers she had met last year could send telepathic instructions to their wyverns, but it seemed the horn was necessary to have such true and open two-way communication.

"I don't need the horn anymore," the giantess explained. "I think it was a side effect of using it for the first time on a dragon. Kind of stretches out your head to touch a mind that large. I can communicate easily with reptiles now." She turned to the wyvern. "How do you know my mother?"

Your mother? Now it was the wyvern's turn to appear shocked.

"What is it saying?" said Sirena.

"Quiet," said Thianna. To the reptile she said, "My mother was Talaria. She fell from the sky over Ymiria. My father caught her."

Your father must have been quite tall.

"He's a frost giant."

The wyvern made a wheezing sound in its long neck. Thianna had enough experience with the reptiles to know it was laughing.

That girl! I thought she was out of surprises. But I am glad to learn that she survived. As humans go, she had courage. How is she?

"She died when I was young."

The wyvern dipped its head.

84

Would that I had died with her. And now they have you here. Is my long ordeal for nothing?

"What is it saying?" Sirena repeated impatiently.

"We're talking about my mother," said Thianna. "How does it know my mother? Why did you bring me here?"

"This is the animal that Talaria rode when she escaped," said Sirena. "I wanted you to see what became of it."

"Why?"

"So you would see how pathetic it is." She glared at the reptile. "How much better off it would have been if it had never fled. If it had stayed here, with its own kind. Staying with your own kind is the better choice." For the second time, she touched the frost giant's arm. "We need you to do the right thing, Thianna. For all of us."

Sirena indicated the door. It was time to go.

Thianna glanced back at the battered creature that had once borne her mother across the world. It had hunkered down into itself. It looked deflated and resigned to its fate.

"I wouldn't be here if it hadn't fled," she said. "I wouldn't exist at all."

The wyvern lifted its head at that.

The horn is kept in a chamber behind the Sky Queen's throne, it said. To Thianna's mind alone.

*   *   *

85

Karn and Asterius were both down roughly half their forces. Neither had lost either Queen or Champion. Karn wondered if they were heading toward a stalemate.

"You could just concede now and get it over with," said the minotaur.

"Or you could give up," said the Norrønur, "and we could start looking for a way out of here. I don't get it. Why don't all your parents join forces and oppose them? There are so few Calderans and so many cities."

"Fire in the sky," said the minotaur. "Once we resisted, and they burned our grasslands." In response to Karn's befuddled look, he explained. "We supply the wheat for Thica. We had no food."

"Don't they need bread too?"

"They feed on other things as well. Things like fish." Asterius spat on the ground in disgust. "A minotaur can't eat such nasty, slimy gunk."

"Hey, I like fish," said Karn. "Anyway, it seems like there must be a better way to do things. If only you'd cooperate with each other."

"Too bad you will never get to show me, human. Since you aren't going to beat me."

The minotaur advanced his Champion toward Karn's Queen. Remarkably, Karn didn't attempt to flee. Rather, he sent one of his soldiers in pursuit of Asterius's Queen.

Play continued for a few tense turns. Karn was able to reach Asterius's Queen first. As he knew that he would, the minotaur used the move called a Prerogative to switch his Queen and Champion on the board.

They rolled the dice. Despite the Champion's advantage, it was a tie. On his next move, Karn immediately retreated.

Asterius laughed and pursued. Karn kept up the retreat for two moves. Then he stopped. Instead, he threatened the Queen in its new location. Again Asterius executed the Prerogative. After the switch, his Champion faced Karn's Soldier.

"Soldier verses Champion," said Talos. "An uneven match."

Karn looked at Desstra.

"You might want to invest in a helmet," she said with a meaningful glance at the minotaur's enormous horned head.

"Thanks for the vote of confidence."

Dice were rolled. Karn scored a six, but even with the benefit of two dice Asterius only received a four. Asterius had lost the challenge and his Champion was forfeited.

Worse, he saw that in exchanging his Queen for his Champion he had brought his Queen in range of Karn's Champion. As the Queen was at the edge of the board, with other pieces blocking possible routes, escape from Karn wasn't possible.

Karn wasted no time moving in for the challenge. This time his Champion won against Asterius's Queen.

"That's the game, then," said Karn.

"You retreated on purpose," said Asterius. "To make me chase you and not pay attention to my Queen. You hornless—"

Karn smiled.

"We drink out of horns where I'm from," he said.

Asterius huffed angrily through his nostrils.

"Play me again," the minotaur demanded.

"I think that's enough for now," said Karn. "We have other business." He left the game table and walked to the door, where he tried the handle. As he expected, it was locked. Then he turned to the dark elf. "Desstra, I think it's your turn."

"Just give me a minute," she replied. Then she bent at the knees and stuck a finger down her throat.

CHAPTER SIX

Weight of Responsibility

Sirena and Thianna arrived at the door to the royal hostage suite. Two guards stood on duty in the corridor outside. Only one of the wall torches was lit, so the lighting was dim, but she saw these weren't the same two who had been posted earlier. Sirena thought it was soon for a shift change, but such routine matters weren't her concern.

She turned to her larger cousin.

"You'll think about the Land Queen's words?"

"Long and hard," said Thianna. "I can promise you that."

Sirena nodded. She seemed satisfied with Thianna's answer.

"We'll talk more tomorrow."

Sirena turned to go. Then she paused. The soldiers

were both young, short. One was sickly pale. And the other—the other wasn't even female!

"What are you doing in that armor?" she demanded, even as the obvious explanation occurred to her.

"Escaping," replied Karn Korlundsson with a grin.

Sirena drew in a breath to raise the alarm.

And the door burst open. Out came the minotaur boy at full charge, bellowing like the bull he was. Sirena was knocked backward, slammed against the opposite wall. As she struggled to rise, the barbarian boy and the sickly pale girl pinned her down.

"I guess that's one way to do it," said Thianna.

"Not the smart way," said Desstra. "Not even the sane way. But one way."

"I said we'd do this 'quietly,'" Karn admonished the minotaur.

"That was quietly," replied Asterius. "You want to hear a really loud bellow?"

"No," Karn replied sternly. "Everyone back inside."

Karn and Desstra dragged the struggling Calderan into the hostage suite. Thianna followed them in.

"You have knees," Karn said smiling, indicating Thianna's Calderan clothing.

"So do you," she replied, poking him affectionately. Then she asked, "I assume Long Ears didn't have any trouble getting the door unlocked?"

"What do you think?" Karn replied.

"It was amazing," volunteered a young satyr. "She had a set of lockpicks hidden in her throat! She gagged them up and . . . I don't know how she carried them there without choking!"

"Practice," said the elf with a smile. "Also, lots of lost meals before I got the hang of it."

Karn laid a concerned hand on Thianna's shoulder.

"You all right?" he asked the giantess. "What was she talking about, 'the Land Queen's words'? And who is she?"

"Slow down on the questions," said Thianna, taking charge of guarding Sirena so that her companions could change back to their regular attire—Karn into his Gordashan tunic and Norrønian trousers and boots, and Desstra into her customary black and orange leathers. "I'm fine. They're trying to recruit me. And she's my cousin."

"Your cousin!" Karn looked at Sirena anew. Beyond the typical Thican features, he thought he could see a family resemblance. Of course, it made sense that his friend might have relatives here. He wondered what knowing she had family in Caldera would do to Thianna. "She didn't convince you, did she?"

"She overplayed her hand," said the giantess. "She showed me my mother's wyvern."

"Oh my gods," said Karn. "It's here? It's alive?"

"They've had it chained up all these years. Punishment

for helping my mother escape with the horn. It told me where the horn is kept." Then something occurred to her. "What happened to the guards?"

For an answer, Karn pointed into the room. Thianna saw that several of the wall hangings had been taken down and used to bind the two unfortunate soldiers.

"Good idea," said the frost giant. She grabbed a tapestry and tore it down in one yank. "Let's bind her with these."

As the heavy material was wrapped around Sirena, Thianna knelt to meet her cousin's angry gaze. "I realize this hasn't been the best family reunion," she said, "but you have to understand that I don't tolerate bullies."

"Bullies?" replied the girl, confused.

"The way the Calderans treat the rest of Thica."

"Weren't you listening? Didn't we teach you anything? The Calderans *saved* Thica. *You* are a Calderan."

Before Thianna could respond, Desstra interrupted.

"We need to move," said the dark elf. "Here, take this." She offered Thianna the sword she had relieved from a guard. The frost giant hesitated.

"I haven't poisoned the hilt or anything—take it!" snapped the elf.

Thianna accepted the equipment.

"We stick to the plan?" asked Karn. Although happily back in his own clothes, he had kept the Calderan sword and shield.

"Yes," Thianna replied. "We're going after the horn."

"And them?" Karn pointed at the hostage princes and princesses.

"What about them?"

"Maybe they want to escape too."

Thianna looked at the odd assortment of boys and girls. Spoiled brats, mostly. Few of them looked like they would be of any use in a fight.

"That's not our problem," the giantess said, even as the sinking feeling in her stomach told her that it was. Over the past half year, she had become someone who didn't turn away those in need. She looked at Karn. "Can they stop bickering, work together, and stay quiet?"

"Maybe two of the three," he said. "I wouldn't guarantee it."

Thianna sighed. "So who's going with us?" she asked.

As it happened, only Asterius and Jasius wanted to leave. As for the rest of the hostages, they were either frightened or worried about what their escape would mean for their cities. Karn didn't waste more words trying to convince them, though he was surprised that the bronze automaton counted among their number.

"You aren't coming?" he asked.

"The time is not right for it," Talos replied cryptically. "But I will be here if you return."

"If things go well, I won't be back," he said, but he added, "Good luck to you, though."

Talos regarded him strangely.

"Luck is not always enough," the metal creature said.

Then Talos placed the Charioteer's die with which Karn had won all his games into Karn's palm. There wasn't time to ponder this, as Desstra and Thianna were herding their small band into the corridors.

Thianna turned back to the room. Several of the children were looking uncertainly at Sirena and the guards, rolled up like fish in pita bread in the wall tapestries. Thianna could see they were debating how much trouble they'd be in if they let them go now versus later.

"Take your time with those," the giantess said. "If I find myself in this chamber again I'll be very unhappy. And you don't want to be locked up with an unhappy frost giant." She indicated her cousin. "Don't bother with her, though," the giantess said. She lifted Sirena, wall hangings and all, and hoisted her over her shoulder. "She's coming with us." Then she left them to contemplate her warning.

Thianna led the way through the Twin Palaces. They were heading for the Court of Land and Sky, where the captured wyvern had told her the horn was. Sirena grumbled at being carried like a sack of potatoes.

"If I shout," she said, "I'll bring the entire palace guard down on you."

The frost giant waved the point of her stolen sword threateningly.

"You wouldn't."

"I'm a desperate barbarian," said Thianna. "You don't know what I'll do."

The bluff must have worked, because Sirena didn't

shout. Karn gave Thianna a look of relief. He knew it had been a hollow threat, but fortunately, Thianna's cousin didn't know the giantess well enough to realize that. Sometimes being viewed as an uncivilized ruffian had its advantages.

The throne room was empty when they reached it.

"Stay here and keep watch," Thianna said to the group.

"Take Desstra with you," suggested Karn.

"What for?" said Thianna, unhappy with the idea.

"She's good at finding hidden things."

"So am I," said the giantess, but she didn't object when Desstra followed her into the courtroom. Karn, Asterius, and Jasius remained outside the doorway as lookouts.

Thianna walked up the stairs to the dais, still carrying her cousin. There was no chamber behind either throne. She turned to the second set of stairs, leading to the balcony.

Sirena shifted in her grip. Had she missed something? The wyvern had said that the horn was in a chamber *behind* the Sky Queen's throne. Not above it or beside it.

Thianna walked to the wall behind Xalthea's throne. Desstra stepped beside her.

"I don't need your help on this," the larger girl said.

"I think you do," said the elf. Then the once-Underhand student ran her hand across the wall.

"Found it," she said, pointing to the faint outlines of a doorway that were visible like a thin seam running through the marble.

Both giantess and elf turned to Sirena when they heard her swear.

"Well, it doesn't matter," said the Calderan. "It only opens for the Keras Keeper. And I won't help you open it."

Thianna thought about this a moment. Then she shifted her sword to her belt and laid her empty palm flat against the wall. A faint light glowed around the seam, then the marble swung outward.

"You were saying?" the giantess said with a smile.

"How did you do that?" Sirena asked.

"Talaria was just your aunt. She was my mother, after all. I figured if it works for you, then it sure should work for me."

Thianna set the bound girl down, then, grabbing ahold of the cloth, she gave it a yank. Sirena spilled onto the floor and Thianna hoisted her to her feet and clamped her arms behind her back before she could catch her bearings. Then she gave Sirena an encouraging shove and together they went into the room, leaving Desstra outside. The chamber was small, barely ten-by-ten feet. The Horn of Osius lay on a stone altar at the other end. Thianna snatched it up and slipped it into her belt.

Sirena stared at her, in shock over her irreverent handling of the relic.

"What?" said the giantess. "These things have been nothing but trouble since I blew the first one."

"What will you do now?" her cousin replied. "You'll never leave this island."

"That's where you are wrong," Thianna replied.

"How?"

"Love to show you, but I'm afraid this is where you get off. But thanks for teaching me about bathing."

Before Sirena could stop her, Thianna bolted from the chamber and slammed the marble door closed. She only had seconds before Sirena opened it from the other side, so she moved to Xalthea's throne and put her shoulder against it. Shoving with all her strength, the giantess toppled the heavy marble seat, which fell against the doorway, preventing it from opening outward.

"So long, cousin," she said triumphantly. But then she added, "Wish we'd had more time."

Sirena didn't waste valuable moments fuming at the actions of her uncouth cousin. She should have known better than to think the barbarian could be tempted by superior Calderan culture. If you didn't know what you were missing, maybe you couldn't recognize it even if it was offered to you. She thought of the wyvern's words: "From a bad crow, a bad egg."

The wyverns. That was how Thianna planned to escape. The same way her mother had.

Sirena ran to the doorway and placed her palm against

it to activate the magical ward. The door was limned in a soft glow but failed to swing open. She gave it a push and realized it was blocked by something heavy.

"Go to the crows, cousin," she swore.

But the Horn of Osius wasn't the only horn her people carried. They couldn't duplicate the magic that Osius had wielded when he forged the three horns, but the Calderans had been able to fashion other, smaller horns. The wyvern riders all carried them. Small instruments that could convey simple messages over great distances. She pulled one from her pocket now, blew a blast. Her Keras Guards would hear it. Hopefully they would be in time to stop Thianna's escape.

Desstra took the lead as the small band made their way onto the streets. She could sneak better than any of them, and her sharp hearing alerted them to signs of trouble before they stumbled upon it. Twice she'd scouted ahead, then returned to steer them in another direction to avoid running into any soldiers.

"I wish we could have persuaded more of the hostages to come with us," Karn said as they waited on Desstra to return from her latest foray. "But at least this way it shouldn't take more than three wyverns to hold us all."

"Flying is no way to travel," snorted Asterius.

"Flying is fine," said Karn. "I'll take a wyvern any day over an ox cart."

"Watch it," said the bull boy. Karn imagined that the treatment of cattle might be a sore point with him.

Fortunately, Desstra returned to say the way was clear. Together they crept to the wyvern roosts that were located near the sky docks where they had first landed. It was a large building, with a central dome flanked by two wings and second in size only to the palace. The wyverns had all gone to sleep for the night and the guards at the door were minimal.

But as the team debated their approach, Desstra's ears twitched. They looked to see a group of women charging through the streets. Thianna spotted Leta and her soldiers just as her enemy spotted them. Something, or someone, had clearly alerted the Keras Guard to their plans.

"Troll dung!" exclaimed Thianna. "Not you again!"

"I could say the same," the Keras captain replied. "Thankfully, this is as far as you go."

"Lady, you turn up like a bad coin," said Desstra.

"For Neth's sake," Karn swore. "This may be a really short-lived escape."

"Let's try not to make it so," said the elf.

With that, all the companions turned and fled.

"After them, fools!" shouted Leta. The Keras Guard shouted and broke into pursuit, with their captain limping along in their wake.

"Why do we not fight?" complained Asterius, huffing as he ran.

"Right," said Desstra. "We'd have the whole Calderan army on top of our heads in no time."

"Are you afraid?" asked the minotaur.

"No," said the elf. "Not stupid either."

"But you fought today in the court?" said Asterius.

"They expected us to resist," said Desstra. "But they didn't anticipate my picking the locks later."

"Not working out so well, though, is it?" said the bull boy.

The group ran as fast as they could. With a steep cliff to one side of them, soldiers to their back, and the palace ahead, their options were limited.

"We need another way off this rock," said Thianna to Karn as he ran along beside her.

"Agreed," he replied between breaths. "I might know a way, but just for one of us."

"What do you mean?" she asked.

"Your mother's wyvern."

Thianna immediately shook her head.

"I'm not leaving you here."

"We have the horn. One of us needs to take it."

"You take it, then."

"I don't know how it works. If I take it, I'll have a squadron of wyverns on my tail the whole way and no magical way to order them to land."

Thianna started to object, but Karn interjected.

"It's the only way. You know that. We'll cover you. If

we fight our way free, we'll take the hostage princes and sneak down the hill. The lower city will be easy to hide in, and we can get a boat and slip away. And if we get captured, once the horn is destroyed you can come back for us."

"I don't like it," she said.

"Remember what you told me in Gordasha? 'If you really care about me, then you have to care about what's important to me.' You don't like bullies, Thianna. This is the only way to destroy the horn."

She didn't answer, but she knew he was right.

Karn dropped out of his run. Behind him, Desstra, Asterius, and Jasius did the same.

Reluctantly Thianna nodded. She turned to the elf. "Just make sure Karn gets out of here safely."

"Go," said Karn. "We'll stay and buy you time." Then he turned to face the approaching soldiers.

Thianna raced into the night in the direction of the captured wyvern.

Karn looked at his companions. He didn't know how the two hostage princes would perform in combat; Desstra was without her weapons, and he didn't have the benefit of Whitestorm's dragon-touched magic either. But he could do something about that.

"Here," said Karn, handing Desstra his sword.

"What are you going to use?" the elf asked.

Karn grinned. He cupped his hand to his mouth,

drew a lungful of air, and shouted as loud as he could, "Whitestorm!"

The sword of Korlundr hauld Kolason came flying through the air, its reddish-gold blade shining. Ever since the dragon Orm had gifted it a magical charge, Whitestorm came when Karn summoned it. Karn held out a hand and his father's weapon settled comfortably in his grip. He grinned at Desstra.

Then the Keras Guard was on them.

The pitiable reptile looked up as Thianna entered the room.

The guards outside my door?

"Are having a nice lie-down," said the giantess.

What are you doing here?

"Getting us out," she said. Then she tapped the horn on her belt.

That got the wyvern's attention.

You have it? it asked. Then it slumped down again. *But I am chained.*

"Chains aren't really a problem," said Thianna. She slipped her sword into her belt alongside the horn and placed her palms on the shackles. "I should warn you, though, this is going to be a little cold."

I've felt the cold before, replied the wyvern.

Thianna nodded. This was the creature that had carried her mother all the way to the Ymirian mountain range. It had suffered a lot since those days, but this time it didn't have to fly so far.

"Skapa kaldr, skapa kaldr, skapa kaldr," she chanted as loudly as she dared. The hoarfrost formed and grew on the metal. The wyvern shifted uncomfortably as its bindings chilled to well below freezing, but it didn't cry out. When the iron links were a nice shade of blue-white, Thianna closed her fingers around them and pulled.

Made brittle by the drop in temperature, the metal shattered like ice. The wyvern lurched to its feet and threw its wings wide for the first time in years. Together the girl and the reptile walked out into the moonslit night.

"Think you can handle it?" Thianna asked.

Freedom will not be difficult to handle, it replied. But when Thianna climbed on its back, its legs shook.

I could lift an ox easier than you. Is that what you had for lunch—a whole ox?

"Hey, you just do your part to get us out of here and watch the snarky comments about my weight."

Hissing in either annoyance or pain, the wyvern flapped its wings. They lifted off the ground, hovered for a moment, then crashed back to earth.

"Come on, quit fooling around!" said Thianna.

It has been over a decade since I did this, the wyvern responded. *If you don't understand that, then how about you flap your arms and I climb on your back instead?*

"Ymir's beard," swore Thianna. "Why is every wyvern I meet such a jester?"

For an answer, the reptile snarled and beat its wings again. This time they managed to stay aloft. Slowly they rose into the air. Together reptile and girl turned toward the edge of the cliff and the yawning depths beyond.

Sirena burst from the door the instant her guards removed the obstruction. Xalthea wouldn't be happy about her throne being upended, but that was nearly the least of her worries.

"You have Thianna?" she asked the women.

"No," a soldier replied. "She ran, but at least she won't be taking a wyvern."

Sirena started to reply, but then an alternative occurred to her.

"With me," she called, leaping from the dais and heading for the door.

"Where are we going?" a soldier asked.

She didn't bother to reply, all her efforts concentrating on moving as fast as she could toward the chamber where the renegade wyvern was kept.

Sirena skidded to a halt when she saw Thianna atop the beast. "Stop her!" she shouted to the guards trailing in her wake. They were too slow, gaping stupidly as the ungainly creature rose and fell in the air. This was ridiculous. Before she was Keras Keeper, she was a better warrior than either of these two older women.

Sirena grabbed a sword from one of the guards lying stunned on the ground before the wyvern's prison. Then she gauged the rise and fall of the animal in the air. Her feet pounded across the earth and she leapt.

She caught the tail of the wyvern, upward of its dangerous barbs. Then she worked her way rapidly onto its back and leapt at her traitorous cousin. Thianna began to turn, but Sirena crashed into the giantess.

Heavy, heavy, heavy! shrieked the wyvern. Sirena was surprised to find that while she was touching Thianna, who carried the horn, she could hear its thoughts as well.

"Just stay in the air!" her cousin yelled.

Too much weight! the creature roared back in their minds. Air whistled through the holes in its damaged left wing.

"I'm doing what I can about that," said Thianna, struggling to shove Sirena off. Below them, the fight between the Keras Guards and Thianna's companions was bringing others. Lights flared on throughout the grounds. They heard the sound of running feet.

"Just get us off this hill!" the frost giant yelled.

"You're not going anywhere," Sirena spat back.

Yes we are! Down! We're all going down!

They hit the ground and the cousins were thrown to the earth. Sirena tumbled over and over, but she came up in a crouch, clutching a sword in one hand. And something else in the other.

Thianna was on her feet just as fast. She saw what Sirena carried and her eyes widened. Then her hand fell to her belt and they narrowed.

"Give that back," Thianna demanded.

Sirena waved the horn in triumph.

"Make me, cousin," she said.

Karn's team was holding its own—he'd put Desstra up against anyone and he had the magical advantage of Whitestorm, but he had seen Thianna and Sirena crash. The Keras Guard had as well, and so both groups were disengaging from each other to attempt to work their way toward the frost giant.

"Thianna's in trouble again," he said. "We've got to help her."

"Why?" said the minotaur. "She has bought us a chance to escape."

Karn looked at the bull boy. He was brash and noisy, but he was brave and strong too. He had come to appreciate those qualities in someone else.

"You have to help *me* escape," Karn said. "Those were the terms of the bet. So you have to help me however I choose to go about it. And I chose to help Thianna."

Asterius blew out an angry blast of hot air. He didn't

like that at all. But Karn knew the minotaur would stick to his word.

"Jasius, you haven't made any promises," said Karn, glancing down toward the young dwarf. "You don't have to come if you don't . . ." His voice trailed off. The dactyl had vanished. Karn looked around, but there was no sight of him. "Where's Jasius?" he asked.

"What's it matter?" said the minotaur. "He isn't any good in a fight. Remember, he hid under a table, and that was only a *food* fight."

"It matters," said Karn, though he wasn't sure he could say why. But the dwarf was well and truly gone. And the fighting had intensified. "But Thianna needs us now," he said.

Thianna swung at Sirena, but the smaller girl was an even far better warrior than she had suspected. The Calderan blocked blow after blow.

"Just give me the horn," the giantess said, scowling. "Then I promise I'll be out of your hair forever."

"If only it were that easy," Sirena answered. "But the die is cast."

The wyvern hovered in the air above them, flapping awkwardly and trying to find a way to descend so Thianna could mount. But the soldiers harried the reptile at every attempt it made to land. And more were racing to join the fight. It wasn't looking good. Regardless of Thianna's size advantage, they would soon overwhelm her with numbers. She was dodging a spear when the tenor of the guards' shouts changed. Thianna gasped in surprise as a woman went hurling through the air, tossed aloft by the horns of a minotaur.

Karn and Desstra were right behind Asterius, racing to her aid. Thianna felt a flash of pride, but also regret. She had hoped that Karn was on his way to safety. There was no way they'd all get away now. And even if the wyvern managed to fly her out, it could never carry the Norrønur as well. She wasn't sure how she felt about leaving the elf, but she knew she wasn't deserting Karn now that he was in the thick of it.

She risked a glance upward to where the wyvern teetered uncertainly.

Get out of here, she thought at it.

What about you?

No sense in us both being captured. You can't help me.

But maybe that wasn't true. Maybe there was something it could do.

Wait, maybe you can.

She leapt into the air, catching the wyvern about the neck. Unbalanced, it teetered and began to fall earthward.

Let go! it cried in her mind, beating its wings furiously but losing height. *I can't carry you!*

"I don't want you to," Thianna whispered to it. "I just need you to carry a message."

The wyvern fought to stay aloft as the giantess spoke rapidly in what she hoped was an ear hole. She couldn't risk their mind-to-mind communication. Sirena held the horn, which meant she would overhear if Thianna traded thoughts with the reptile. But good old-fashioned speech was another matter. When Thianna had packed as much information into as few words as she could manage, she let go. Freed of her weight, the wyvern shot into the sky, and the frost giant fell to earth.

CHAPTER SEVEN

Slip and Slide

Thianna watched the wyvern soar into the night sky. Then angry Calderan forces moved to encircle her. But as they approached, the roar of an angry bull filled the air.

Asterius charged. Head down and bellowing exactly like Thianna would have expected a bullheaded person to behave, the minotaur plowed into an unwary soldier, catching her from behind. The boy lifted his head, tossing the poor woman high in the air. Then he swung his horns to drive back another.

Thianna shook off the surprised soldiers and ran to meet Karn and Desstra.

"I didn't make it," she said.

"Yes, we already know that," said Desstra. "So not very helpful."

"But what do we do now?" Karn asked. "We need a new plan to get out of the city."

"I've got an idea," Thianna replied. "Follow me."

Together they fought their way free of the soldiers. They ran through the streets, Asterius emitting a deep, loud roar every so often.

"Can't you shut him up?" the giantess asked.

"Not so far," Karn replied. "Where are we going?"

"New plan," she said. "Something I spotted from the tower. Do you remember the ride we took into Gordasha?"

Karn did. They had blasted in on an ice sled through the pipes of an aqueduct.

"Fastest, wildest ride of my life," he said.

"Well," Thianna continued, "this will be even more fun."

"That doesn't fill me with confidence," said Karn, but he was smiling.

Thianna steered them toward an open square where a large fountain spouted water into the air. The water fell into a pool, then flowed out in a stone-carved channel that wound through the city. Karn instantly knew what she had in mind. His stomach twisted in anticipation.

"Who's first?" said the frost giant. Then Thianna reached into the fast-moving stream and muttered the hoarfrost chant. A block of ice quickly formed atop the water, like a single-occupancy fishing skiff. Beside her the minotaur watched her magic in amazement.

"Ah, our first volunteer," Thianna said.

"What? No!" protested Asterius, but the giantess had already hoisted him onto the block.

"Hang on tight," she said, letting go.

"But my bottom's cold!" the bull boy objected. Then the impromptu little boat shot away, carrying the minotaur swiftly down the stream. His shout of alarm rang loudly in the night.

"You're next," said Thianna, with the second ice boat already fashioned. "I'm not going to enjoy this, am I?" said Karn.

"This ride is open-air," she said with a grin. "Much more exciting than shooting through a brick pipe. See you on the other side, Norrønboy." She gave Karn a slap on the back to send him off, then turned to Desstra. "Guess that leaves you, Long Ears."

"I'm surprised you remembered me," the dark elf replied. But as she took her place, shouting emerged from the street beyond. The soldiers had caught up with them. Desstra glanced their way, hesitating. With Karn and Thianna separated, she wasn't sure which one to protect.

"Go, go," said Thianna. "I'll be right behind you."

Thianna slipped into the stream just as her cousin came around the corner. She waved a merry goodbye. The Keras Keeper swore and ran after the giantess. Dead Ymir's head, thought Thianna, the girl was fast!

"Come on," Thianna urged her little boat. Ahead in

the watercourse she saw Desstra disappearing through a hole at the base of the first of the intercity walls.

Sirena made a grab for Thianna and missed.

The giantess started to voice a witty goodbye when her cousin leapt again. This time she sailed into Thianna and almost knocked her off the ice boat. Sirena clutched her tightly, refusing to be dislodged. Then it was their turn to pass under the wall.

The slope of the watercourse tipped severely as the stream hit the steep embankment. They tottered in the air for an instant, Thianna and Sirena sharing a look of panic. Then their craft tilted nearly forty-five degrees, and they were racing down the hill.

The wind blasted Karn in the face as he fought to stay atop the slippery frozen block. He actually left the watercourse entirely when stepped cascades sent him briefly airborne. He landed with a splash, feeling like his stomach wanted to flee his body through his mouth.

At the forefront Asterius continued to holler, but the tone of his yells seemed to have shifted to be more excited, less terrified. The minotaur was enjoying the ride.

Karn saw Desstra behind him. The elf seemed to be having the hardest time of it, clinging to her craft for dear life. Then he spotted wyverns in the air over her head. It was going to be close!

Karn passed a befuddled man standing with a clay jar, blinking at the strange procession speeding along his source of drinking water.

"Be healthy!" Karn called to the man.

"Uh, good fortune," the man replied, confused.

Then the watercourse veered to the right. They were heading to the southernmost tip of the island, near the south gate and the land bridge to freedom. Though what they would do to outpace the wyverns when he arrived, Karn hadn't a clue. Figuratively and literally, he would cross that bridge when he came to it.

Thianna and Sirena battled atop the ice craft. Neither had time to draw a weapon, so they swung at each other with their fists. Each tried to stay aboard while shoving the other off the side. The little boat rocked precariously as the two girls struggled.

Ahead of them Desstra watched as the cousins fought. The houses were thick enough here that the wyverns could only be glimpsed intermittently between the buildings, but they'd be upon them soon enough. If Thianna fell off, she'd be lost.

The elf looked to Karn. He had a strong head start. And he wasn't the one the Calderans were truly after. Karn was smart too. He'd reach the lower city and either escape or hide until he could get away. The stubborn frost giant was in the most trouble. Desstra made up her mind.

She leapt nimbly into the air, spreading her legs to land atop the sides of the watercourse. Her little boat flew away without her. Desstra bent at the knees and raised her hands in anticipation, watching Thianna and Sirena zooming toward her.

She'd have to time it perfectly.

Desstra hurled herself at Sirena. She struck the Calderan hard, and the two of them fell splashing into the water. They slid down the hill, but without the ice raft they weren't moving as fast.

The elf pushed away from the girl and sat up in time to see the frost giant's confused look as she realized what Desstra had done. Thianna was safe.

No, the frost giant was standing on the ice block, looking back in puzzlement. And the last of the intercity walls loomed ahead.

"Duck, duck!" Desstra shouted, but Thianna couldn't hear her. She slammed into the wall as her craft sped under it. Thianna fell to the edge of the watercourse and rolled to the street. Desstra cursed out loud at Thianna's stupidity. Her sacrifice had been for nothing. Neither of them was getting away.

Thianna groaned and clambered to her feet.

"Stupid, stupid, stupid!" she berated herself. The wall had knocked the wind out of her, but she'd struck it flat-on. It didn't seem like anything was broken, though it had certainly hurt. Worse, she had almost gotten away. Even worse, she had Desstra to thank for it. If the elf hadn't surprised her with that stunt, she would have seen the wall coming. Of course, Sirena might have gotten the better of her if Desstra hadn't sacrificed herself. "It was still a dumb thing to do," Thianna said, unwilling to concede the point.

At any rate, now she'd have to go help the elf. She just needed a minute to recover. She shook her head to clear it and leaned back against the wall. The stones shifted behind her as a section of the brickwork fell inward. The portion of the floor she stood on tilted upward, pitching her over. Then Thianna was sliding again, through the newly revealed hidden doorway and down into the dark heart of the island.

"You stupid, pale"—Sirena hesitated, glaring at the girl who had ruined her victory—"whatever you are!"

"Elf," said Desstra.

"I don't care," the Calderan shot back. "You're not going to be around long enough for it to matter."

Sirena charged at the elf, but Desstra was faster. She twirled aside, thrusting out a leg and shoving with her shoulder. Sirena was sent splashing face-first into the trough of water. She sputtered in rage as the current carried her downstream. Desstra didn't wait to continue the fight. She needed to get to Thianna, and quickly. But the direct route wasn't the best. If there was one thing the dark elf knew, it was how to hide in the shadows. She ducked into an alley before Sirena could recover. Then, moving swiftly but silently, she worked her way to where the giantess had fallen.

But there was no sign of the big girl. Had she managed to get away? In the moonslight it was easy for the dark elf to spot Thianna's large footprints in the dirt. They traced a path to a section of bare wall. Thianna had rested here. But where had she gone next? The footsteps didn't continue. The giantess was a good climber. She might have gone up, though there wasn't much in the way of handholds.

The elf's ears twitched. Company was coming. Reluctantly she moved back into the shadows, settling in and holding perfectly still. If she didn't move, no one would find her unless she wanted them to.

Sirena came around a corner. Desstra repressed a smile at the girl's drenched clothing. Her own fire salamander leathers were more resistant. Water beaded on them and shed quickly. Then the elf heard the beat of wings and saw two wyverns land beside the girl.

"Don't let her get away!" Sirena yelled. "Get back into the air and go!"

"She's in the lower city now," one soldier protested. "It will be like looking for a pebble in the sand."

"She's seven feet tall, you moron!" Sirena replied. "Go!"

The soldiers rose back into the air. Thianna's cousin

scowled as they departed, then ran in a direction Desstra assumed was toward the next gate.

The elf waited to be sure the coast was clear, then she rose, determined to search the wall some more for any clue to Thianna's whereabouts. But then her ears twitched again and she hesitated. What she had thought was a potted plant on the side of the street had just moved. Were her sharp eyes playing tricks on her? Surely not. As she watched, the clay pot lifted off the ground and the plant shuffled a few feet farther down the road. Then it settled down and sat still. A heartbeat later, the plant again shuffled a few more paces. Desstra was intrigued. She crept forward, moving soundlessly, and approached the ambulating vegetable. When it began to walk again, she tapped it on the shoulder.

"Yikes!" the plant yelped. Then its leaves rearranged, some of them parting to reveal a face and others settling into the shape of Thican-style clothing. Desstra found herself looking at a young girl. Her skin was patterned like tree bark, while hornlike branches grew from a head that also sported long, slender green leaves in place of hair. The elf saw that the girl had camouflaged herself by fluffing out the leaves of her clothing and brushing her hair across her face.

"You're a hostage princess," said Desstra. The plant girl didn't answer. She cast her eyes around looking for a way to flee, eyes large with panic. "I don't want to hurt you," the elf continued. "My name is Desstra. I'm looking for a way out of here."

The girl relaxed a little at this.

"My name is Daphne," she said. "I'm looking for a way out too."

"Forgive me for asking," said Desstra, "but are you a tree?"

"No," Daphne replied with a nervous laugh. "I'm a dryad. Though some people call us 'tree folk.'"

"I've heard there are dryads in Araland," said Desstra. "That's the country next door to Norrøngard. But I've never met one before."

"I've heard that too," said Daphne, "though we lost touch with the dryads of Araland a long time ago. But—if you don't mind my asking—what are you?"

"I'm an elf," said Desstra.

"But I thought elves were more glam . . . ," Daphne trailed off. Desstra's eyes narrowed.

"Glamorous? Beautiful? Enchanting?"

"I'm sorry, have I offended you?"

"My scowl's not giving it away?" replied the elf. Daphne looked like she wanted to disappear back into her camouflage. "No, it's all right. You're thinking of the wood elves. Or the light elves. Or maybe the sea elves— they've got green hair like yours. Well, not exactly like yours. But I'm a dark elf. I guess we got the short end of the elf stick."

Daphne tilted her head in puzzlement.

"Aren't you're awfully pale to be dark?"

"It's because we live in the dark," Desstra explained. "And our hair is dark. And our eyes. And, well, other people don't really like us very much. Not that we've given them much reason to. Anyway, we call ourselves the Svartálfar, "the swart elves.""

"Doesn't *swart* mean dark too?"

"All right, look," said Desstra irritatedly. "It's not important. What are you doing here?"

"I'm looking for the passageway," said Daphne, then clamped her lips tight, bringing a small hand to cover her mouth.

"There is a hidden door!" Desstra exclaimed. "I knew it. Come with me!" She dragged the protesting dryad to the wall. "It's got to be right here. Show me."

"What?" said the dryad. "No, I don't know anything about that."

Desstra's eyes narrowed. "My friend—okay, we're not exactly friends—but Thianna disappeared right on this spot, and I'm going to find her. So show me what you know."

"I don't know anything!" whined Daphne.

"Tell me," hissed Desstra.

The dryad quaked at her anger. "You said you weren't going to hurt me."

"I said I didn't want to. That's not the same thing!"

Desstra pushed the girl against the wall. "Now show me where the hidden door is!"

"I don't know about any door. I'm looking for a passageway," Daphne wailed.

"Quiet," said the elf. "You'll bring the guards back." She turned to the wall. "It's got to be here somewhere." Desstra ran her hands over the brickwork. Tricks and traps were her specialty. If anyone could find a hidden switch or lever, it was her. "Ah," she said, her fingers finding a loose brick that shifted at her touch. "Here you are."

"Here is what?" asked the dryad.

"This," replied the elf. She depressed the brick, which slid back into the wall. Then the wall itself fell inward, a section of the floor at their feet rising up. Desstra and Daphne were pitched into the opening. Then they were both crying out as they tumbled into the darkness.

Karn sent a spray of water into the air as he slid to a halt in a small pond. The ice raft was very nearly melted. Fortunately, he was at the foot of the hill, near the gates to the land bridge. Karn splashed his way to shore, where Asterius was just climbing onto the land.

"We need to find a place to hide," he said to the minotaur prince, "until Thianna and the others get here." Karn looked up the slope. Desstra should have been right behind him, Thianna on her tail. The fact that neither of his friends was in sight worried him. Had they been captured?

"No hiding," snorted the minotaur. "Fighting! Escaping! Not hiding."

Karn sighed. Was the bull boy always going to be this much trouble? Then he noticed the wyverns overhead. They were still searching the city, but they weren't following the watercourse. Obviously the soldiers thought Thianna had abandoned it.

"They think she's left the stream for the city streets," he observed.

"Then she's fine," said Asterius. "Searching for her in the city will be like looking for a flea in the straw."

"We need to be the same," Karn replied.

"I don't like fleas," said Asterius. He swished his tail involuntarily.

Karn pointed to a nearby building. "We can hide there and wait to see if Thianna and Desstra make it down."

"No!" Asterius stamped a hoof. "I will go to my father in Labyrinthia. When he hears how I was attacked by the Calderan soldiers, he will raise an army and come back!"

"We wait for Thianna," said Karn.

"We escape!" demanded Asterius.

"Wait!"

"Escape!"

"Honestly," spat Karn. "You're as stubborn as a—as a—"

Asterius glared at him.

"Go ahead," the boy growled. "Say it!"

"As a frost giant!" yelled Karn.

The minotaur blinked.

"All right, I admit, I wasn't expecting that."

Karn glanced hopefully at the watercourse. Still no sign of his friends. He didn't want to acknowledge it, but it didn't look like they were coming. Their plan to seize the horn had failed. He needed new options.

He looked at the bull boy. Asterius was strong and eager for a fight. Were all minotaurs like that? Asterius had been the cause of the food fight with the other royal hostages, too proud to get along. But if the minotaurs could be convinced to stand alongside others, maybe Thica would rise up against the Calderans.

"Look," said Karn, "will your father really help you?"

"I'm sure of it," said the minotaur.

"Then I don't mind going to him. But, um, let's just take a moment to collect ourselves before we escape."

"That's okay," said the minotaur. "As long as we're clear that we're not hiding."

They reached the building, which was a long, rectangular one-story structure. Sliding open a large door, Karn saw that the interior was dark. There was a familiar earthy smell, and something crunched under their feet. Karn reached into his shirt and pulled out the phosphorescent stone that he wore on a necklace. He shook it to life and it cast light around the room. They were in a stable. He could see the stalls running along each wall. The floor was littered with hay but also with grass seeds and vegetable scraps. The hay, although it should have been in a feeder, was clearly for horses, but why someone would strew chicken food in a stable Karn couldn't imagine.

He walked to one of the stalls, lifting the glowing stone to shine its light inside.

"What in the world is that?" Karn said. Unfortunately, his light woke the stall's occupant.

"Kikiriki!" it crowed.

The rest of the stable occupants woke up too. Suddenly, they were all crowing and neighing, poking their muzzles out of their stables and beating their feathered wings, stamping hooves and scratching in the dirt with claws. The noise was deafening.

"Now can we escape?" said Asterius.

The elf and the dryad slid to a halt at the bottom of the slide, tumbling onto a hard stone floor. They were in a cavern, a natural basalt cave. Desstra picked herself up, then noticed that Daphne was crawling on her hands and knees. The girl was feeling her way gingerly with her palms and quivering in fear.

"You can't see in the dark," the elf realized.

"You can?" said the dryad in amazement. She began questing toward the sound of Desstra's voice. "It's pitch-black. Where are we?"

"You tell me. This was the hidden door you were searching for."

"No, it wasn't," objected Daphne. "I told you, that's something else. Please, I can't see a thing."

Desstra studied the girl. She appeared terrified. And helpless. She didn't want to be burdened with the dryad, but she couldn't just leave her groping in the dark. She sighed in exasperation. Karn and Thianna were Desstra's responsibility. Not this leafy plant girl at her feet. Now that she was one of the "good guys," was she going to have to help every unfortunate case that came along?

"All right, calm down," said the dark elf, assisting Daphne to her feet. "I've got you. I've got you. We're in a cavern—no surprise there—but I see a tunnel leading out of it." She glanced down at the shards of clay at the girl's feet. "Also, I think you broke your pot in the fall."

"It isn't mine," said Daphne. "I was just borrowing it. You don't think I walk around with that thing around my ankles all the time, do you?"

"I don't know what tree people do," said Desstra. "You could eat dirt for all I know. You don't eat dirt, do you?"

"No, of course not," said Daphne. "Don't be silly. We just stick our feet in it from time to time." She wriggled her toes at a pleasant memory.

Grumbling, Desstra led the dryad toward the exit. The girl was clinging tightly to her arm, and the elf already felt hampered by her presence. She shifted Daphne's grip.

"Take my hand. I'll get us out of here, but I've got to find Thianna first, and I can't do that with you tugging on me. Fortunately, there's only one way she could have gone."

The tunnel went mostly northward, descending as it did so. Despite having to lead the blind surface dweller, Desstra found that she was breathing easily and a smile had come to her face. It felt wonderful to be under the earth again. She had grown up in the caverns of the Svartálfaheim Mountains of Norrøngard and, apart from the fact that her own kind probably wanted her dead, she was enjoying this taste of home. Not so much the girl beside her.

"Not having fun?" she asked.

"I miss the woods," Daphne replied. "The great forests are all in the west and north. They don't have anything like them here. The trees don't grow very tall in the south, and they cut down most of them anyway."

"I bet that goes over well with your kind," said Desstra. "Why do the tree folk put up with it?"

"Thican fire," said Daphne. "What choice do you have when you're made of wood?"

"I can see your point," said Desstra.

"I wish I could see anything," said the girl. Despite herself, the elf laughed at this, and the dryad laughed as well.

"Come on, tree girl, let's get you out of here. Then we can see what trouble Thianna's gotten herself into now."

CHAPTER EIGHT

Cock's Crow

"What are they?" marveled Karn.

The creatures were the strangest things he had ever seen. They had the front half of a horse, including the forelegs, but it was attached to a rooster's wings, tail, and legs. They had yellow plumage, but their horse's coats and manes varied in color.

"They're called hippalektryons," said Asterius. "And they're fast!" he added enthusiastically.

Karn heard shouts from outside the stable walls.

"Good," he said. "We're going to need fast."

He turned to the hippalektryon in front of him. Its hair was a lustrous black with a gorgeous yellow mane that blended smoothly into its feathers.

"Okay, nice horse-rooster," he said. "Don't bite me. Or peck me. Or whatever you do."

He opened the stall and guided the animal forward. Although its front looked like a horse, it cocked its head at him in a birdlike gesture. Taking this as his cue, Karn scooped some of the chicken feed off the floor and held it for the animal. It nibbled from his palm appreciatively. He let it eat for just a few moments.

"Sorry, no time for a long meal," Karn said. "We need to be on our way."

He steadied himself on a wing, then hopped up onto the creature's back. It trotted toward the doorway.

"Don't just stand there!" Karn yelled to Asterius, who was still gaping at the creatures in admiration. "Come on!" Then he patted the hippalektryon. "At least you seem to know what you're doing."

Karn and Asterius galloped out of the stable just as two soldiers were approaching the door. The women fell back, surprised. The bull boy whooped enthusiastically. Karn didn't think he'd be satisfied until he'd alerted the whole city to their location.

Instinctively, they steered toward the south gate to the land bridge. In their wake, the soldiers shouted ineffectually at them to stop. The ride was surprisingly smooth given the creature's mismatched legs. Karn couldn't suppress a grin. Growing up, most of his riding had been in ox-drawn carts. This was something else entirely!

As they neared the southernmost exit from Caldera, Karn's expression soured. Five soldiers stood blocking their path, and the portcullis was lowered for the evening.

"We're cut off!" he hollered to his companions.

"Keep going!" shouted Asterius.

"The gate is down!" Karn yelled. "What are you going to do, ram it?"

He pictured the minotaur battering at the steel bars with his thick skull. No matter how stubborn Asterius was, the results wouldn't be pretty.

"Trust me," Asterius shouted, "I know what I'm doing!" Then the minotaur dug his heels into his hippalektryon's flank. The mount responded with a burst of speed. Karn did the same, and his own hippalektryon quickened its pace.

The soldiers spotted them and raised weapons and shields. Karn was close enough now to see the anxiety on their faces. He shared it. The hippalektryons weren't slowing down or turning aside.

Karn looked at the array of sharpened swords. They might barrel the guards over, but they would be skewered in the process, then smash against the gate. And still the hippalektryons ran. Karn forced himself not to close his eyes.

Suddenly the hippalektryons sprang on their rooster

legs. They rose into the air, beating their wings in an ungainly manner. Karn and Asterius sailed over the wall.

"They can fly?" asked Karn, laughing through his amazement.

"Only short distances," replied Asterius.

Flapping, clucking, and neighing, the hippalektryons soared for a few hundred yards, then came down heavily in the dust of the land bridge.

"Kikiriki!" his mount crowed in triumph.

Karn patted its neck.

"I know just how you feel," he said. He had never ridden any animal that could move so fast. Not the wyverns. Not even the dragon Orma. He looked at the rocky ground racing under his feet and felt a wave of dizziness.

"Hippalektryon Riding: lesson one," he said. "Don't look down."

"Nervous?" shouted Asterius beside him.

"Yes!" Karn called back.

"Don't fall off, then."

"Lesson two," said Karn. Then he worried about the probable lesson three—fighting on a horse-rooster. He didn't doubt they'd experience that lesson soon enough. And so, despite holding on for dear life to the neck of the hippalektryon, he risked a glance back at the city. He wasn't surprised to see a cloud of dust rising into the air, and under it four mounted soldiers in pursuit.

"We've got company," he said.

"And they're gaining," replied the minotaur.

"They know how to ride these things," said Karn. "We're just learning."

The Norrønur looked at the terrain ahead, searching for any features he could use to their advantage. Asterius was leading them southwest. The foothills of the enormous central mountain range were to their right, open grasslands to their left, and straight ahead only low-lying hills.

"They'll overtake us on flat ground," he said. "We're outnumbered and out-armed." He pointed to the foothills of the mountains on their right. "We head there. It'll even the odds and maybe give us a chance to hide."

"Who put you in charge?" said Asterius, but the minotaur was already steering his mount in the direction Karn suggested.

At the speed the hippalektryons were moving, the companions reached the foothills just as the first burst from a Thican fire lance blasted a boulder beside them. Karn's mount squawked and veered sharply, nearly slinging him off. Karn clung tightly to the animal's neck.

"Don't stop!" he yelled. Karn hoped that the speed and the uneven ground would combine to make aiming the long lances difficult. "Faster!" he cried. The hippalektryon must have understood, because it let out another cry of "Kikiriki" and tore forward.

At these speeds, the terrain was changing almost faster than Karn could blink. They entered a valley strewn with boulders. The moon and her satellite above cast strange patterns of light and shadow. The northern boy set his mouth in a grim smile. The game board had just become more interesting.

"Weave and dodge!" he shouted as another burst of flame arced over his head. Feathers singed at the tips of the hippalektryon's wings. Karn steered as close to the rocks as he dared, whipping around the stones with only a tight margin of error.

A Calderan soldier appeared on his left. She smiled evilly at him as she brought her fire lance to bear. Karn drew Whitestorm and the woman laughed. He wasn't close enough for a sword to be any good. Or so she thought. Karn hurled his father's blade at the soldier's face. Surprised, she batted at it and the sword fell away. Her expression said she didn't understand why he would throw his weapon away so needlessly. He smiled in return and pointed. The woman looked up just in time to see the boulder. She struck it at speed, feathers flying everywhere.

"Whitestorm!" Karn shouted over his shoulder, and was rewarded when the sword returned to his grasp. Then he had to duck quickly as his mount ran under a large slab of rock that lay at an angle across a pile of boulders. Behind him, he heard a squawk that suggested another soldier hadn't been so lucky. Sometimes being the fugitive had its advantages. It was easier to run than to aim, chase, and steer all at the same time.

The terrain changed again. They were riding through

what looked like an abandoned city nestled in a broad valley. Karn noticed several buildings that looked like dilapidated sports arenas. Then his attention was diverted by Asterius's bellowing.

A soldier was chopping at the minotaur with her sword, but the boy was fending her off with deft slashes of his horns. Then, as Karn watched, Asterius launched himself off of his hippalektryon onto his opponent's. He and the soldier wrestled atop the squawking, braying mount. Then both combatants tumbled to the ground.

Karn steered his animal into a tight turn, and went back to help. He screeched to a halt and dismounted. Asterius had the soldier pinned down.

Karn removed the woman's weapons.

"Let her up," he instructed.

"But . . . ," objected Asterius.

"She's the last of them. And she's disarmed." Karn looked at the struggling soldier. "You're outnumbered. Give me your word you'll head back to Caldera and I'll let you go." He looked around. "Or we could tie you to a rock here and you can hope one of your friends finds you in a couple of days."

The soldier looked around at the ruins, made ghostly in the moonlight. The prospect of being left there obviously didn't appeal to her.

"I swear by Sestia, goddess of war," she said. "I will return to Caldera."

"Sounds good to me," said Karn. He motioned for

Asterius to let the soldier rise to her feet. She glared at the bull, then turned and mounted her hippalektryon.

"We'll be back," she said.

"We won't be here," said Karn.

The woman kicked her heels into her mount's sides and streaked away. In seconds, she had vanished.

"Well, that was fun," said Karn. He looked around at their surroundings, studying the ruins. It was easy to imagine creatures lurking amid the crumbling stones, watching them from the shadows. Karn shivered. "Let's get out of here," he said.

Regrettably, the hippalektryons seemed to have other ideas.

Digging his heels into its flanks didn't produce any result. The mount stood steadfast and refused to move.

"Why'd they stop?" he asked.

"Because they're stupid," Asterius replied unhelpfully.

Then Karn noticed his mount's hind legs. The oversize rooster feet were clawing at the dirt. He had grown up caring for chickens at Korlundr's Farm. He recognized this gesture immediately.

"They're hungry," he said. "Moving as fast as they do surely burns a lot of energy. That's the price of their speed. You get a quick burst, then you have to fill them back up."

Unfortunately, they had left Caldera in too great a hurry to grab saddles and bridles, let alone hay or chicken feed. Karn was unhopeful as he looked at the rocky soil.

"Not much for them here," he said. Karn struggled again to get his mount to move, but the hippalektryon wouldn't budge. "It looks like we're stuck until we find some feed." He looked around at the ruins. "Any idea what this place is, anyway?"

"I know," a sultry voice purred.

Karn closed his eyes briefly before he looked up. He'd met a dragon the last time he'd taken refuge in a ruined city. Who knows what this was going to be? He turned to face the speaker.

"Welcome to the Sanctuary of Empyria. Or what remains of it, anyway."

Sitting on a nearby rooftop basking in moonsbeams was a bizarre creature. It had the haunches of a lion but the face of a woman. Her long black hair fell down to shoulders that appeared human but became a lion's forelegs before ending in paws.

"Pardon me for asking," said Karn, "but are you by any chance a manticore?"

"Filthy beasts," said the creature, hissing in disgust. She swished a very lionlike tail, perhaps to show that she lacked a manticore's scorpionlike stinger.

"She's a sphinx," said Asterius. "And we're in serious trouble."

CHAPTER NINE

The Hammerfist

"This is me getting impatient," said Thianna to Jasius.

"Just a little farther now," said the beardless young dactyl. "We're almost there, and believe me, everybody wants to meet you."

Thianna grumbled and tried to get comfortable, but it was difficult. She was riding on a litter being carried by a small band of dwarves. And it was hardly a smooth ride. They jostled her up and down while a chorus of curses and complaints issued from beneath her chair.

When Thianna had first tumbled through the hidden door into the cavern, Jasius had been waiting with a torch to greet her. Then he had whistled and more dactyls had come scurrying out of the dark, bearing the litter along with gifts of food. Jasius had promised her answers if only she'd come with them.

Beneath her, one of the dactyls stumbled on a stone in their path.

"I can walk, you know," she said.

"It's no trouble," said the dwarf. Then he grunted. "Actually, it's a little trouble."

"I told you she was big," said Jasius. "It's your fault you didn't bring more dactyls." To Thianna he said, "Go on, try a grape."

Feeling somewhat awkward, the frost giant bit into the little purple fruit. Sweet juice squirted into her mouth. She gobbled several more.

"Good, yes?" said Jasius, smiling. "Bet you don't get those where you're from."

"We don't," said Thianna. "Not much grows in Ymiria, though we do trade with the humans for fruit." She ate another grape. "Strawberries, bilberries, lingonberries, cloudberries."

"How did you get so big on berries?" asked one of her litter bearers. "What else do you eat?"

"I hope it's not dwarves," said another.

"I have had apples," said the giantess. "Cheese. Occasional fish. Also goat, but, um, don't tell any satyrs I said that."

There was a general muttering of agreement at the

wisdom of this. Then Jasius turned and made an exaggerated bow.

"Lady Frostborn," he said, "welcome to Caldera Under Caldera."

Thianna was snickering at the title of Lady when the litter passed through an elaborately carved archway.

"Dead Ymir's head," she swore.

They stopped on a balcony before an enormous cavern. What must have once been stalactites and stalagmites had been expertly carved into angular columns and buttresses supporting the dome of the roof. Enormous stone faces adorned their surfaces or gazed sternly out from the walls. A river of lava flowed slowly in the depths below, twisting amid buildings that rose past the height of where they stood on the balcony. The lava bathed everything in a red glow. Bridges ran between the various structures at multiple points with staircases leading up and down everywhere Thianna looked. She saw dwarves going about their lives throughout.

"This is a whole city! Right here! Under the ground!" The giantess was in awe that such a place existed. Smiling with pride, her escort allowed her to briefly take in the view, then the litter moved forward, bearing her out onto a narrow walkway that wound toward a large stone palace at the far end of the cavern.

Thianna gripped the sides of her chair tightly. The dactyls were showing signs of exhaustion, and she didn't want to be tipped into the lava flow beneath. She could take heat better than a full frost giant, but she drew the line at magma.

They reached the palace and finally the litter stopped. The dactyls lowered it so that Thianna could step off.

"Jasius," she asked, "where are we?"

The young dwarf puffed up his chest.

"We are in the True City, and this is the realm of King Herakles Hammerfist."

"Shh, stop complaining," said Desstra sharply. Daphne had been whining about the lack of sunlight for the past five minutes.

"I can't help it," said the dryad, stifling a yawn. "My foliage is diurnal." She patted down her leaves. They seemed to be trying to curl up around her, making it difficult for her to walk. They also gave off a rustling noise, a constant irritation to Desstra's sensitive ears. "They think it's nighttime."

"It is nighttime," said the dark elf. "Anyway, try to hold on. I see a light up ahead."

In fact, there was a warm reddish glow coming from farther down the tunnel.

"Lava flow," said the elf. Then she lifted her long ears. "But I hear voices too. Lots of them. Oh, Thianna, what have you gotten yourself into now?"

"I'm starting to see a little," said Daphne, letting go of Desstra's hand. The dark elf shook her fingers to restore blood flow. The panicky dryad had a strong grip.

"Do you think whoever it is will be friendly?" the tree girl asked.

"I wouldn't bet on it," replied Desstra. "At least, that hasn't been my experience with people who live underground."

"Maybe we should turn back?" said the dryad, looking longingly the way they had come.

"Not without Thianna. Anyway, there's no way up in that direction."

"I hate this," said Daphne. "I'm not brave. Not like you. I've been timid and fearful ever since I was a seedling."

Desstra was surprised to hear the dryad's praise. She found herself softening to the helpless tree girl.

"Being brave doesn't mean you're not afraid," the elf said. "It just means you don't let the fear stop you from doing what you have to do." She took the girl's hand again. "I'll get you out of here, I promise. But you have to do what I tell you. And for Malos Underfoot's sake, try to keep your leaves from rustling."

"Food, drink, grapes?"

King Herakles was one of the stoutest dwarves Thianna had ever seen. He was possibly even broader than he was tall. The king had an enormous aquiline nose, and his beard, oiled and curled into heavy black ringlets, dropped nearly to his sandaled feet. He wore a cape made entirely of golden links, which jingled like coins when he moved. His large hands, however, left no doubt as to why he was called Hammerfist. Even as big as she was, Thianna didn't think she would enjoy being on the receiving end of one of the king's punches.

"Cheese and spinach pie?" asked Herakles.

"No thank you," said Thianna, who wanted to understand what was going on before she accepted any more food. She still wasn't sure whether she had been rescued or kidnapped.

"Are you sure?" asked the king. "Every slice has a diamond baked inside. Some have two."

"That sounds like a good way to break a tooth."

The king frowned at her, and beside her Jasius coughed. Thianna realized she might have inadvertently insulted them. The dwarves back home were known to be a tough breed and proud of that reputation.

"Not a dwarf's tooth," she added hastily.

"Oh, of course," the king said, brightening. "I forget how soft you big folk's teeth are. No offense taken where none's intended." He gazed up at Thianna. "Well, how do you like it?"

"I haven't tasted it yet."

"No, I meant my city. Caldera Under Caldera. The True City." He spread his arms and did a complete turn, then gave a little bow.

Since no one was forcing her to do so, Thianna bowed back.

"I had no idea it was down here," she said.

"Of course not," said the king. "No nondactyl has been here in centuries. The Calderans above don't even remember it exists. They don't have a clue."

"But you live above, in the middle district of the city, don't you?"

"Yes," said Herakles. "We're the perioikoi. Noncitizen freedmen. We do their metalwork, repair their armor, sharpen their swords, and sometimes serve as auxiliary troops and military support—but for all that, they grant us no say in their government. The two queens aren't even aware there is a dactyl king. They know nothing of my underground kingdom nor the true size of the population living under their feet."

"How is that even possible?" asked Thianna.

"We all look alike to them." The king shrugged. "We take turns living on the surface, and they've never noticed that the faces of the dwarves around them keep changing. Big, stupid fools never look down at their feet." Herakles laughed and wiggled his toes.

"Why do you put up with it?" Thianna asked. "You obviously outnumber them."

"Ah yes," the king replied. "Straight to business. Good, good, good." He took Thianna's wrist in one of his large hands and led her to another chamber in his palace.

"Dactyls were here first," he told her. "In fact, it was in

these very caverns that dactyls hid the infant god Cratus the Smith, when his divine brother and sisters wanted to kill him for his deformity. We taught him to use his first anvil and hammer. Good times."

Herakles stopped before a large mosaic on the wall. It depicted a map of Thica, with cities marked out in precious stones.

"Ithonea, Naparta, Zapyrna, Creos, Labyrinthia, Lassathonia . . ." He read off the names of the Thican city-states. "Pymonia, Dendronos—they're all too far if you have to walk it. Or even sail it. The only way to control such a vast territory is to fly over it."

Thianna stepped away from the map.

"You're talking about the wyverns."

Herakles grinned.

"Sharp as a pickax you are," he said. "I'm talking about the wyverns. So here's the deal, big girl. We help you get the Horn of Osius. You use it on our behalf. Instead of Xalthea and Melantha on the twin thrones, it could be Herakles and Thianna. What do you say?"

"Me?" Thianna couldn't help but laugh at the idea of wearing a crown.

"Why not you?"

The frost giant shook her head.

"The wyverns are enslaved. Just like the helots are enslaved. It isn't right."

"Someone has to be on top," said the king. He began to pace around the room. "We've lived under their feet for too long. It's time we had our turn at the crown of the hill, so to speak. Is that such a bad thing?"

"I don't like bullies," said the giantess.

"I'm a good king," said the dwarf, puffing up his chest.

"It's a bad system," said Thianna.

"Maybe," said Herakles. "But if it collapses, the city-states will go back to fighting among themselves. I'd make a much better Sky King than the current Sky Queen. We dactyls aren't warlike by nature, but we've watched the humans mess things up for too long. It's time we had our chance."

"To mess things up?" she asked.

"Ha, funny," said Herakles. "Just think it over." He stopped in the doorway to the chamber. "You'll have time." Then he pressed a jewel set into the wall.

Thianna leapt as she heard the grinding sound of heavy stone. She wasn't fast enough. Two enormous slabs of rock slid into place. They sealed off the doorway, leaving only a slit that ran horizontally a little below waist level.

She dropped to her knees and looked through the gap. Herakles's eyes stared back at her.

"What are you doing?" she demanded.

"There's a Thican expression," the king said. "It's better to tie your donkey down than go searching for it afterward. I want what's right for my people, Thianna Frostborn. You'll stay here and stew until you agree to help me get it."

"Troll dung!" Thianna swore.

"Don't worry," said the king. "We'll send in some cheese and spinach pie. And I'll have Jasius fish out the diamonds for your soft teeth."

As it turned out, however, Thianna didn't have much of an appetite.

"But I picked the gemstones out and everything." Jasius's eyes shone with disappointment through the slit in the stone.

"I told you I'm not hungry," Thianna grunted. That wasn't entirely true. She'd actually eaten very little other than grapes. And a half giant could eat a lot. She should probably keep her strength up so that she'd be ready to escape when the opportunity presented itself.

The dwarf tossed something into her prison. It fell to the ground. Thianna, already kneeling to see through the gap, picked it up. A small, uncut precious stone.

"See?" said Jasius. "Diamond-free."

"All right," said Thianna. "Pass me the pie."

Jasius handed her a triangle-shaped wedge through the horizontal opening.

Thianna tried a bite. It had a flaky crust and was drenched in olive oil. The cheese was from goat's milk—she recognized the taste—and there were onions and spinach too. She made an appreciative noise.

"You like?" asked the dwarf hopefully. "It's called spanakopita."

"Not bad, whatever it's called," Thianna admitted. "Not so good that I'm forgiving you, though."

"I'm sorry about that," said the young dwarf. "I really did imagine I was helping. I thought you'd be thrilled with the offer. I mean, who wouldn't want to be queen?"

Thianna snorted. "Who has time for that? There's a whole world to see. Why would you want to be stuck in one place where you had to tell everybody what to do all day long, day after day. I can't think of anything more boring than being a monarch."

"Gee, when you put it that way," said Jasius. His eyes moved away from the gap. "I was looking forward to it."

Thianna stopped chewing.

"Herakles is your father?"

"Yes," said Jasius. "But I won't be king for a century at least. I don't even have my beard."

"I didn't realize." The giantess thought about that. "Hey, wait," she said. "If the Calderans don't know about the dactyl king, what were you doing with the other hostage princes and princesses?"

"I wasn't a hostage," said Jasius. "I just slipped in. Nobody notices another dactyl underfoot."

"So what were you doing there?" the giantess asked, but she jumped to the obvious conclusion before the dwarf could respond. "You were after me from the start, weren't you?"

For an answer, a slice of spanakopita slid through the gap.

Thianna took the pastry wedge.

"You didn't have to abduct me," she said. "You could have asked. For that matter, why doesn't Herakles speak to the queens? They might feel different if they knew there was a whole city down here."

"They would feel threatened is how they'd feel," said the dwarf.

"I don't know. Melantha doesn't seem as bad as Xalthea."

"She isn't," Jasius replied, "but she's afraid of the Sky Queen too."

"Some co-monarchy if one's afraid of the other," said Thianna. "But what happens when the two queens argue?"

"Did you see that large Queen's Champion board in the Twin Palaces courtyard?" asked Jasius.

"Karn pointed it out when we arrived."

"Well, that's how they settle disputes. If one of the monarchs feels strongly enough about something, she can challenge the other to a game. Technically any citizen can challenge the queens as well. But you have to have seven supporters to play on your side, see? They figure that if you can't rally a team, your objection must not be very important, right?"

"Makes sense," said Thianna. "I guess the supporters have to be citizens, all Sky and Land soldiers?"

"Usually. Though I've heard of perioikoi being drafted into the game. They'll let us fight for them. They just don't give us a say in governing the city."

"Listen, Jasius," she said. "I was picked on my whole life."

"You?" The dwarf was surprised.

"For being short," Thianna explained with a laugh.

"You're joking."

"I'm not. I grew up with frost giants. So I know what it's like to be disregarded. I really wanted to take those giants down a peg or two. Actually I did a few times. But that made me no better than they are. Karn showed me that I could be more than that."

"Hmm," said Jasius. "You're still bigger than most."

"Not giants. Not dragons. Not trolls. But how you treat others counts for more than how tall you stand."

"Is that why you're so rude to that pale elf? Sure looks to me like you are disregarding her when she wants to help."

Thianna glowered.

"Shut up and hand me another piece of pie."

Desstra stared down at the dwarven city. There were way more people milling about than she had planned on dealing with. She had expected to find only a small group of dwarves with her friend, not an entire population.

"This complicates things," she said. "I need a distraction. We'll never get in or out otherwise."

"We have to go down there?" said Daphne beside her. "That seems like a really, really bad idea." The dryad gripped her arm again in panic.

"It's where we're going," replied the elf crossly. When they had emerged from the tunnel into the larger cavern, it had taken quite a bit of cajoling to get the fearful dryad to climb to the higher ledge where they now hid. They were in the lip of a small, natural lava tube near the ceiling of the cavern. It narrowed as it receded, so it wasn't useful as a way out, but Desstra suspected it served as a ventilation shaft. She pointed at one palatial structure in the city below. "They must be holding Thianna in that central building."

"Why do you say that?" asked Daphne.

"It has the most guards, and, well, she's a frost giant. So they're needed."

Desstra reached unconsciously for her leg sheath. She didn't have her darts on her. Nor did she have any other weapon.

"If only I had my satchel," she mused.

"Why? What's in your satchel?" asked Daphne.

"Useful things," replied the elf. "Gas bombs, smoke bombs, incendiary bombs."

"You have a thing for bombs, do you?" asked the dryad.

Desstra shrugged. "They'd come in handy now. As would some good rope."

She eyed the dryad's leaves. Daphne guessed her thoughts and stepped backward quickly.

"Don't even think it," the tree girl said.

"I've woven cord out of plant fiber before," replied the elf.

"Well, these are much too delicate, I assure you," Daphne protested. "Also, they're all I have to wear, and they take forever to grow."

"Okay, relax," said Desstra. "I'm just considering all the angles. I hate going in there naked."

"Naked is what I'd be if you plucked my leaves and wove them into ropes!"

"I got it," said the elf. "Quiet down." She motioned for the dryad to join her at the tunnel's edge. Daphne stepped forward, then stopped when her foot landed in something with a squelching noise.

"Oh gross," said the dryad. She looked down, lifting her foot gingerly from an unpleasant pile of something sticky and stinky. "I think I've stepped in fresh bat droppings," she said, her nose wrinkling in revulsion.

Desstra's ears perked up at this.

"Bat droppings?" she repeated.

"I don't know what you're so enthusiastic about," said the dryad. "It's disgusting."

"It's just what we need," said Desstra. She grabbed the tree girl's ankle, lifting her foot to look at the sole. The elf nodded, pleased with what she saw. She let go of the ankle. "Here, help me scoop up as much of that as we can get."

"Scoop?" said Daphne uncertainly. Her upper lip curled back in revulsion. "You mean with . . . with . . . with our hands?"

"I thought plants liked dirt," Desstra teased.

"I like rich, healthy soil," said the tree girl. "Not fresh bat poop."

"Well, healthy soil isn't what we need right now," said the elf.

"And bat poop is?" asked Daphne uncertainly. "This is going to save your friend?"

"Oh yes," said the elf, smiling. "I don't know that she'd say we were friends, but we're going to save her, and this is how we're going to do it—in style! Now let's get scooping."

CHAPTER TEN

Cat's Conundrum

"Manticore. Sphinx. I've got to say," said Karn, "I don't really see the difference."

"I'm not a manticore!" protested the sphinx. "We're nothing alike."

"They have lion bodies too," said Karn.

"We're nothing alike!" The sphinx lashed its tail angrily.

"They have human heads."

"We are nothing alike!" It shook its mane.

Karn thought about this.

"So you don't eat people?" he asked hopefully. The sphinx scowled.

"Well, occasionally. But otherwise, we're nothing alike!"

"I think we'll agree to disagree on that," said Karn. "But we'll be on our way—don't want to trouble you any more than we already have—and you carry on with not being a manticore."

He put a hand on his hippalektryon to steady the animal. The presence of a large feline creature seemed to be agitating its rooster half.

"Not yet," the sphinx said. "You don't get to leave here quite so easily."

"Of course not," said Karn with a resigned sigh. He dropped a hand to the pommel of his sword.

"Not that way," said the sphinx. Then she let out a roar.

Hundreds of little figures came swarming from the ruins. They burst out of doorways and climbed from holes in the ground. They clustered like birds on the rooftops. They reminded Karn of descriptions he'd heard of the ice goblins of the Ymirian.

"We're surrounded," said Asterius.

"Allow me to introduce my friends, the kobalos," said the sphinx. "They are impudent, mischievous, thieving little knaves, really, but like me, they are very fond of games."

"Games?" said Karn.

"Oh yes," replied the sphinx. "Don't you know what the Sanctuary of Empyria is?"

Karn shook his head. "Should I?" he asked.

"She's talking about an ancient neutral city," Asterius explained. He looked around with awe on his face. "Do

153

you mean *these* are the ruins of Empyria? We're *standing* in it?"

The sphinx nodded. "Centuries ago," she said, "this was the host city-state for the Empyric Games—sports competitions held every year to honor the Twelve Empyreans, the chief Thican gods and goddesses. It was quite something. The city-states of Thica were all free. Athletes came from all over to compete in tests of physical prowess." She purred in appreciation. "The games were also a way to forestall wars. The city-states channeled their rivalry into friendly competition."

"So what happened?" Karn asked.

"Timandra the Magnificent happened," said the sphinx bitterly. "She conquered the whole island-continent and founded the Thican Empire. But she didn't see a need to unite the city-states in games when they were already gathered under her banner. And then the Gordion Empire came along. Of course, now we have a new empire." She hissed in evident disgust. "I had hoped that, as in love with the past as the Calderans are, they'd get around to reinstating the games. But they seem to have forgotten us."

"Us?"

"We sphinx," she replied. "We were always the masters of ceremony. It was a great honor, and it satisfied our love of competition and challenge. The kobalos were our assistants. Referees, scorekeepers, et cetera. They love a good game as much as we do."

"I'm sorry," said Karn. "I understand. I'm a gamer my-self, though I like board games better than athletics."

"It's the challenge you appreciate, yes?" asked the sphinx. She smiled, showing two rows of very sharp teeth. "Nothing like competition and stakes to get the blood flowing."

Karn felt his stomach sinking. "We're not going to play a ball game, are we?" he asked. "Because I have a friend who is really good at knattleikr. I could run and fetch her."

"No, no," replied the sphinx. "These days we play a new kind of game. Not as physical. More of an intellec-tual challenge."

"Like Thrones and Bones or Queen's Champion?" Karn asked hopefully.

"Not so much," the feline creature replied. "Tell me, how are you with guessing riddles?"

"Riddles?" said Karn. "Is that what we're going to do? How's that work, then? We ask each other a few riddles, share a laugh, fun times, we wish each other well, and we're on our way?"

The kobalos all snickered at this. The sphinx smiled.

"Human life is short," she said. "It's good you have a sense of humor about it. Especially at the end."

"The end?" said Karn.

"Of course," she replied. "I said I only ate humans *oc-casionally*. Well, it just so happens that the specific *occasion* on which I indulge that appetite is when someone can't guess my riddles. I wouldn't want you to think I just go around feasting on humans indiscriminately. I always give them a sporting chance."

"Humans," said Karn. "Not minotaurs?"

"Hey, you're the one in charge," objected Asterius.

"Oh, now you think so," said Karn bitterly.

"So here are the rules," said the sphinx. "I ask you a riddle. You guess it, you and your friends go free. You get it wrong, or stand there gaping like an idiot for so long that I get bored, and I eat you. And probably your minotaur friend too. Sound fair?"

"No," said Karn and Asterius at the same time.

"Too bad Thica's not a democracy," said the sphinx. "Now here we go."

She leapt from the roof to land atop a nearby column. Karn noticed that the stone was actually worked into the shape of a huge foot, broken off just above the ankle. If a complete statue had once stood here, it must have been colossal, its stance striding the valley. From this new perch, the sphinx puffed out her chest and sat up straight, clearly enjoying the moment. Then she cleared her throat.

"I attract the worst and corrupt the best," she said. "They say I reside in the blood, but blood spills when I change hands." The sphinx paused to lick her lips, then she finished, "What am I?"

Asterius leaned over to whisper in Karn's ear.

"It's got to be some sort of sharp object. She said it

cuts your hand when you grab it. Say a knife, or maybe a really sharp fork."

"What's a fork?" asked Karn, softly so the sphinx wouldn't think that was his answer.

"No helping!" the sphinx chastised them.

"Believe me," the Norrønur replied, "he isn't."

"I think I'm offended by that," snorted the minotaur.

"Quiet!" said Karn and the sphinx together.

Karn thought about the things he found attractive. He wondered if any of those things could rust or decay. He wondered at what could be inside his veins and still be something you could pick up. Around him, the kobalos hopped about, chittering in annoyingly shrill voices. A few of them waved eating utensils at him in derision. Probably forks, he thought. They looked like they might be handy at mealtime but not helpful here. "Worst, best, blood, hands . . . ," he muttered.

"Time is running out," said the sphinx.

"It always is," Karn replied. He felt a burst of exasperation. "What is it with you people? There's always some draug or dragon, some secret society or imperator, who thinks his way is the only way. Do this or else. Do that or else. Just once I'd like to meet a monster or a ruler who . . ."

Karn's voice trailed off, and he smiled.

"Power," he said. "The answer to the riddle is 'power.' It attracts the worst people and it corrupts those who have it. Kings and queens pass it down their bloodline to their children, and no one ever lets it go or seizes it without a fight."

The sphinx clapped her paws.

"Very good," she said. "Excellent, really. Most impressive."

Karn was surprised.

"You're not upset I guessed your riddle?"

"Why would I be upset?" she replied.

"You don't get to eat me."

The sphinx batted her tail in irritation.

"I told you, I only do that *occasionally*. It's not like people are a favorite food or anything—that would be spanakopita, actually; the kobalos make a delicious spinach and cheese pie if you want to try some. They could whip one up in half an hour."

"No thank you," said Karn. "But—the riddle?"

"As I said, it's the challenge that's fun. I love contests of brain or brawn. I don't really care who wins or loses. It's why we sphinx were such good moderators when the Empyric Games were up and running. We're impartial. We just love watching people compete."

"Oh," said Karn, relieved that he was still alive and the sphinx seemed happy. Then he had a thought. They were heading to Labyrinthia to find allies. But maybe they could gain a few more. He held out his left hand.

"Does this ring mean anything to you?"

"Is it valuable?" asked the sphinx.

Karn shrugged. "I'm told there are other measures of its worth."

"Too bad, then, that I don't have hands," she said. "But no."

Karn was frustrated but not ready to give up.

"My friend is a prisoner of the Calderans. Will you and the kobalos help us rescue her?"

"Absolutely not," said the sphinx. "We don't get involved in local politics. We're impartial."

"We're desperate."

"Nothing doing," said the sphinx. "We could cook you some nice spanakopita instead, if you like?"

"Could you make it without the cheese?" asked Asterius hopefully.

"No," said Karn, scowling at the minotaur. "We don't need spanakopita!" He turned to the sphinx. "But maybe you have something that our hippalektryons would eat?"

"I think we could manage that," said the sphinx.

"Good," Karn replied. "The sooner we reach Labyrinthia, the sooner we can return and rescue Thianna."

CHAPTER ELEVEN

Tangled Webs

Thianna was leaning against the wall of her prison when she heard the explosions. The stone walls rocked with the force of the blasts. This was followed by lots of shouting and the sound of running feet.

She peered through the gap between the slabs. Into a familiar pair of dark eyes.

"What are you doing here?" she asked Desstra.

"I'm glad to see you too," replied the elf. "Now stand back. I'm going to blow the door."

"There's a switch on the wall, actually. You just press a jewel."

"Hmm," said the dark elf. "An explosion would be more fun."

"Didn't you already set one off?" asked the giantess.

"I set off several."

Desstra stood up, passing out of Thianna's narrow view. The frost giant heard her fumbling at the wall, then the huge stone slabs slid away with a loud grating noise.

Desstra stood leaning against the wall of the doorway with a very satisfied look on her face.

"Where's Karn?" Thianna asked.

"Last I knew, he was escaping," said Desstra.

"I thought you were protecting him."

"I was protecting you both. You needed it more."

"I told you I don't need your help."

"Yes, you're really doing a bang-up job without me, I can see. Been in this cell long?"

Thianna grunted. "It's not so bad. There's a big map on the wall, so I was brushing up on my geography. And the food here is pretty good."

"I've noticed that about Thica," said the elf. "They do feed their prisoners well. If you'd like, I can close the door again."

"No, no," said Thianna. "I think I'm ready to go."

Desstra led Thianna toward the exit. The giantess noticed the elf's palms. "What's that on your hands?"

"Bat droppings," the elf explained. "Highly explosive."

"Ah," said Thianna. "Things make sense now. It's gross, but it makes sense."

The giantess paused when she noticed the odd plant standing in one corner of the next room. She was fairly certain it hadn't been there on her way in.

As Thianna stared, the foliage of the plant relaxed, and suddenly she was staring at a strange girl with skin of bark and hair and clothing of leaves.

"Wood elf?" asked Thianna, though she didn't think so.

"There are elves made of wood?" the plant girl asked.

"This is Daphne," the elf explained. "She's a dryad. One of the hostages. She's with us."

"Great," said Thianna. "Welcome aboard. Can you fight?"

The dryad shook her head.

"I'm good at hiding," she volunteered.

A dactyl guard noticed the three girls as they emerged from the palace. He shouted to catch the attention of others who were busy battling flames. Several of the guards turned their way, brandishing hammers and axes.

"Unfortunately, I think we're through doing that," said the giantess.

King Herakles appeared, shouting, "Take the big one alive!" and suddenly Thianna found herself struggling under the weight of a pile of dwarves.

However, taking the frost giant at all was proving to be a problem. Even gripped around the legs, arms, and waist, she was managing to stumble forward. Luckily, the frost giant was also drawing the most attention, allowing Desstra to pick off Thianna's attackers. Behind the elf, Daphne quaked and tried to slip into her camouflage.

"It's a little late for hiding!" Desstra yelled.

"But never too early for a somersault," said Thianna, who dove to the ground and tumbled head over heels. She came up laughing, which was more than could be said for the unfortunate dactyls who had either been shaken off or rolled over. Thianna picked up a discarded hammer and handed it to Desstra.

"What am I supposed to do with this?" said the elf, eyeing the unfamiliar weapon. "Because if you want me to build you a longhouse, I'm a little shy of nails."

"Very funny," muttered the giantess. "It's a hammer. You hammer things with it."

Desstra adjusted her grip on the weapon, frowning skeptically.

"Just like the stupid dwarves to make a weapon without a pointy end," she muttered. "I'm really missing my darts about now."

Hastily the three girls made their way across a narrow footbridge. They allowed Daphne to take the lead, while Thianna came last. She swept her sword back and forth to keep the dactyls at bay. Below them the river of lava bubbled ominously.

"Nobody fall," Thianna advised.

"Good thing you pointed that out," said Desstra, "because otherwise that would have been my plan."

"By all means, don't let me stop you," the giantess replied.

Desstra was preparing a retort when Daphne interrupted her.

"They're cutting us off," the dryad pointed out. Sure enough, another group of dwarves were charging at them from the other side of the bridge. "Oh, this is the worst rescue ever!" she wailed.

"Let's make sure it's not the shortest," Desstra replied. She moved to take the lead, readying her hammer to engage the first of the new dactyls. Behind her, several brave dwarves rushed Thianna at once. They were being pressed from both sides, forced together into a tight knot with nowhere to go.

"We need a way out, elf," said Thianna.

Desstra looked upward, but the ceiling was far too high to offer any solutions. She glanced at the lava flow below. There was no way to go there and survive. Then she noticed a narrow ledge on a rocky wall, about fifteen feet down and ten feet out. A door set into the wall on the ledge, secured on the near side with a heavy metal bar.

"There's our way." She pointed with her free hand while bringing her hammer down on a hasty dwarf. "I can make that. Thianna, I'm sure you can. Daphne?"

"You don't have to tell me twice," the dryad replied. Without waiting for further instruction, she leapt from the bridge. Thianna drew in her breath as she watched the arc of the girl's fall. The dryad wasn't going to make the ledge. Then, to her and Desstra's wonderment, two large leaves spread from under Daphne's arms. They caught the air like wings. Buoyed by her foliage, Daphne sailed the rest of the way to land safely on the ledge.

Thianna shoved a dwarf away and turned an amazed look on Desstra.

"You didn't tell me she could fly!" she exclaimed.

"I didn't know. Anyway, that was more of a glide."

"Well, it's our turn," said Thianna.

Desstra nodded. The giantess didn't hesitate. She leapt across the gap, landing heavily on the ledge below. Her impact dislodged a few stones, which fell splashing into the lava.

The dark elf hesitated. The distance looked farther than she'd first imagined. Beside her, the dactyls seemed as daunted as she did. They paused, watching their chief quarry waving at them from the ledge below. Then they realized they could still trap the elf, and they reached for her.

Desstra sprung into the air. She glided across the gap, the lava hissing far below her feet. And fell shy of the ledge.

This is how it ends, she thought.

Thianna caught her and pulled her to safety. The two girls stared at each other for a second. Then Thianna released her and turned to unbar the door.

"Oh, I wouldn't go that way!" King Herakles shouted down to them from above.

"We're not asking you to!" yelled the frost giant.

"No, I mean, I wouldn't go that way *if I were you,*" the dwarf monarch corrected himself.

"We got it," snapped Desstra. "But you're not us."

Thianna pulled the door open. They gazed into a dark lava tube, which led downward.

"We barred the north exit for a reason," said the king.

"So it's an exit, then, is it?" said Thianna.

"A curse on my big mouth," said Herakles when he realized his mistake. "Still, it's really in your best interest that you don't go that way. Believe me."

"Maybe we should listen to him," suggested Daphne.

"You can stay if you want," said Thianna. "I've got places to be."

She marched into the darkness. Desstra followed. The dryad hesitated, and then with a shudder she hurried after the two girls.

"There's a light up ahead," said Desstra.

The going had been extremely slow, with the elf having to lead both Thianna and Daphne through the pitch-darkness. The frost giant had stubbornly tried to walk on her own, but after the third time she struck a wall or bumped her head on a low arch, she relented and let Desstra lead her. Daphne clung to the elf's other arm, her bark nails once again gripping Desstra's bare flesh too tightly.

"I don't see anything," said Thianna.

"You will in a second. It looks like they've carved shafts to let light in."

"Why just at this end?" asked the giantess.

"They probably did it throughout," replied the elf. "But it was nighttime when we set off. It must be dawn now."

As if in response, a beam of sunlight fell through a shaft before them. Daphne relaxed her grip on Desstra's arm and stepped into the warm golden column. A smile grew on the dryad's face as her foliage stretched out appreciatively to catch the light.

"I was getting hungry," she explained.

"That's convenient," said Thianna.

"Very," said Desstra, whose stomach had begun rumbling. Then she voiced a small "ooh" of excitement. The elf bent to examine a patch of mushrooms growing beside the tunnel wall.

"Find something you like?" asked Thianna.

"Very much so," said Desstra, plucking a variety of different fungi. "Several of these are quite tasty."

"If you say so."

"And these," continued the elf, uprooting a strange purple mushroom, "these have other uses." She smiled wickedly. Thianna wondered just what sort of nasty potions the Svartálfar could concoct with the weird fungus. Desstra dusted off and ate a few and slipped others into her pockets. "You never know when they'll come in handy," she said.

They continued on their journey. The tunnel widened into a larger chamber, where the basalt stone walls and columns had been elaborately reworked by the dwarves.

Impressive facades were carved into the walls, and large stone dactyl faces gazed down at them from the corners of the room. Numerous passages opened onto balconies on either side, though the main tunnel continued at the opposite end from where they had entered. Water issued from the mouth of a larger-than-life dwarven statue in the center of the room. It collected in a small pool and doubtless flowed out through a drain at the bottom, though a break in one section had caused a large puddle to form over a good deal of the floor.

"It's a shame they don't use this room anymore," said Thianna. "I wonder why they abandoned it. It must have been nice before it was deserted."

"Nice?" protests Daphne. "No soil, no sun. I don't call that nice. Though I could stick my feet in that fountain if we have a moment. I'm still thirsty."

"Suit yourself," replied the giantess. Daphne gave a little squeal of excitement and went to splash in the pool.

"Glad someone's having fun," said Thianna.

Beside her, Desstra had grown very still.

Thianna looked to her companion.

"I don't think this room is abandoned," the elf said quietly.

"You saw the bar on the door," said the giantess. "They don't come this way anymore."

"I know," said Desstra. "I think it has other occupants." She pointed. Thianna followed her gaze to a corner of the room, where, under the shadow of a large dactyl head, she saw a cluster of round objects. Some were fist-sized, others were larger.

"A pile of rocks?" Thianna asked, puzzled.

"Not rocks," said Desstra. "Eggs. We need to get out of here. We need to get out of here now."

"I think it's too late," said the giantess.

"Why?"

"Your ears are twitching."

Desstra felt the muscle convulsions in the tips of her long ears. Her sixth sense always warned her of danger—unfortunately never more than a few seconds ahead of time.

Both girls readied their weapons. Watching the tunnels to either side, they began to move cautiously across the room. They headed for the dryad, still happily soaking her feet in the shallow water.

"Daphne," said Thianna, "we're leaving."

"So soon?" said the tree girl, disappointed. Her foliage seemed darker, which in the dim light probably meant it was becoming more green, and her leaves appeared fuller and bushier than before. "Can't we stay a little longer? The water here is deliciously pure. And rich in minerals."

Something emerged from a tunnel at the opposite end of the cavern.

"Don't worry," it said. "You're going to stay a lot longer. In fact, you're never going to leave."

The speaker emerged fully into the chamber. The creature had the legs and body of a large spider, but

169

where a head should have been a human torso grew, with human arms and a human face. Instead of two human eyes, however, eight beady black orbs glared at them. More of the creatures scuttled from out of other tunnels. Scarlet markings in the shape of an hourglass were visible on their lower abdomens.

"You've got to be kidding me," said Thianna. "Goat men, bull boys, now spider women?"

"Arachne," said Daphne in a small voice.

"I'm pleased you have heard of us," said the spider woman.

"It is said," explained the dryad, "that the chief goddess Casteria cursed a mortal woman for her vanity, turning her into a spider. The first of their kind. They're really nasty."

"Nasty is in the eye of the beholder," said the arachne. "Nasty is a fearful little plant girl with bad manners and no red blood for us to drink." The arachne turned her multiple eyes on Thianna. "But don't worry, sisters. This one looks like a meal big enough for all of us." She dropped to block the far exit from the room, while her so-called sisters fanned out in an attempt to flank the companions on both sides.

"Fall back," ordered Thianna, withdrawing the way they had first come.

"I don't think so," said the arachne. "Oh, boys!" she called.

The hairs on the frost giant's neck crawled at the scurrying sound behind her. Reluctantly, she turned to look. The "boys" were only spiders, without any human bits. But they were enormous, easily the size of large dogs. And there were dozens of them. The spiders swarmed all over the room, cutting them off and blocking any hope of retreat.

"I guess the bugs want to fight," said Thianna.

"Spiders aren't bugs," Desstra corrected her, then hastily added, "I know, you don't need to know what something is called—"

"To stomp it," said Thianna, bringing her foot down heavily on one of the males that had scuttled too close.

"Careful," warned Desstra. "They're venomous."

"Of course they are," said Thianna resignedly. "At this point, I'd be surprised if they weren't."

One of the arachne hurled a web at the giantess from overhead. It struck her sword arm. Thianna cried out but couldn't disentangle herself. On the ceiling, the spider woman attempted to draw the line in.

"Sisters, help!" it called. "This one is even heavier than she looks."

Desstra ran to Thianna's side.

"Be still a moment," the elf said. Then she quickly set to work unsticking the webbing from Thianna's forearm. "Special gloves," she explained. "Made from spider hide back home."

"You know these things?" Thianna said in amazement.

"No," replied the elf. "We have large spiders but nothing like these twisted creatures."

"Manners," chided one of the arachne. "You may look like a pale, bloodless thing, but we can smell the juice inside. We'll eat you first if you don't behave."

"Don't do me any favors!" Desstra shouted. She yanked hard on the webbing, dislodging the arachne on the ceiling. It dropped at her feet, and the elf brought her weapon down hard on its head. With a groan the spider woman fell unconscious.

"I think I could learn to like hammers," said the elf. Then the spiders were upon them.

Thianna and Desstra chopped and hammered while dodging threads of spider silk and avoiding bites of the males' savage fangs. Despite the giantess's reluctance to admit it, she and the elf were a formidable team when they were forced to work together. Crumpled spiders piled up at their feet and another of the females was taken down. But the numbers were too great. It wasn't a fight they could win.

The spiders appeared to be ignoring Daphne. The dryad stood quaking in the pool of water, her leaves turned up around her in a useless attempt at camouflage. Desstra thought the arachne were ignoring the tree girl because of her lack of red blood, but when quick dodging maneuvers splashed some of the puddle water onto her bare skin, she understood. The pool was freezing cold. Of course, the elf realized. The spiders of the Svartálfaheim Mountains back home were sluggish in the cold. They only ventured aboveground into the Wyrdwood in the summer months and remained belowground for the rest of the year. Extreme cold could paralyze or even kill them.

"Thianna," she called, "freeze the room."

"What?" said the giantess.

"They can't bear the cold," the elf explained. "Drop the temperature in this room."

"Hard to do that and still fight," Thianna replied.

"It's our only chance," said Desstra. "I'll cover you."

"I've got four sides," said the giantess.

"I know," said the elf. "You just do your thing and I'll do mine."

Then the Svartálfar was moving as quickly as she ever had. The little elf was nearly a blur as she danced around and even over the frost giant. She struck at arachne before, behind, beside, and above the giantess.

Thianna was amazed, but she couldn't afford to waste the breather Desstra was buying her. Drawing a great gasp of air, she put as much force into her frost charm as she ever had. "Skapa kaldr skapa kaldr skapa kaldr," she chanted.

The air around Thianna misted. The puddle at her feet froze over. Norrøngard-born Desstra had no trouble keeping her feet, but the arachne weren't so fortunate. Those that scurried across the ice slipped and slid and were easy to squash with a hammer.

"It's working!" shouted the elf. "Pour it on."

"Skapa kaldr skapa kaldr SKAPA KALDR!" roared Thianna. A spider woman lost her grip on the ceiling overhead and fell to the floor, striking with a dull thud.

Thianna laughed.

"Don't stop," said Desstra.

As the giantess continued her invocation, the spiders slowed. They rolled over to their backsides and curled their legs up. More of the females dropped to the floor. Thianna stopped chanting. She and Desstra stared around the chamber at their vanquished foes.

"Thanks for the tip, Long Ears," said Thianna.

"Did I hear that right?" said Desstra. "Did you just thank me?"

"Don't get used to it," said the frost giant. "It did work on the bugs really well, though."

Desstra looked toward the dryad. Daphne had grown quite still, her foliage curled up around her. "That's not all it worked on," said the elf.

"Is she dead?" asked Thianna.

As if in answer, the dryad let out a loud snore.

"Doesn't sound like it," said Desstra. "Though one of us is going to have to carry her, and that one isn't me."

Thianna grumbled, but she lifted the dryad easily, tossing the girl over one shoulder. Desstra bent and selected a long strand of spider silk from the cavern floor. She looped it into a tight coil and fixed it to her belt. "For later," the elf explained. Then, as she straightened up, Desstra noticed something on the giantess's exposed calf.

"Thianna, your leg," she said.

"Yes, those are my bare legs. Karn has already re-marked on it. They don't seem to like pants here very much. Or haven't you noticed?"

"No," said her companion, pointing. "You've been bit-ten."

Thianna glanced at her calf. Blood oozed slowly from a small puncture. The wound was slight and already scab-bing.

"That's nothing," she said. "Just a scratch."

"But, Thianna," said Desstra, worry filling her dark eyes. "You saw the red hourglass markings. These spiders are venomous. I don't have my satchel . . . my antidotes."

"Oh. How venomous are they?" Thianna asked.

"Even tiny spiders can be deadly," the elf replied. "And these are giant."

"Yes, well, I'm a giant too." Thianna began march-ing toward the far cavern exit. "Come on," she said. "No sense waiting around here for the bugs to wake up."

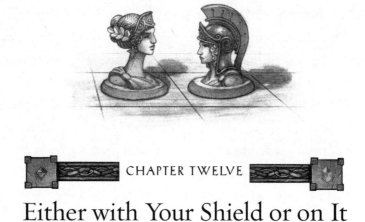

CHAPTER TWELVE

Either with Your Shield or on It

Sirena marched sullenly through the palace. She had returned from an all-night and utterly fruitless search of the lower city. There was no sign of the troublesome giantess anywhere. As unbelievable as it seemed, the enormous girl had simply vanished. She'd heard the reports from the south gate, the theft of the hippalektryons, but Thianna was not among the fugitives.

"Crows take you, cousin," she swore. The barbarian had betrayed her, betrayed her hospitality. Sirena had treated Thianna like an equal, afforded her the pleasures of a full Calderan citizen. But even shown the trappings of civilization, Thianna had rejected her. And in so doing snatched away any chance of a return to Sirena's former life. She shuddered to think they were related.

Sirena reached the central courtyard of the palace complex, where a broad patio was surrounded on three sides and opened to the steep cliff on a fourth. The courtyard was unusual in that it was dominated by a life-sized Queen's Champion board, complete with theater seating. Spectators could choose to sit in either the Sky Queen's or the Land Queen's stands. She saw that Queen Xalthea walked across the checkered board now, in the company of three soldiers.

A guard stood nearby in the shadow of the palace.

"To whom does the queen speak?" Sirena asked.

"Hippalektryon units," the guard replied.

"Melantha's soldiers?" Sirena was surprised. Xalthea commanded the wyvern troops who held sway over the skies, but Melantha was in charge of ground forces.

"They wear their earrings on their right," the woman said. Sirena nodded. Calderan soldiers only wore one earring. Those who served the Sky Queen pierced their left ear; those who served Melantha, their right. Her own ear had been pierced on the right, but she had had to pierce her left when she was elevated to the position of Keras Keeper. The hole in her right lobe had yet to close.

"They did not report to the Land Queen?" she asked.

"Xalthea intercepted them," the guard replied, her previously impassive face growing uncomfortable with discussing the rivalries of her monarchs. "They had just returned from chasing the escaped hostages."

Sirena raised an eyebrow.

"Returned empty-handed?" she asked.

"So it appears," said the guard, stone-faced.

"I would not walk in their sandals," said Sirena. The guard diplomatically said nothing, but her eyes said she agreed. The Sky Queen was not known for her mercy.

Sirena walked out into the courtyard but took a seat in the stands. She could see that one of the three soldiers was badly injured. She was clearly in need of medical attention but had come to report first. Perhaps this would mitigate the queen's displeasure. As Sirena watched, the woman fell to the ground. She lay where she had fallen, struggling to rise.

"Be still," Queen Xalthea said. "You have clearly given your all in the service of Caldera. We will see your injuries treated shortly. And you"—she turned to the other wounded soldier—"do not seem much better. Your effort is commendable."

Xalthea turned to the remaining women.

"Step forward," she commanded. The women did so. This placed them each upon a separate square on the Queen's Champion board. Xalthea looked to a woman with a dark bruise on her face.

"Knocked from your mount and rendered unconscious," the Sky Queen said. "Not an ideal performance."

"My queen," said the nervous soldier, "I was incapacitated."

Xalthea harrumphed. "Chasing after children," she said. Then she addressed the last soldier.

"Where is your sword?" she asked.

"It was taken from me, my queen," the woman responded.

"And your fire lance?"

"Also taken."

"And your pelta?" Xalthea was referring to the distinctive crescent-shaped half shield that marked Calderan soldiers. The woman did not immediately answer. "Are you going to say that it was taken from you too?"

"Yes, Sky Queen," the soldier said. Sirena wondered if the use of Xalthea's title was a desperate attempt to remind the queen that they served the Land Queen, not her.

"And yet you are not injured," Xalthea said, frowning.

"I was overcome and disarmed."

"By a beast boy," said the queen. She sighed theatrically. "What do we say in Caldera where our shields are concerned?"

The woman did not answer. Xalthea turned to Sirena, though she hadn't taken any notice of her before.

"Keras Keeper, you were once a soldier."

"I was, my queen," said Sirena. It stung to be reminded of the life that was denied her.

"What is the slogan that they drill into you concerning your pelta?"

Sirena hesitated, as if saying the words made her complicit in the soldier's fate.

"Come now," said the queen. "Surely you have not forgotten already?"

"Either with your shield or on it," she called quickly.

"Either with your shield or on it," Xalthea repeated. "You are not with your shield, and yet you walk unaided and uninjured."

"My queen," said the woman, desperation mounting in her eyes. Sirena felt her own pulse quicken in sympathy with the woman's.

"I am not *your* queen," Xalthea replied coldly. "I would be ashamed to have such cowards in my ranks."

The Sky Queen suddenly stepped forward onto a square beside the frightened soldiers. In Queen's Champion, this would constitute a challenge. The woman opened her mouth to speak.

Gears under the checkerboard turned. The square the doomed soldier stood upon fell inward like a trapdoor. She disappeared through the hole in the board. Sirena heard her screams for a brief moment; then they were cut off abruptly as her body collided with the cliff and tumbled to the waters below. The section of checkered square slid back into place with a mechanical click. It rang loudly in the stunned silence.

The remaining soldiers looked at Xalthea in horror. Sirena turned her face away. The penalty for failure in Caldera was always strict. It should not bother her so. She knew that strength of the city came at a high cost.

The queen turned to the one with the bruise on her face.

"Don't fail me again," she said.

The queen left the soldiers on the board and walked to where Sirena sat in the stands. Her look sent a chill down Sirena's spine. For a moment, she worried that her futile search for Thianna might also be counted a failure in Xalthea's judgment. But she was no longer a soldier. She carried no pelta.

"When this is over," the queen said, "I think we'll send a squadron of my wyvern riders to Ymiria and burn that pathetic frost giant village to the ground. A long overdue payback for harboring our enemies."

Sirena nodded. If she worried for a distant village of inhuman strangers, that concern paled against her relief that Xalthea's temper was focused elsewhere.

The Sky Queen started toward her wing of the Twin Palaces, then paused. She fixed Sirena with a cold stare.

"And, Keras Keeper," she said, "if for any reason I am unable to command my wyverns then, you will follow this soldier down the mountain."

The sphinx was luxuriating in a patch of sunlight. She was loving the feel of the warmth on her belly while she pondered new riddles. Obviously her material was getting a bit dated and she needed to up her game. She should have asked that blond-haired boy to tell her a few riddles before letting them go.

Around her the kobalos began chittering excitedly. The noise was distracting.

"Keep it down," she ordered. "I can't hear myself think." She rolled over onto her belly and arched her back in a long stretch.

The din the kobalos were making only got louder. Several of them came scurrying up to her where she sat atop a broken roof.

"Honestly," the sphinx complained, "I don't know why I keep you wee folk around. If you weren't such excellent cooks—"

She stopped talking when she saw the dust of the ground rising in little swirls. The sphinx raised her eyes and saw three wyverns dropping out of the sky. Not for the first time, she was jealous of their power of flight. Thican sphinx were wingless, unlike her winged cousins across the sea in Neteru. It was hardly fair.

Then she noticed that the wyverns had riders. Soldiers in black leathers and bronze armor. They wore helmets with black plumes. One of them wore a black cape. The sphinx supposed this one thought she was the most important.

The black-caped woman stepped down from her wyvern. She approached the sphinx on her perch, walking with a slight limp. The woman took off her helmet.

"My name is Leta," the woman said. "I am the captain of the Keras Guard."

The sphinx shrugged. Politics and soldiery weren't

nearly as interesting as sports competitions and riddle contests.

"We are tracking two fugitives," the woman named Leta continued. "We know that they came to these ruins."

Now the sphinx had her back up.

"These ruins, as you call them," she said, sitting up and puffing out her chest, "are the Sanctuary of Empyria. One of the most sacred spots of all Thica."

Now it was Leta's turn to shrug.

"Ancient history does not concern me," she said. "The whereabouts of my quarry does."

The sphinx thought about this.

"Perhaps I could ask you a riddle," she said. "It's a really good one. It goes like this: I fall when I am born. I die when I am warm—"

"Let me ask you one instead," the guard captain interrupted. She was really quite rude. "What burns when it doesn't do as it was told?"

The sphinx considered for a moment. Then she noticed that the two guards on either side of the black-caped woman had both aimed their lances right where she was sitting. Their fingers were on the triggers, ready to shoot the deadly Thican fire at a moment's notice.

"Well, that's an easy one," said the sphinx. She waved a paw at the soldiers. "You really shouldn't have given me such a strong hint. It spoils the challenge."

"Would you like an even stronger hint?" Leta asked. She nodded at the soldier on her right, who shot a burst of flame from her lance. The fire passed right over the sphinx's left shoulder, singeing the hair of her mane.

"Hey," she objected, "I just had that combed!"

"I will burn the rest of it, and you with it," said the woman. "Along with as many of your irritating little friends as I can, if you do not answer my question."

"Sphinxes burn. That's the answer."

"Not that question," said the woman. "The one about the fugitives. Where did they go?"

"Well, that's not a proper riddle," said the sphinx. "You didn't even actually ask it. You just implied it."

Leta sighed.

"Light her up," she said to her soldiers.

"No, wait!" cried the sphinx. "I can do this. You're talking about that blond-haired boy and the minotaur?"

"Yes," said Leta. "It's the blond I am most concerned with."

"They left here yesterday."

"And they were heading . . . ?"

"South." One of the kobalos chattered. "No," said the sphinx. "It was southwest. Straight southwest."

Leta smiled. It wasn't a nice smile.

"Thank you. I believe I know where they are heading."

She donned her helmet and mounted her wyvern.

"Have fun in your ruins," she said. Then all three beasts rose into the air. The kobalos chittered angrily at the cloud of dust.

"Well now," said the sphinx, "who's a self-important harpy with no appreciation for history?"

Around her the kobalos twittered.

"It was a rhetorical question!" said the sphinx. "I didn't expect an answer. I'm just saying that things aren't like they used to be."

CHAPTER THIRTEEN

Head Games

Karn's backside was starting to seriously ache. His second day on the hippalektryon riding without a saddle was taking its toll. On the plus side, he was getting to be a much better rider. But he wasn't sure he would ever be able to sit down again.

They were moving at phenomenal speed across the open grasslands, having left the mountain range behind them in the north. Karn shook his head.

"I've never been anywhere so flat," he said.

"Flat?" the minotaur replied.

"The ground," said Karn. "Norrøngard—where I'm from—is mostly mountains. We've got flatlands, but they're wooded and hilly. This is, well . . ."

"As flat as a pancake," suggested Asterius. "That's what the northerners say."

"What's a pancake?" Karn asked.

"A waste of good wheat," said Asterius. When Karn frowned, he added, "Flour, olive oil, honey, and milk. Mixed together and cooked in a frying pan. I've never had one, of course, but some people seem to like them."

"Remind me to try one when this is over," said Karn. He turned to the bull boy. "You are sure your father will help us?"

"Absolutely," said Asterius. "You'll see. My father is the bravest minotaur that ever lived."

"Guess we'll find out soon enough," said Karn. A city had appeared on the horizon.

"Home," said the bull boy enthusiastically. He spurred his mount forward.

At the speed the hippalektryons traveled, spotting a destination and reaching it was a matter of heartbeats. Karn marveled at the sight that came into view.

Labyrinthia was a round city surrounded by a high wall. A massive gate loomed up before them, flanked by two towers with stone protrusions carved to resemble horns. Asterius explained that the gate was one of four, each set at one of the cardinal points. As the hippalektryons halted, they were challenged by a soldier.

"Who goes?" the soldier called, peering down at them from a tower.

"Open in the name of the prince!" demanded Asterius to the guard. "Or do you want me to tell my father that you kept us waiting?"

"My prince," the guard hastily apologized. "We did not expect you. Are you not a guest of the Calderans?"

"More like a prisoner!" yelled Asterius. "Now open the gate."

The portcullis rose, and Asterius turned to Karn and grinned.

"Now you can see what a real city is like," he said.

Karn wanted to reply that he had been in many real cities, but he could tell the bull boy was proud of his hometown, so he kept his mouth shut. However, he couldn't help but let it fall open when they rode through the entrance.

The high walls that surrounded Labyrinthia continued inside the city itself. They lined the street, which was empty at ground level. Instead, homes and other structures hung from the sides of the walls, stopping about a story shy of the earth. Retractable ladders and staircases folded down from their lowest floors. While the streets were crowded with people—all of them minotaurs—there were no structures at this level.

"Why are the houses on the walls?" asked Karn.

Asterius gave him a look that said the question was a dumb one.

"For defense, of course," he said. "Even if someone breaches the walls and gets inside, they are still at a disadvantage. At least, someone who can't fly," he added, a bitter note in his voice.

Karn looked upward at the buildings. Some seemed a part of the wall; others were precariously hung upon it. While the walls were of stone, many of the buildings were wooden. The streets themselves were often covered with grass rather than paved, and they seemed to be laid out in an odd pattern. He couldn't make sense of it at first, but then he remembered the name of where they were.

"Asterius," he asked, "are we in a maze?"

The minotaur smiled.

"Labyrinthia is a giant maze," he said. "My father's palace is at the heart."

"Labyrinthia is a labyrinth," said Karn. "Of course. But how do you find your way around?"

"A minotaur is never lost in a maze," said Asterius with a snort. "We love walking their paths. And anyway, it's another layer of defense if the city walls are breached."

As it turned out, however, Karn thought the benefit was far outweighed by the monotony of treading the circuitous route to the city center. Labyrinthia was certainly an interesting place, but he couldn't imagine having to switch back and forth so often every time you wanted to get from one side of the city to another. Unless you were a minotaur, it would be too much hassle. Eventually, they reached an open square at the center of the maze, where an enormous building stood.

"My friend," said Asterius, "welcome to the Palace of the Double Ax."

Crack!

The noise rang out in the courtroom. Karn couldn't see for the crowd of minotaurs in his way, but it sounded like some sort of fight was taking place before the throne. Asterius grinned.

"You're going to love this," he said, pushing his way through the spectators and urging his companion on.

Karn was unnerved by the herd of bull folk in the room, all cheering and snorting and stamping their hooves. He couldn't help but think what would happen if they decided to stampede. Nor was such a thing impossible indoors.

The courtroom was large and high-ceilinged, which Karn supposed made sense for a people who loved the open plains. Moreover, it was decorated with elaborate tile mosaics that formed an intricate maze running across the walls, floor, and ceiling. Throughout the design, minotaurs were depicted engaging in battle with foes and monsters. Karn found the pattern dizzying to look at. It drew his eyes and distorted his sense of depth. He felt a headache coming on, but none of the minotaurs seemed bothered. Karn kept his eyes forward as he followed Asterius through the crowd.

Crack! Pushing to the front, Karn saw that two enormous bull folk were butting heads in a contest of strength. The sound of their skulls crashing into each other rang out in the courtroom. The male warrior staggered under the blow, but the larger female bellowed a challenge at him. They lined up again, pawing the earth, then lowered their heads and charged.

Crack! This time both contestants went down, dropping to the floor, stunned.

"Marvelous!" King Asterion roared. He was seated on a large metal throne, the back of which was cast to look like a gigantic double-bladed ax. "Did you see that?" he said, grabbing his nearest warrior-advisor by the horn and pulling the man's ear to his mouth. "I thought she had him, but he rallied brilliantly, and they took each other out! A tie!" He pounded a fist on the table before him in joy, then grabbed a wide drinking cup and tossed a large gulp into his mouth. The red wine spilled and ran down his chin.

"Next!" the king hollered. He looked to his warrior-advisors, seated four on either side of his throne. "Where is our next challenger? Come now, don't be shy. Who will be next?"

"I will!" called Asterius, stepping forward from the crowd to approach his father.

"Who?" said the king, looking for the latest volunteer. The joy faded from his eyes as he recognized his son.

"Asterius," he said. "What are *you* doing here?"

"I escaped, Father," said the boy. "I fought the Calderans and won my freedom."

Standing slightly behind the bull boy, Karn coughed.

"With my companion," Asterius amended. "He helped a little bit too."

"A little bit?" said Karn.

"You fought?" said the king, ignoring Karn. "You escaped?"

"Yes," said Asterius, puffing out his chest. "I am a brave warrior, like you."

But King Asterion shook his massive horned head.

"I am not pleased, my son," he said. "Not pleased at all. This is a most difficult situation you have placed me in. Most difficult."

Asterius was taken aback.

"You're not happy to see me?" he said. The bull boy's bottom lip began to quiver.

"It is not my unhappiness," said the king, "but Queen Xalthea's that should concern you. It was not my wish, but her command, that you were to be left as hostage in Caldera."

"I'm not afraid of her," said Asterius, trying to put some bluster into his voice but failing. The minotaur had been so sure that his father would be glad to see him. Karn realized that he was devastated by the king's reaction.

"Then you are foolish," said the king. "The twin

queens rule all of Thica, and we follow their decrees lest fire rain from the sky. You must return at once."

"I saw you in the court," said Karn, speaking up. "You don't like being under their rule. You're practically . . ." He paused. He had been about to say "champing at the bit" but realized that a bridle metaphor might not go over with a bull man. "Bursting to fight them," he finished.

King Asterion turned his gaze to Karn for the first time.

"And I will one day," said the monarch. He lifted a large ax from beside his throne and shook it in his mighty fist. "This I swear by Teshub, god of sky and storm. But not today. For now we must pretend obedience while we bide our time."

"Wear their yoke, you mean," said Karn. This time he was being deliberately provocative, and it worked. The king stood, hefting his ax again and stepping down from his throne. Beside him, his warrior-advisors lowed angrily.

The king approached Karn, swinging his ax in a deceptively casual way. Karn swallowed. Maybe he had misjudged his approach.

"You are one of the hostages?" the king said.

"No," said Karn.

"A foreigner?" said the king. "Your hair is like wheat."

"I'm from Norrøngard," said Karn. "My name is Karn Korlundsson."

The king snorted. The hot breath blew in Karn's face. Karn raised a hand to shield himself from the smell. His eyes fell on his own ring finger. Karn held up the symbol of the Order of the Oak. When he had parted from Leflin Greenroot in the city of Castlebriar, the wood elf had told him it would open doors for him, maybe prevent a knife in the back. He wondered if it might also stop an ax in the head.

"Does this mean anything to you?" he said to the king.

The minotaur monarch squinted at Karn's finger.

"It's a pretty ring. Silver, is it? A bit too small for my finger, though." Asterion held up one of his thick digits and laughed.

"It was worth a shot," said Karn. So the minotaurs weren't aware of the Order of the Oak. But maybe there were other reputations he could leverage. "I came here with Thianna Frostborn," Karn said, "to find the Horn of Osius and destroy it."

There were exclamations of alarm throughout the court.

"You came with the Frostborn?" said the king, looking at Karn with new respect. "Is it true she can use the horn?"

"Yes," said Karn. "But she's already destroyed one of them. Help us, and she'll destroy the other. You're planning to rebel eventually. Help us now."

"An interesting conundrum," said the king, lowering his ax. "Most interesting. I will think on it." He waved for two of his warrior-advisors. "Take him away for now. Hold him somewhere secure."

"Wait," said Karn. "We can fight the Calderans. We can fight them together."

"I will think on it," said the king again, a threatening note in his voice. "But for now I desire more head-butting! Who's next?"

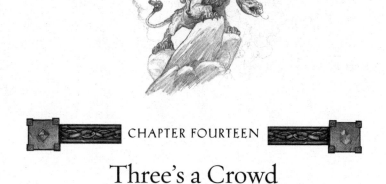

CHAPTER FOURTEEN

Three's a Crowd

"Thianna, are you okay?" asked Desstra.

"I'm fine," the giantess answered brusquely. She'd stumbled on the rough tunnel floor. And not for the first time.

"You don't look fine."

"I told you, I'm okay," she said.

"You're slowing down," said the elf. "I think the venom is finally getting to you."

Thianna frowned. "It takes a lot of venom to knock me out," she said. Then she glared at the elf. "You should know."

Desstra nodded. She did know. Thianna had an amazing constitution.

"You also respond to antidotes remarkably fast," she said. "If only I had some."

"None of those mushrooms you picked are any good?" the giantess asked.

"I wish," said Desstra.

"Then we keep walking. If I'm going down, at least I can get you two as far from those bugs as possible." Thianna's face set into a stoic grimace and she marched on, but she stumbled now as often as she stepped.

"Take it easy," complained Daphne, uncurling a leaf from over her eyes and attempting to stretch her arms from atop the giantess's shoulder.

"Look who's finally awake," said Thianna, but the relief she showed in setting what should be a slight burden down worried Desstra.

"You can wwwalk for yourssself," the giantess said, slurring her words. Desstra gasped when Thianna dropped to one knee.

"What's wrong with her?" Daphne cried out in alarm.

"She was bitten," said Desstra.

"Told you, I'mmm okkkay," said Thianna. Then she fell down heavily on her bottom. "I waz okay. Maybe I'mma not okay. Maybe I'll juss lie down."

"No," said Desstra, who knew that Thianna shouldn't give in to the venom. "You've got to get back on your feet." She turned to Daphne. "Give me a hand, will you? Come on, Thianna, show me that stubborn streak we all know and love."

"Stubborn?" said the giantess with a loopy grin. "Who you calling stubborn, Long Ears?"

"I said help," snarled Desstra at the dryad.

"I am," Daphne replied.

The elf looked at the dryad. Daphne seemed to have sprouted a cluster of small red berries. She pinched them off, wincing slightly as she did so.

"What are you doing?" said Desstra.

"Saving your friend," the tree girl replied.

"Nah frinz," said Thianna.

Daphne crushed the berries in her hand, rubbing them into a paste. By this point Thianna had slumped to the ground. The dryad bent over her where she lay and pried her lips apart.

"Ge yuhr finners outta my mowf," muttered the giantess. But Daphne shoved the berry paste to the back of Thianna's throat.

"Yuck, bitter!" said Thianna quite clearly. She made a face.

"Don't spit it out!" Daphne yelled. "Help me make her swallow," she said to Desstra.

"Making her do anything isn't easy," said the elf, but together the two girls clamped hands over Thianna's mouth and stroked her throat. The giantess tried to shake them off weakly, her lips screwed up at the unpleasant taste under their fingers. Eventually, however, the herbal medicine went down.

Then Thianna bolted upright.

"Make way!" she shouted, pushing past them.

Desstra turned a questioning look on the dryad.

"She's going to, um, well, you know," Daphne half-explained. "The venom is going to work its way out of her, pretty much every way it can."

"Oh," said Desstra.

"Yes," said Daphne. "We should probably stand clear."

They walked a little ways away, while behind them Thianna began making unpleasant gulping noises. Soon the tunnel echoed with nauseating spattering sounds broken by intermittent shouts of "Troll dung!" and "Sweet Ymir's feet!"

Desstra gave Daphne a wry grin.

"She may not thank you for this," the elf said, "so let me. You saved her life."

"It's nothing," said the dryad.

"No, it's *something*," said Desstra. "I admit I thought you were pretty useless when we got into a fight, but you've just proven how valuable you are."

Daphne smiled.

"Thank you," she said.

Thianna staggered up to them. "Come on," the giantess said, wiping a palm across her mouth. "Let's put some distance on this section of tunnel, why don't we?"

The seagull squawked in surprise. The statue that it most loved to perch and poop upon had quite unexpectedly moved. The bird rose into the air, flapping its wings in irritation. It screeched angrily to let the stone figure know that its new conduct wasn't appreciated. Then it flew to a nearby grove of trees, from which it expected better behavior.

Thianna Frostborn crawled out of the gap revealed as the statue slid aside. She looked at the marble, which was carved into a dactyl dwarf. He held a mathematical compass in one hand and a scroll in the other.

"That's the famous inventor Damnameneus," Daphne explained, climbing up to stand beside her.

"I keep hearing about him," Thianna replied. "He made the death rays . . ."

"Also the Claw of Damnameneus," said the dryad. "It is said that it can pull ships right out of the water. And he sketched plans for lots of other mechanical devices, most of which never got built. He even designed a flying machine."

"You'd think as much as this dwarf did for Thica," said Desstra, stepping up beside her companions and slipping glasses over her eyes, "they'd put his statue at the *top* of the hill."

"I don't know," said Thianna, "I think this neighborhood seems more fun." They were apparently in the northern part of Caldera, just upslope of a large amphitheater in the helot district. Eateries and drinking houses clustered nearby. To their left they saw a small grove of olive trees.

"We're on the opposite side of the island from where

Karn was heading," said the frost giant. "And I've got no idea if he's still here or he made it out."

"We need to get out of sight," said the elf.

"We need to find Karn," Thianna replied angrily.

"Which we can do better if we're not captured again, yes?" Desstra said.

"I suppose that's right," said Thianna. "Let's find somewhere to hide and take stock. I guess you're better at the sneaky stuff than I am."

"You guess?" said Desstra pointedly.

"Fine. You *are* better at sneaky stuff." Thianna looked around. "Where'd your little tree friend go?"

Sure enough, Daphne had vanished. It didn't take them long to spot her, however. They saw a strange-looking plant—the dryad had returned to camouflage mode—shuffling its way toward the grove.

"We'd better go after her," said Desstra.

"Must we?" the giantess said.

"She's pretty helpless on her own," the elf replied. "And she did save you."

They followed the dryad down the slope, entering the cluster of olive trees a few minutes after she did. It was pleasant inside the grove. The noises of the crowded district were muffled, and the dappled sunlight falling through the leaves was easier on Desstra.

"It reminds me of the Wyrdwood in summer," she said. "Only without all the elf-eating monsters."

They found Daphne standing before a tall elm, the only one amid all the olive trees. Strangely she seemed to be in conversation with it. Even odder still, it appeared to be answering her.

"Daphne," said Desstra, "what are you doing?"

The dryad yelped as the elf and the frost giant approached.

"Nothing," she said. "Just leave me here. Better yet, just go away. Better still, I'll go away." She bolted around the tree.

Puzzled, Thianna and Desstra sprang after her. Daphne ran a circle around the large trunk of the elm. Desstra switched directions, circling back to cut her off. But instead, she and Thianna collided.

"Where'd she go?" Thianna asked. "She can't have vanished."

"Shh," said Desstra. She cocked her long ears, listening. Then she let the tips drop. "She's not in the woods. Or anywhere near here."

"Are you sure?"

Desstra gave Thianna a look that said she thought the giantess was a moron.

"Okay, Long Ears, I get it. You're sure. But where did she go, then?"

The girls looked around the grove, then turned in unison to the large elm.

"Don't look at me," it said. Then it clasped a hand over its mouth.

Thianna and Desstra both gaped in amazement.

"A talking tree?" the giantess said.

Large amber eyes looked from one girl to the other. Then the tree clamped its eyes shut under brows of knotty bark.

"We know you can talk," said Desstra.

The elm stayed stock-still. This in itself was odd, because a slight sea breeze was rustling the olive trees around it.

"We heard you do it," said Thianna.

Still the tree didn't move.

Thianna grabbed two limbs near the trunk and started to shake the elm. As she continued to shake the tree, several leaves became dislodged and floated to the ground, along with little seeds that whirled around them on leafy wings.

"Stop that," said the elm, taking its hands from its mouth.

"Aha!" Thianna said in triumph. The tree frowned miserably.

"Are you a dryad like Daphne?" asked Desstra, though she didn't think so. This creature was rooted in the earth, and its branches rose a good ways into the air.

"Of course not," it said. "I'm a hamadryad."

"Never heard of you," said Thianna.

"We keep our existence fairly secret," the hamadryad explained. "We can't move around like the dryads. Being stuck in one spot our whole lives makes us vulnerable.

Also, there aren't as many of us as there are dryads and drus."

"It must be terrible to be stuck in one location," said Desstra.

"Moving is overrated," said the hamadryad. "Anyway, this is a rather pleasant place. And I can keep tabs on the Calderans and report—oops!" The hamadryad clamped its hands over its mouth again.

"Report to who?" said Thianna.

The elm closed its eyes tight.

"I think it needs another good shake," Desstra said. "Thianna, if you'll do the honors."

The giantess again gripped the hamadryad's branches, but the tree opened its eyes.

"Thianna," it said. "Are you *the* Thianna Frostborn?"

"You've heard of me?" asked the giantess.

The tree nodded.

"Oh yes," it said. "Well, that changes things. That's quite a different story."

"Changes things how?" asked the elf.

"For starters," said the hamadryad, "I think you'd better come inside."

"Inside where?" Thianna asked. But a doorway had suddenly appeared in the elm's trunk, the bark sliding open to reveal an interior of glowing green light. As Thianna and Desstra peered inside in amazement, the tree reached out with its long branches and swept them forward. They tumbled through the door, which slammed shut behind them.

Up in the elm's higher branches a seagull cried out angrily at all the sudden motion and flew away.

Thianna and Desstra stumbled through a green void. They could see Daphne quite clearly moving ahead of them. But there was nothing but diffuse emerald light between their position and the dryad's. It was disconcerting to see her so sharply while everything else was fuzzy and indistinct. It made judging distance impossible.

Thianna sniffed the air.

"It smells," she said. "I don't mean badly. It just smells—" She hunted for the right word to describe the rich, verdant scent in the air.

"Green," said the elf. "Like growing things."

"No breeze, though," observed the giantess.

Something moved, or maybe swam, in the space beside them. They glimpsed nebulous forms that appeared and disappeared before their shapes could be fully grasped.

"What are they?" Desstra asked.

"Don't take an interest in them," the voice of the hamadryad sounded in the space around them.

"Why not?" asked Thianna, searching for the elm, though its voice came from everywhere and nowhere.

"Because then they'll take an interest in you," the

hamadryad replied. "Just follow Daphne. We can't have you getting lost here. Or worse."

"Where is she—where are we going?" Desstra asked.

"You'll see," said the hamadryad. Its voice sounded more distant now.

"Are you going away?" Thianna asked.

"You are," it replied. "You've traveled quite a distance from Caldera already. Only a little ways more to go."

"Where?" Desstra called, but the hamadryad was silent. Either it had faded away or it had decided to keep its mouth shut.

When the two girls caught up with Daphne, the dryad exclaimed, "You're not allowed in here!"

"Tell that to your hamadryad friend," said Desstra. "We weren't really given a say in the matter."

"Where is here, anyway?" Thianna asked.

Daphne paused before she answered. "I suppose since you're already inside, I might as well tell you. This is a Greenway, one of the Roads Between."

"The Roads Between?" repeated Desstra.

"Like the Darkways and the Shimmering Paths."

"Still not following you," said Thianna.

"Bridges between distant places," the dryad explained. "Tunnels through the material world that open only to those who know how to find them. The Greenways are for the tree folk. Once, they connected lands all over the world. Now we can only travel across Thica."

"Why? What happened?" Desstra asked.

"The hamadryads control the portals. When a road fades, it's because a hamadryad has died."

"They died all over the world?" said Thianna, struck by the scale of the loss. Daphne nodded sadly.

"The portal to Araland was the last to go," she said. "My people used to commune with the druids there. But even that Greenway withered before I sprouted."

"I'm sorry," said Thianna, who didn't know what else to say.

"It is what it is," said Daphne. "The world moves in cycles. New things grow and old things die. Anyway, we're here."

A column of live wood stood before them. It was devoid of bark and dotted with rings that were scattered up its length. Daphne circled around it, looking for something.

"What is this?" Thianna asked.

"Wait, I get it," said Desstra. "We're inside another tree. Those rings are its branches. This is the tree—only turned inside out!"

"Ah," said Daphne, smiling. "Here's the door." She pushed and a small section of the column opened inward.

Thianna bent and peered inside. Or rather outside. The frost giant saw a forest through the doorway. She straightened up in shock, then walked completely around the column. She crouched and looked again. The impossible woods were still there.

"Come on," said Daphne. She walked through the door. Desstra and Thianna followed.

They emerged into the forest. Turning around, Thianna found that they had stepped out of an ash tree. A doorway in its trunk was just sliding closed. The face of another hamadryad looked down at her from above.

"Welcome to the city of Dendronos," it said. "You are expected."

"How could you know we were coming?" asked Thianna. "We didn't know it ourselves."

The hamadryad laid a hand on its trunk in a gesture like a person patting their belly.

"You have gas?" asked the giantess.

"You cannot move through the Greenways without our sensing your passage," it explained. "And we are all connected, one hamadryad to the other. News of your arrival has been passed to the Council of Elders."

"Council?"

"The ruling body of Dendronos," the talking tree explained.

"Look," interrupted Desstra, pointing. "Here comes the welcome party." Thianna followed the elf's gaze. From out of the woods ahead, twelve large figures emerged. Each resembled a different type of tree in their bark and foliage. The giantess and the elf recognized fir, oak, olive, laurel, and date plum. But the girls' fascination was tempered by the very obvious threat of their long, sharpened wooden spears and large round shields of bark.

"Daphne," said Thianna warily, "your people don't look very glad to see us."

"I'm sure it will be all right," said the dryad. "We're just careful about visitors. You have to understand, the other Thican cities have cleared a lot of wood over the centuries. In the south they felled a whole forest to make their farmlands."

"Good thing I never learned to use an ax," said Thianna. The weapon was a favorite in the north, but she had always preferred the sword.

"It doesn't seem like something that would go over well here, no," agreed Desstra.

"You will come with us," said a female tree person who strode up to them. She stood as tall as Thianna, though she was not as broad. Her stern green eyes glared at the giantess from below a patch of oak leaves that she bore in place of hair. In addition to her shield, her bark had grown into formidable armor.

Thianna's hand fell to her blade.

"Please don't do that," said Daphne quickly. "Let's go with them, and I'll explain who you are."

Thianna and Desstra met each other's eyes. Neither liked the odds of the fight. Thianna relaxed her stance. Then the oak woman motioned for them to follow.

The girls were led farther into the forest. Thianna and Desstra saw that what they thought were oddly shaped trees were actually dwellings. As they walked they picked up followers. Little green children, their bark not grown fully in, frolicked at their feet, laughing at the strange visitors.

"I've seen a lot since I left my mountaintop," said Thianna, "but this has got to be one of the strangest places I've ever been to."

"I've heard the wood elves sometimes live in villages full of tree houses," said the dark elf, "but those are homes built into the branches. Not houses that were built out of trees themselves."

"*Built* is the wrong word," said Thianna. "This city looks more like it was grown."

"I think it's still growing," observed Desstra, looking at a miniature house that seemed to be in the process of sprouting from the earth. A dryad was watering it from a can while singing softly. All around them, the homes they saw were clearly made of still-living wood. Walls and rooftops sprouted branches with leaves and flowers, even fruit. Doors and windows opened in fat trunks. Long limbs became elevated walkways connecting buildings in streets above their heads. Often, clusters of trees were entwined to create larger structures.

"But how do you coax the trees to grow into the shapes you want?" asked Thianna. She looked at a particular tree home that seemed to be a multistory apartment house, and beside it one with high wooden arches that recalled a church or temple.

"How do you think?" asked Daphne. "We sing to them."

"Silly me," said Thianna. "Of course you do."

The three girls continued, their escort leading them

toward the center of the city. If the houses were unusual, then the citizens of Dendronos were even more so. Everywhere, dryads and drus went about their lives in a bustling green world. The tree folk were as varied as the plants around them. They passed one fellow who had roses blooming all over his body, while the crown of his head was covered with spiky thorns where hair should be.

The procession arrived at a glade where neatly trimmed grass formed an open-air space. It was ringed by trees that were taller than any they had seen so far. The trees' limbs twined together over their heads, making the space seem like a cathedral or a court. Dryads and drus watched them from between the trees or from perches on their branches.

Thianna noticed that the children had left their side. The tree folk warriors had also fanned out to the edges of the glade, circling the girls from a distance where their spears would be the most useful. The set of Desstra's jaw told Thianna that the dark elf had noticed this too.

"It's okay," said Daphne, seeing their tension. "That's just a precaution for our protection, I'm sure. We'll talk to the Council of Elders now. I'll tell them who you are and how you helped me escape."

"There will be no audience with the council," said the tall oak woman. "We already know who this one is"—she eyed Thianna menacingly—"and the council has already pronounced their judgment."

"What do you mean judgment?" said Desstra, a note of warning in her voice.

The woman ignored her. "You are the horn blower?" she asked Thianna.

"I've been called a lot of things," replied the giantess.

"You are the one who wields the Horn of Osius? The only one alive to do so successfully?"

"I blew that horn a few times, yes," said Thianna. "But I don't like what it does or how it's used."

"Perhaps," said the oak warrior. "But you are still a threat to us. If you were captured again, you could be persuaded, or forced, to use the horn for the Calderans."

"She wouldn't do that," objected Daphne. "Thianna wants to fight the Calderans. She's been fighting them all along."

"Look at her," said the woman. "She *is* a Calderan. A big one, perhaps, but still one of them."

"You didn't see her in the capital," said Daphne. "She stood up to the two queens. I'm telling you, she's our friend."

"Then I am sorry," said the tall dryad. "We have had enough of tyranny in the skies over our woods. The elders have ordered that we remove the threat entirely."

Thianna and Desstra instantly drew their weapons, but the circle of warriors didn't seem concerned. The oak woman stepped away from them, pulling Daphne with her as she did so.

"We cannot harm a hostage princess nor a Calderan for fear of retribution," she explained. "And you are either one or the other. But we have a visitor who is under no such compunction."

She gestured to one edge of the glade. In the dappled shadows of the tree limbs, something approached. Something large.

"What is that?" said Desstra, ears alert.

"Good hosts should always see to their guests' needs," said the oak woman. "But we didn't know how to feed this one until now." She bowed slightly in mock thanks and moved to the edge of the ring.

The creature that stepped into the clearing was like nothing Thianna or Desstra had ever seen. It had the body of a lion but three heads. One head was that of a lion, the other of a goat, and the third a serpent.

"What is it with these hybrid creatures around here?" said Thianna. "Everything is half this, half that. Whatever happened to good old trolls and dragons? Who sticks all these monsters together?"

"What *is* it?" said Desstra, readying her stance as the animal approached.

"It's a chimera," called Daphne from the edge of the ring. "I'm so sorry!" She looked miserable, not that her feelings were much consolation for either of the girls.

"How many times do I need to say this?" called Thianna. "I don't need to know what it's called—"

The goat head suddenly opened its mouth and a burst

of flame shot out. Thianna and Desstra dodged aside; the grass of the glen sizzled where they had been.

"Troll dung! This thing breathes fire!" the giantess realized. "Now that, I did need to know!"

"Stand apart," advised Desstra. "Divide its attention and don't give it a single target to focus on."

"I know how to fight," said Thianna.

"Then stop fighting with *me* and start fighting *with* me," said the elf.

The chimera bounded into the glade, roaring and bleating and hissing all at once. It swiped at Desstra with wickedly sharp claws, but the little dark elf surprised it by tumbling out of harm's way at the last second. She scored a touch on its forearm as she did so and the goat's head let loose a plaintive cry.

While this occurred, Thianna attempted to lunge forward and strike at the animal's other side, but the lion head spotted her and bared its jaws. The giantess retreated, then circled in a bid to get behind the chimera. The goat's head twisted its neck around in an impossible 360-degree turn and belched a gout of flame.

"What?" roared Thianna. "You can look behind you? That's so not fair!" As she dodged the fire burst, the chimera took another swipe at her.

Desstra rolled under a strike from the serpent's head and came up to slash at the lion, pulling its focus away from the giantess. It tried to bite her, but the elf was too quick. "Not fair is my saving your big butt again without any thanks," she said.

"Hey," said Thianna, kicking the chimera in its flank. "My big butt has already thanked you once today. Which is once more than I wanted to."

Both girls had to retreat as the creature struck at them each simultaneously. With the chimera's three pairs of eyes and two types of attack—claw and fire breath—they were finding it impossible to get the jump on the creature. Desstra glanced to the edge of the glade, but a drus guessed her intention and pointed a spear warningly her way. There'd be no escape in that direction. Their only choices were to defeat the chimera or die trying. She worried it would be the latter option.

Thianna tried to circle behind the animal again, but the goat's head wasn't having it. It blew its burning breath at her. Thianna noticed as she skipped aside how quickly tree folk appeared to toss buckets of earth on the sizzling grass. She wished they were tossing water instead, but they had obviously heard about her frost magic. And simple cold on its own, without ice, would just be an annoyance to a creature that breathed its own flame.

So ice magic was out. And her strength alone wasn't enough to fight so large and powerful a creature. Thianna tried to think as Karn would have if he were here. He had told her a story once, about a time he outwitted a two-headed troll. Well, this creature had three heads and one of them was a reptile. She should be able to work something there.

While she waged a defensive fight, keeping the deadly claws away and dancing aside from the flames, Thianna expanded her mental awareness, trying to find the thoughts of the chimera's snake head. It was like picking the lock on a door, then having the door open.

Watch for the little one on our right. I've got the big one covered. She's not as clumsy as she looks.

Thianna realized she was hearing all three heads thinking at once. When she had met the cockatrice in Gordasha—an animal with a rooster head and a snake head—she had only been able to communicate with its reptile half. But that had been a creature at odds with itself, with a head on either end of a body. Here the three heads were set in a row, and the chimera was clearly used to them all working together as one being. She was hearing the goat and lion heads' thoughts conveyed through the serpent head. The experience would be fascinating if it wasn't life-threatening.

I'll swallow the little one whole. I'll rend the big one with my teeth. I'll cook them both, the heads thought. *I hope the giant tastes better than she smells.*

Thianna started to object to the insult, but then she paused. She made a feint with her sword and listened as the goat head warned the lion of her approach. The heads were passing information between them, preventing any surprise from their prey. But they didn't know she could hear them. Karn would say that gave her an advantage.

Watch it, Thianna thought, doing her best to sound like a goat. The little one is behind you.

The snake head whipped around at that, searching for Desstra where she wasn't. The elf took advantage of the opportunity to stab the chimera's forearm.

Ouch, yelped the snake in Thianna's mind. *You said the pale one was in back of us!*

I did not! came the reply.

It's the giant that's in back of us, Thianna thought.

What? exclaimed the lion head, twisting to protect its rear. Thianna delivered another savage kick to its side.

Attack right! thought the snake in sudden panic.

Attack left! Thianna countered.

The chimera attempted to spring in two directions at once. Instead, it tipped over its own legs and fell to the ground. Desstra leapt in and out, leaving a red gash on its side. The chimera leapt up at once, roaring and bleating and hissing in anger.

Keep it together, thought the goat. *What is wrong with us?*

We attack left, the serpent thought.

We attack right, Thianna shot back.

This time the three heads knocked together as the confused animal tried to cross itself. Caught in the middle, the goat head suffered the worst of the collision. It wobbled on its neck dizzily.

Thianna used the chance to leap from behind, landing

on the lion back and gripping the goat head by its horns. It tried to twist around to burn her, but she was too strong for it.

Get it off! Get it off! Get it off! all three heads thought in unison.

The lion head tried to bite her, but unlike the goat it couldn't manage to reach so far around. The snake, with its longer neck, could, but Desstra stabbed at it and it had to face the elf instead.

Thianna pulled back savagely on the goat's neck. It bleated and shot fire into the sky.

Give up, Thianna thought, revealing herself to the chimera's mind at last.

What? Where? Who?

Give up, she thought again, putting as much force into her mind as she put into her arms.

I think we should give up, thought the snake. The lion growled at this.

Thianna had once brushed against a dragon's mind and not backed down. There was no way she wouldn't beat a chimera. She felt her mind pushing across the serpent's awareness to reach the goat and the lion through it. It was a feeling of incredible power, her will forced on another's.

Give up! the giantess roared. Thianna felt the chimera's resistance dissolve, felt her mind take control of its minds.

Okay okay okay! the animal replied. *We surrender.*

Then the beast shocked her with its next words.

We are yours to command.

Thianna let go of its horns and slid from its back. Confused, Desstra looked to her, ready to strike a killing blow at the deflated creature. The giantess waved her away.

"I don't want to command anyone," she said. "You can do whatever you want. Just don't eat the elf and me, all right?"

Freed of her weight, the chimera leapt clear and turned around.

We won't eat you, all three heads thought at once. *Thank you for our life. Thank you for our freedom.* Then it bolted from the clearing and disappeared into the woods.

One of the trees in the clearing suddenly pulled its limbs out of the tangle of branches that formed the ring around the glen. It clapped enormous wooden hands. Thianna realized that it was a hamadryad. All the trees that surrounded the circle were. Eyes were opening on every trunk, and more hands joined in the clapping.

"You're the Council of Elders, aren't you?" asked the giantess. "You watched all of this. We've been in your presence the whole time."

"Yes," said the hamadryad. "We are the elders of Dendronos. And we congratulate you, Thianna Frostborn. You have surprised us when you refused to kill or command the chimera. We are not accustomed to surprises. Or to displays of mercy. And we have reversed our judgment."

CHAPTER FIFTEEN

Strong Blasts Carry Far

Sirena wandered outside the palace grounds. She carried the Horn of Osius, which meant that a small detachment of Leta's guard followed her. Since the hostage escape, they were taking no chances. But Sirena hadn't practiced with the instrument since Talaria's wyvern had fled, and time was short. She would have to take another creature from the roosts. While she felt no sympathy for the rebellious wyvern that had created all their troubles, she did feel a twinge of pity for whichever loyal reptile would be subject to her experiments. But only a twinge. This situation was not her fault or doing. If she couldn't master the horn by the Great Hatching, she wouldn't be the only one to topple off the mountain. The Calderan way of life would fall as well. To preserve that, there was little she wouldn't do.

Crows take Thianna. How could a girl who was only one-half Calderan be better at using the horn than she, a full-blooded female born at the summit of their city? How could someone raised in an ice cavern best someone raised in the palace? It was ridiculous. It was infuriating.

Sirena found herself outside the hatchery. The woman guarding the door didn't challenge their Keras Keeper as she marched into the round domed structure. Inside, Sirena found herself on a circular balcony that followed the circumference of the room. The floor descended in a series of concentric circles until it reached the small stage where she would be expected to perform for a very unique audience. Hundreds of wyvern eggs were nestled like spectators in the stands of an amphitheater. In just three days she would play the horn upon that stage, weaving the notes that would compel the newly birthed wyverns to a lifetime of obedience.

She descended the balcony stairs to the center of the room. Sirena faced the rows upon rows of eggs, waiting silently upon her performance. She lifted the horn and placed it to her lips. She blew a tremendous blast.

I bet that rattled them in their shells, she thought of the eggs. Then something the traitorous wyvern had said floated to the front of her mind.

Strong blasts carry far.

When Thianna had first blown the horn in Ymiria, the wyverns in the roosts here had felt it even though they were thousands of miles away. Other things felt it too. The wyvern had been trying to warn her not to blow such forceful notes, but perhaps it had given her a clue. Thianna was part of the magic of the horn now. Could the horn be used to track Thianna?

Sirena sucked in a huge lungful of air. She raised the horn once again. And she filled it with all her rage.

The eggs in the hatchery shook violently. Outside the walls she could hear shrieks from the roosts. She was certainly upsetting the reptiles in Caldera, but how far was the soundless note traveling? Would it reach her cousin?

An image descended on Sirena's mind like a thunderclap.

She reeled under a vision of Thianna Frostborn. Incredibly her barbarian cousin was battling a chimera. Amid a circle of tall trees. The vision was brief but powerful. She was touching Thianna's mind! And Thianna's mind was touching something else! The half giant was communicating with a reptile, the serpent head of the chimera. The horn was letting Sirena eavesdrop on that conversation.

She ran from the hatchery. First she would have to return the Horn of Osius to its chamber for safekeeping. Then she would go to the Sky Docks. She needed the fastest wyvern available and she needed it now. She knew where her cousin was. And this time Thianna wasn't going to escape.

Stranger things than fish swam in the waters south of Thica.

Amid the range of islands known as Sarn's Teeth, something very large and very unusual glided under the waves. The other sea creatures gave it a wide berth. They knew how much it ate, and they didn't want to be next.

But the creature wasn't hungry. It had feasted on a large trading vessel earlier this morning. The screams of the unfortunate crew had been delightful, as had been their futile efforts to defend themselves. Shredded bits of meat still trailed from its many, many teeth. It had many mouths but only one belly. It drifted along at an almost leisurely pace now, digesting its breakfast and watching tiny prey dart away from it in fear. The creature enjoyed its unchallenged mastery of the sea.

A sound that wasn't a sound stabbed its many minds like spears through the eyes.

The creature roared, lashing its tail and flailing its necks at the sudden pain in its heads. The other denizens of the sea didn't understand what had caused its agitation. They didn't want to know. They fled.

Alone in the waters, the titanic creature writhed and twisted. So great was its size that its thrashing sent hundred-foot waves rolling across the ocean. Boats miles away would soon be capsized. Several nearby villages would be wiped off their islands entirely.

The creature didn't care. All its attention was focused on the sound in its ears. And it had a lot of ears. It had heard the agonizing reverberations before. But on that occasion the noise had come from far away, deep in an icebound land. The sound had ceased long before the creature could reach the source. But this time the sound was closer, louder, stronger. This time it could be tracked. One by one it turned its heads in the direction of the hated noise. Then it began to swim with purpose. It would find whatever, or whoever, was making this terrible sound. And it would silence it. Forever.

CHAPTER SIXTEEN

Family Squabbles

Thianna awoke from her first decent night's rest in a long while, having slept late into the morning. She was in a pleasant guest cottage grown from the trunk of an apple tree. While the enormous flower petals that she lay on weren't as comfortable as her preferred bed—a frozen block of ice piled high with furs—they were soft and silky and she had slept like a giant baby. She reached to the wall and plucked breakfast, a shiny red apple.

"You trust that?" said Desstra. Thianna glanced and saw that the elf was awake. She sat on a stump that rose from the floor. All the furniture in the cottage was part of the tree. The dark elf was nibbling on some of the mushrooms she had collected from the tunnels beneath Caldera.

Thianna shrugged. She took a bite of her apple and munched loudly.

"What if it's poisoned?" continued Desstra. "After all, yesterday they were trying to feed us to a chimera."

"And now today we're honored guests," said the giantess. "I've noticed that people trying to kill me have a habit of changing their minds," she added pointedly.

"Only some of them," said Desstra, who certainly qualified for the distinction.

"The lucky ones." Thianna grinned. "Anyway, we might as well enjoy it while it lasts." She took another bite of the apple, then rose from the flowery bedding and strode to a window. Pushing aside a leafy curtain, she bent down and gazed out through a near-transparent petal at the city outside. She wasn't surprised—or even offended—that the oak woman stood guard in the street outside. She turned from the window and leaned against it.

"How long does it take these hamadryads to come to a decision?" she wondered.

"You're asking them to rebel against their overlords," replied Desstra. "It's not something they should take lightly. They are all made of wood, after all. And your people are really trigger-happy with those fire lances of theirs."

Thianna frowned and tossed her apple aside.

"What's wrong?" asked Desstra.

The giantess straightened up—though not all the way, as the cottage was low-ceilinged—and began to pace.

"My people," she said. "It was bad enough when I thought my mother's people were after me. But we get here and discover they've enslaved a whole continent. 'My people' really aren't very nice."

"Your frost giants sound nice," said Desstra. "Most of them, anyway."

"Yeah, but that's Dad's side of the family. I came off the mountain to find out more about being human, and now I learn that my mother's family is a bunch of jerks and bullies. How do you feel proud about that, when your people are all evil?"

"No one is all evil," said Desstra.

"Says the dark elf," replied Thianna. Desstra gave her a sharp look.

"Says the dark elf," Desstra repeated. "The Underhand are nasty—no one knows that better than me, believe me—but not everyone in Deep Shadow is like they are. They are supposed to exist to protect us from the surface world, but they've grown too powerful. They control too much of the underworld as well. But there are plenty of wonderful people, most of whom live in fear of the Underhand themselves. I see that now, all the poor shopkeepers, mushroom farmers, leather workers, children, and parents . . ." Desstra's voice trailed off as she thought of her own family. She wondered what lies the Underhand had spread about her after her desertion. They didn't even have to lie. The truth was she was a traitor to her kind. Her family was probably suffering humiliation now. They would be ostracized. Or worse. "Anyway," she said, pulling her thoughts back to the present. "You can't blame everyone for a bad government."

"Can't you?" said Thianna. "When every citizen is a soldier and every soldier works to keep Thica under Caldera's thumb? How can I be proud of my human half if this is what I am?"

"You do the best you can for yourself," said the elf. "You do what you know is right."

"But what if I don't know what right is?" said Thianna. "What's right about my coming here a stranger and turning everything on its ear?"

"You don't like bullies," said Desstra. "You know that."

There was a knock at the door.

"Come in," Thianna called.

Daphne stepped into the room.

"The council want to speak with you now," said the dryad.

"They're going to help us?" Thianna asked.

"I don't know," Daphne replied. "Only that I am supposed to fetch you."

She led them through the city to the glen where the ring of hamadryads stood. Once again their branches were clustered with interested citizens who wanted to see the spectacle of the frost giant and the dark elf.

"I hope we don't have to fight anybody this time," Desstra muttered under her breath as they stepped into the circle of trees.

"Welcome to the Council of Elders this morning, Thianna," said the same hamadryad who had addressed them the day before. Thianna guessed that it was the spokesperson for the group. She nodded.

"You've considered my suggestion?"

"We have," the hamadryad replied.

"And you'll rise up and help me fight the Calderans?"

The hamadryad shook its branches. "We cannot help you now."

"But you know I won't side with them," protested Thianna. "You know the Hatching is coming. I can help you be free!"

"Free from fire that falls from the sky?" asked the hamadryad. "But patience—I have not said that we will not help you. Only that we will not help you *now*."

"What do you mean?" Desstra asked.

"Dendronos cannot be the only city to rise up. We would suffer too heavily in such a fight while others hung back and awaited the outcome."

"But if we can get others?"

The hamadryad smiled.

"If you can convince other cities to join in this battle, then Dendronos will fight as well."

Thianna looked at Desstra, then back to the hamadryad.

"I don't know if you've noticed," she said, "but we don't exactly have a lot of time here."

The hamadryad held up a hand to forestall her.

"The minotaurs of Labyrinthia are the most capable warriors. They are also the most stubborn. If King Asterion could be convinced to join your crusade, other cities would follow. Persuade Labyrinthia to join the fight and the dryads and drus of Dendronos will take up your cause as well."

"How are we supposed to do that?" asked the giantess. "How do we even get there in time?"

"How you change the minotaur's mind, I cannot say," the spokesperson replied, "but as to how you get there, we have a hamadryad in the palace gardens at the heart of Labyrinthia."

"You have a spy!" exclaimed Desstra. "Like the one in Caldera."

The hamadryad smiled sadly.

"It was not always so. Once we called them ambassadors. But times change." It motioned with a branch and Daphne stepped forward.

"This one will accompany you," said the spokesperson. "She will guide you to Labyrinthia and return to us with news of your success or failure."

"I will?" asked Daphne uncertainly. The little dryad didn't look thrilled with the prospect of more adventure. The hamadryad coughed. "Oh, I mean I will," Daphne amended.

*　*　*

Thianna and her companions were preparing to depart. The hamadryads had equipped them with food and other necessities. Everything was loaded into backpacks made of woven grasses.

The frost giant took stock of their supplies. She held out a pouch full of strange, pebblelike objects. They were yellow, transparent, and droplet-shaped.

"What's this?" she asked.

"We call it the Tears of Dendronos," Daphne explained. "It's resin from the mastic tree."

"What do I want with tree resin?"

"It's a gum. For chewing," the dryad said. "It tastes good. And you use it to freshen your breath."

"My breath smells as fresh as my feet, tree girl."

"That might be her point," said Desstra, joining them.

"Give it a try," urged Daphne.

Thianna was skeptical, but she placed the resin droplet into her mouth. Daphne nodded encouragingly. After a few bites, the gum began to soften as she chewed. The flavor was a not-unpleasant pinelike taste.

"Well?" the dryad asked.

"Not bad," Thianna confessed. "Not that I am admitting I need it or anything."

"Of course not." Daphne offered a piece to the elf.

"No offense," said Desstra, "but that looks like something that fell from your nose."

The dryad looked hurt.

"Maybe Karn will like it," Desstra added.

"If we find him," said Thianna. "Which we will."

The girls were taking their leave of the Council of Elders when a young drus broke through into the glade.

"They're coming!" he cried. He had been running hard and was panting.

"Who are coming?" asked a hamadryad.

"From the skies." He pointed.

A shadow fell across the grass.

Three wyverns descended. Sirena rode on one, flanked by two soldiers. As they touched down in the glen, the hamadryads became still and silent. For all the newcomers knew, they were simply a ring of trees.

"Good to see you, cousin," said Thianna sarcastically.

"No more playing around, *cousin,*" Sirena replied. "You will come back with me to Caldera now."

"And if I have other plans?"

Sirena gestured to the woman on her right. The soldier leveled her fire lance and shot a burst of flame at a tree beside the giantess.

The hamadryad shrieked and beat at the fires with its branches. A drus ran forward to toss sand on it.

"The tree—" said the woman. "It talked!"

"It screamed!" said the other soldier.

Before Sirena could react, a hamadryad behind her party sprang to life. It reached out long limbs and plucked the offending soldier off her mount. The woman hollered, kicking and squirming. A door to the Greenways opened in the hamadryad's trunk and it shoved the pro-testing soldier inside. Her screams cut off abruptly as the door closed. The green glow ceased as the bark sealed.

Thianna took advantage of the confusion to rush Sirena. She didn't attack the girl, however, but put her shoulder to her mount's torso and heaved.

Sorry about this, she thought to the reptile.

Then she upended the wyvern, dumping Sirena to the grass. The Calderan had to roll away to avoid being trapped beneath her own mount as it tumbled over.

The remaining soldier leveled her fire lance, then yelled as it was jerked from her hands on a spool of spi-der silk.

"Told you this stuff would come in handy," said Desstra.

Then the soldier was lifted into the air and tossed into a door in another hamadryad. It didn't stop with the soldier but grasped the wyvern by the tail and dragged it into its trunk. The beast was slightly too large for the opening, but the tree pushed and prodded.

"I can't believe I ate the whole thing," it said with a wink.

Then the hamadryads stuffed the remaining wyverns into doorways.

Sirena witnessed this in horror, then suddenly realized she was the only Calderan left. She made to bolt from the clearing, but she was snatched up in a branch.

"Don't hurt her!" Thianna called, but her cousin was

hurled through a doorway just as her soldiers had been. Her shouts of protest vanished as the doorway closed.

Thianna stood staring at the glen. One minute there had been Calderan soldiers there. The next they were gone, as if they never were.

"Time is now of the urgency," said a hamadryad. "Or so it would seem." It opened a door in its trunk. "Go now."

"Hold on a moment," said Thianna. "Didn't you just stuff the soldiers in there?"

"Different pathways lead to different places," the hamadryad explained. "Do not worry for them. They will be unharmed. Though they will find themselves somewhere they did not expect to be." It pointed at the glowing hole in its own trunk. "Now go. You must bring Labyrinthia to your cause before news of our actions reaches the capital. We will be punished severely for this. You are now our only hope, Thianna Frostborn."

Thianna nodded. "Ready, Daphne?" she said.

"No," said the dryad. "Of course not. But let's go."

Thianna grinned. Beside her Desstra rewound her spider silk.

"You know I'm ready," the elf said.

The three girls entered the Greenways, leaving Dendronos behind.

CHAPTER SEVENTEEN

Running of the Bulls

Karn was having a hard time avoiding looking at the walls. The labyrinthine mosaic ran throughout this room as well. It still gave him a headache, though he appreciated the craftsmanship in its design. But like everything else in Labyrinthia, it was meant for minotaurs and not outsiders.

"I wish there was something to eat other than wheat," he said aloud. He had passed the night in very nice quarters. That is, if you were a minotaur. Karn was lying on a large pile of straw, which was set beneath a four-poster canopy. He did have to admit, it was the freshest, cleanest straw he'd ever seen, though he wasn't sure if he was supposed to sleep in it or eat it for the day meal. Probably both.

The door to their room opened. Asterius barged in, snorting and pawing the ground in agitation. The bull boy was clearly in a huff. Karn looked at him expectantly. He noticed that Asterius had a large pack over his shoulder.

"I—" Asterius began. "Well, I—look, this is hard for me to say, but I'm sorry. Okay? I thought my father would help us. I don't understand why he won't fight the Calderans. I know he wants to."

"He has to think about his city," said Karn. "I'm sure he will stand up for Labyrinthia when he feels the time is right."

Asterius swished his tail, knocking a vase from a nearby stand. It crashed on the ground.

"The time is now," he said adamantly. "Only he doesn't see it." He stopped pacing and unshouldered his pack. "I'm to be sent back to Caldera. He's hoping it will buy him more time."

"I'm sorry," said Karn. Then he added, "What about me?"

"He hasn't decided." Asterius looked miserable. "He may send you back as well. Or he may decide to do away with you and pretend you never came here."

"Do away with me how?" said Karn in alarm.

"Don't worry," Asterius said. "I'm going to get you out of here."

The minotaur tore open his pack and pulled out an oversize helmet. Cattle horns had been fixed to the sides.

"Here," he said, handing Karn the odd headgear. "Put this on."

Karn looked at the strange helmet.

"Who wears horns on their head?" he said. He glanced apologetically at the minotaur. "I mean, if they don't grow there naturally." It didn't seem to make good sense. "An opponent could grab the horn and pull the helmet over your eyes or expose your neck for the stroke of an ax."

"You don't have to fight in it," said Asterius. "I'm trying to disguise you to look like a minotaur."

Karn was skeptical, but he donned the unwieldy headgear. He walked to a dresser, where a highly polished shield of white steel served as a mirror. He gazed at his distorted reflection.

"This looks ridiculous," he said. "It's not going to fool anybody."

"Just keep your head down," said the bull boy. "Hopefully nobody will pay attention. If I can get you to the hippalektryons, you can be miles away before anyone notices you are gone."

"What about you? Aren't you coming with me?"

Asterius shook his head.

"What is the point? I thought my father would rise up. If he's not going to, I might as well be a prisoner on a mountaintop as anything." The minotaur stamped a hoof in frustration, then flung open the door. "Let's not stand here chewing our cud," he said. "Let's move."

Asterius led them out into the corridor, choosing back passageways through the palace.

"My father is a brave man," he said softly to himself. "A brave man."

Karn left him alone in his thoughts for a bit, but after a while he couldn't keep quiet.

"I feel stupid," he said. He was trying and failing to keep his head still. The oversize helmet was a loose fit and every single movement sent it sliding. At present, the horns had slipped halfway around. If anyone was observing him and genuinely thought he was a minotaur, it would appear that he had one horn growing from out of his forehead and the other from the back of his skull.

Asterius sighed and adjusted Karn's helmet.

"You're supposed to be a minotaur, not a unicorn," he said.

"Don't you think I know that?" said Karn. Then he added, "Not that I know what a unicorn is."

"Stop complaining," said Asterius. "At least I'm getting you out of here. And I'd like to see you do better on short notice."

The two companions exited the palace and began working their way through a garden outside. Predictably, it was a hedge maze. The tall shrubs kept them from seeing anything but the path in front of them, but at least it hid all but their horns from passersby. Regardless Karn grumbled at what felt like a ridiculous waste of time. All the twists and turns and doubling back wasn't putting enough distance between them and their captors, but Asterius swore that he had chosen the least conspicuous way for them to depart. And Karn was grateful to the minotaur, who negotiated the maze effortlessly. If Asterius weren't guiding them, he was sure that he would be hopelessly lost.

Eventually they stepped from the hedge maze onto the streets of Labyrinthia. An orderly row of trees marked the gate where they emerged, but across from where they stood they saw the familiar city walls with its houses, shops, and eateries hanging from the ramparts.

Unfortunately, a squadron of soldiers stood atop the wall gazing down at them. King Asterion glared at them from their midst.

"Son," said the minotaur ruler, "I am very disappointed in you."

"Father—I—"

"Get up here now!" roared the king. A stairway lowered.

"I tried," said Asterius. Head hanging, he trotted up the stairs to join his father. The king snorted at him, then turned his attention to Karn.

"You're in a difficult situation, wouldn't you say?" said the king.

Karn opened his mouth to answer, but at that very moment one of the trees by the gate suddenly began to glow around its midsection. A doorway opened in its trunk and a frost giant stumbled out.

"Thianna!" Karn exclaimed, rushing to his best friend's side. The giantess's face lit up when she saw him. She grabbed Karn in a bear hug.

"Ribs—easy," he gasped. But he was smiling as broadly as she was. Gradually each let go of the other. Thianna looked around her to see where she was, but Karn was noticing the glowing green hole in the trunk she had so recently vacated.

"You, um, you came out of a tree," he said.

"Surprised you, didn't it?" she replied, smiling. "Actually, it's a hamadryad, but I'll explain what that is later. We've been to Dendronos."

"We?" Karn asked hopefully. "Is Desstra with you?"

"Here I am," said the elf, stepping from the Greenway. She held up a small pouch. "And look, we've brought gum."

Karn didn't know what *gum* meant, but he laughed, relieved to see that she was all right. Then he noticed the bark-skinned girl climbing from the tree. She was blinking brown eyes and gaping at the walls around her from under leafy bangs.

"Who is that?" he asked.

"Daphne," said Thianna. "She's a dryad. They're like little hamadryads that aren't planted in one spot."

"There's more to it than that," objected Daphne.

"Anyway," said Thianna with a shrug. "She's been helping us. She saved me, actually."

Karn gave the dryad a quick wave of thanks.

"I'm glad we're back together," he said.

"So am I," Thianna replied.

"This is all very touching," shouted King Asterion, who until this point had been watching the conversation with a look of amusement on his face, "but if your reunion is over, perhaps we can get on with the matter of your recapture?"

Thianna looked up for the first time at the king and his retinue of soldiers.

"You remember Asterion, king of the minotaurs?" said Karn.

Thianna nodded.

"What's he want?"

"He's been keeping us prisoner, trying to work out whether to kill us and cover it up or hand us back over to the two queens."

"I see you've been having as much fun as we have," said the giantess. She shouted to the king. "I have a message for you, Asterion!" she said. "The Council of Elders in Dendronos say they will join our rebellion if Labyrinthia does as well."

"What's this?" said Karn beside her. "I leave you alone for two days and you start a revolution!"

"Imagine what could have happened if we'd stayed away a week," said Desstra, stepping up beside them.

Above them King Asterion was considering Thianna's words, rubbing his chin with a large fist and swishing his tail.

"What do you say?" Thianna called to him.

"Father?" Asterius said hopefully.

"Bah!" roared the minotaur. "It's a ploy. Some trap of the tree folk."

"How can it be a trap?" asked the frost giant.

"The Dendronosi are timid, careful people. Vegetables can play a long game, after all. They want to trick us into attacking first, let Labyrinthia suffer the brunt of Caldera's retaliation, then come into the fight to mop up the survivors."

"That's actually not a bad strategy," observed Desstra.

"Not helping," said the frost giant. To the king she said, "That's not the case here. The Calderans saw them aiding us. They have only a matter of days before they'll be punished. They can't afford to wait."

"Even better," said Asterion. "We can let them fight first, and we can mop up later." He twirled his double-bladed ax. "Which only leaves me the conundrum of whether to disappear you children or hand you over."

"There's a third option," said Thianna.

"What's that?" said the king, still twirling his ax.

"We run for it!"

She took off down the street. Karn and Desstra exchanged a glance, then charged after her. Behind them Daphne did the same.

Above them King Asterion roared, but not in anger.

"A chase!" the minotaur monarch yelled gleefully. "Thank Teshub! It's been years since we've had a good old-fashioned chase through the labyrinth." He laughed and beat his free hand on his side. Then the king turned to the soldiers beside him.

"Well," he said, "what are you waiting for? After them!"

Sirena struck the ground hard. But at least it was ground. She gripped the grass between clenched fingers, struggling to get on top of her anger. Then she lifted her head and looked around.

She was in a park in the middle of a city. A normal, human city from the look of the nearest buildings. She didn't recognize it, but it was neither Dendronos nor Caldera. She needed to get back, and fast—before her cousin escaped. Sirena turned around. Several trees grew in a cluster behind her. None of them moved or spoke. No magic doorways were visible in any of their trunks. It was impossible to tell which one was the tree she had come through.

"Was it you?" she said to a date plum tree. The tree did not respond. She turned to the one next to it. She kicked the trunk. "Open up!" she yelled. She kicked the tree again, but the only response was that several fruits were dislodged and fell to earth.

Sirena turned and pounded her fist on the next-nearest tree. "I know it was you," she said. "You're only making it harder on yourself by keeping mum."

She turned to a third tree, studying it. Then she

snatched a leaf and tore it off savagely, hoping to provoke a reaction. None followed. "Argh!" she exclaimed in frustration. "If I had a fire lance, I would set every one of you ablaze!" She grabbed another tree and began to shake it. "Open up! Open up! I know you can open up!"

"Child, are you all right?"

Sirena spun around. A soldier was gazing at her as if she were crazy.

"I'm not a child," she barked. "I'm your Keras Keeper."

"Keras Keeper?" said the woman, confused. "Shouldn't you be in Caldera? The Great Hatching is in two days."

She marched up to the soldier.

"Don't you think I know that? Tell me, what city is this?"

"What city? Don't you know?"

"Yes, what city? It's a simple question, you witless grunt. What city is this?"

"There's no need to be rude," the woman said, her cheeks coloring.

"There's every need," barked Sirena. "Now shut up and answer my question."

"But if I shut up, how will I—?" the soldier began. Seeing the menacing look in the Keras Keeper's eyes, she stopped and swallowed. "This is Lassathonia," she said.

"Thank you," said Sirena with exaggerated politeness. "That wasn't hard, was it?" She considered her location. Lassathonia was the southernmost city on the Thican island-continent. She was hundreds of miles from Caldera, even farther from Dendronos. There was no point in trying to reach the city of tree folk. Thianna would be long gone before she could get there. She needed other options. Sirena turned to the soldier.

"Take me to your garrison," she said. "I'm going to commandeer a wyvern. And I need reinforcements."

As they walked from the park she turned to the cluster of trees.

"Crows take you all," she said.

The soldier gave her a funny look.

"I don't think crows eat trees," she said. Then, when she saw the murderous glare that Sirena turned her way, she amended, "Of course, I could be wrong about that."

The loud peals of cowbells rang in the air. Those citizens of Labyrinthia who were at ground level rapidly ascended staircases, drawing them up in their wake. As the streets emptied out, doors and windows opened and groups of the bull folk strode onto balconies to look down at them. Alerted by the noise of the bells, bull men and kine women were preparing to enjoy the spectacle.

"Looks like we have an audience," Karn said.

"What do they want?" Daphne asked fearfully.

"I think we're the morning's entertainment," said the Norrønur.

"Then let's give them a show," Thianna replied.

The elf spun around and lobbed something at their

pursuers. When it hit the ground it exploded. The soldiers reared away from the resulting smoke and flames.

"It's mostly flash," Desstra apologized. "Not a lot of bang."

"At least it buys us time," said Karn.

"Nicely done!" shouted King Asterion. Thianna looked for the source of the voice and found the minotaur monarch perched atop a nearby wall. Someone had brought him a wide drinking bowl while an attendant stood by with a plate piled with fresh grasses. The king wiped wine from his chin, then grabbed a handful of vegetation and munched. Beside him, his son Asterius seemed less pleased with the events of the morning.

"I'm glad somebody is having fun!" Thianna shouted at the king.

"Yes, indeed, thank you," Asterion replied good-naturedly. "But don't worry, your own fun is just beginning."

Thianna gritted her teeth and led the charge through the streets of the city. After the third switchback, she threw her hands wide and exclaimed, "What is this, some sort of maze?"

"Well, yes," said Karn. "It is called Labyrinthia, after all."

"Who builds a city shaped like a maze?"

"I would think the answer was obvious," said Desstra.

Thianna raised a warning finger at the elf.

"I just want to get out of here," said Daphne. "Which way do we go?"

"I don't know," said Karn. "I only got here yesterday, and we didn't come in this way."

"I thought you were good at games," said the frost giant.

"Board games," he replied. "Strategy games. Not mazes. Mazes aren't games."

"Sure they are," said the frost giant.

"A maze is a type of puzzle," said Daphne. "And a puzzle is a type of game."

"See?" said Thianna. "She agrees with me."

"Never mind," said Desstra. "Just go left."

"Why left?" asked the Norrønur.

"We take every left turn," the elf said. "That's how you avoid getting lost in a labyrinth."

"It is?" asked Thianna.

"I think. I've never been in one before."

"Oh great," said the frost giant, but she led them along the leftward street. A few more twists and turns and the group found themselves in a small open square. It was dominated by a marble minotaur statue. Water issued from both of its horns into a small pool. Fanning out to either side of the fountain was a second troop of minotaur soldiers.

"We're boxed in," said Thianna. She readied her sword, trusting that her companions would do the same.

"Let's even the odds," said Desstra. The elf lobbed another incendiary at the approaching minotaurs. The explosion drove several of the soldiers back, then the rest fell upon the companions and the fight began in earnest.

Swords, hammers, and axes clashed. From the houses above, the citizens of Labyrinthia variously cheered and booed. Some threw flowers and others tossed stones and rotten apples. The bull folk seemed not to favor one side or the other as long as the entertainment was good. Weaponless and terrified, the dryad ran about as her leaves tried to curl up over her head.

Dodging a quick stroke from an ax, Thianna tripped and fell into the fountain. Seeing this, Karn hollered in alarm, but the giantess emerged from the water. As she stepped from the pool, Karn noticed that she had frozen the water in her clothing. Her Thican robe was now hard and stiff.

"Instant ice armor," she said with a grin. "Now I don't have to be so careful." With the benefit of this extra layer of protection, the giantess dove into a group of three soldiers and soon had them on the ground. Thianna smiled as a bouquet of flowers was thrown at her feet.

She picked it up and waved at the crowd.

"Somebody's popular," noted Desstra.

"I just hope they don't expect us to eat those," Karn said.

Having driven back or overcome their opponents, the

companions continued through the square and onto another street.

Unfortunately, the next intersection led them to a dead end. They had to backtrack, which meant their pursuers gained ground. When the soldiers spotted their prey, they shouted and charged.

"Here we go again," said Thianna.

"Wait," said Desstra, laying a hand on her arm.

Suddenly the entire group of minotaurs stopped and flipped over onto their backs. It was as if each of them had been yanked backward by an invisible rope.

The giantess gave the elf a questioning look.

"Spiderweb," Desstra explained. "Stretched across the street. Hard to spot. That's twice it's come in handy."

"What will you do for a third time?" asked Thianna.

"Are we getting anywhere nearer to the city gates?" Karn asked.

"Impossible to tell," Desstra said. "A maze winds in and out before leading you to its exit."

"We could be heading right back to the center!" wailed Daphne. The timid dryad was definitely not having fun.

"Exactly!" King Asterion called down from the wall above. "How do you know whether you are making progress? A fascinating conundrum, isn't it? But carry on."

Karn reckoned that they were somewhere roughly halfway between the central palace and the outer walls when events took a turn for the worst. As they neared a bend in the streets, they heard a loud scuttling sound. He grabbed Thianna's arm and slowed her run.

"Something's coming," he warned.

"More soldiers?" she said.

"I don't think so," Karn replied.

Something indeed felt its way around the corner. It was a long leg, covered in a shiny black carapace.

"Not more spiders!" exclaimed Daphne. But the dryad was mistaken.

An enormous scorpion rounded the corner. It was bigger than a horse. Bigger even than an Uskirian war pig. Its claws were so large they looked like they could snip a person in half. An enormous stinger curled up from its hindquarters and towered in the air. A minotaur rode upon its back with reins affixed to its head.

"I don't think we can fight that," said Karn.

"Oh, but wouldn't you like to try?" King Asterion shouted at them. He laughed and called for another bowl of wine. Then the king pointed. "And look this way."

More soldiers were approaching from behind. They were boxed in again.

Desstra lobbed an explosion. Riderless, the scorpion fell back in the wake of the flames. Then Daphne surprised everyone by racing forward. As the creature reached a claw for her, she leapt into the air. Spinning, the dryad fanned out her leaves. She whirled upward, soaring above the grasp of the deadly pincers. Rising up after her, the scorpion exposed its underbelly. Thianna took the opportunity to charge it, throwing her shoulder into its midsection and toppling it over. Desstra passed Karn one end of a spiderweb, and the two of them ran at the beast. The Norrønur wore one of the former Underhand student's specially treated gloves so that the sticky silk wouldn't snare his hand. Between the two of them, they tangled the legs of the scorpion and pulled the strong thread tight.

Atop the wall, the king of the minotaurs seemed pleased.

"This is the best day we've had in Labyrinthia in ages," he said to his son. "What do you say, Asterius? Should we invite foreigners to the palace more often?"

"They work together, Father," said the bull boy.

"Yes," the king agreed. "They are putting on quite a show. All the more fun because they have no idea which way to go. And more soldiers come!"

Asterius gave his father a reproachful look.

"That's not what I mean," he said. "Look at them, Father. Really look at them. A giant, a pale human, a dryad, and whatever the pointy-eared one is. They are all different, from different places. But together they are beating your soldiers."

The king frowned.

"What are you implying?" he said.

"If you were to join Dendronos and the other city-states, you could beat the Calderans now. You wouldn't have to wait."

"Leave politics to the adults, son," said the king. "Just shut up and enjoy the maze."

Asterius hung his head, but not in shame. In mounting anger. When he had fled Caldera, he had been so sure that his father would stand up for Labyrinthia, the first of the peoples of Thica to rise. Now he realized that the king would always hesitate. If someone were to lead the charge, it wouldn't be King Asterion.

"Enjoy the maze," repeated Asterius, a hoof unconsciously pawing as he gathered his energy and his nerve. "Good advice, Father. I think I will."

The minotaur prince leapt from the wall. He bounced once on a large awning, then sprang to the street below.

"Asterius, get back up here!" roared the king, but the son ignored his father.

"Follow me," the bull boy called to his friends and companions. "I am a minotaur, and I can lead you out of the maze."

CHAPTER EIGHTEEN

Casting the Dice

"Open in the name of the prince!" Asterius ordered the guard atop one of the two horn-rimmed towers.

"My prince?" said the minotaur soldier. "But—didn't you only just arrive yesterday?"

"And now I am leaving again. Raise the portcullis."

The guard stared from his platform at the motley crew of young people before the gate.

"Raise the portcullis," repeated Asterius, "or I'll come up there and knock you off your post." He glanced sideways at Thianna. "Or she will."

The guard quickly bent to the task, turning the wheel that wound the heavy chain that in turn would raise the gate. The huge portcullis slid upward. Then the noise of their pursuers thundered down the street. The soldier saw a half-dozen minotaurs charging toward the children. And behind them three scorpion riders, one of which was his monarch. He stood up, mouth agape, and released the wheel. The gate began to fall.

Thianna leapt forward, catching the heavy portcullis before it closed completely. She heaved, raising the gate to the level of her shoulders and holding it open.

"Quickly! Heavy!" the frost giant grunted. Karn ushered his companions through. When the last of them was clear, Thianna leapt aside. The metal clanged as it crashed down, blocking their pursuers' exit.

Or so they thought. The three scorpion riders went right up and over the wall. The legs of the creatures found holds in even the smoothest stone. They scurried down the other side and fanned out around the fugitives.

"Haven't you had enough fun for one day?" yelled Thianna. "We beat everyone you tossed at us *and* we got through your maze. Why don't you give up and let us go?"

King Asterion didn't reply. He sat on the scorpion, gazing at his son standing amid all the strange folk. He raised his double-bladed ax, spinning it around. The two blades caught the bright sunlight. Then he tossed the weapon to the ground, where one edge stuck in the dirt.

The king slipped from the back of his scorpion and approached the group.

"Quite an assortment you are," Asterion said. "Human, minotaur, Dendronosi, and . . ." He paused when his eyes fell on Desstra.

"Elf," she said.

"And elf," finished the king with a smile. "One so different from the other. And all fighting alongside each other against a common foe. You surprised me when you left my side to join them, son."

"Father, I—" began Asterius, but the king waved him to silence.

"Sometimes it takes a real surprise to shock a stubborn bull into changing his mind." He strode to stand before the frost giant. "Thianna Frostborn," said the king, "you have shown us the path we must tread. Thank you and congratulations. Labyrinthia has taken up your cause."

"You mean it?" said Thianna, her face breaking into a grin.

"Let the dice be cast," said the bull man. "They will fall where they may." He ruffled his son's hair, and this time Asterius didn't shake off his hand. "Let us all return to the Palace of the Double Ax as allies," he said. "We will feast with my warrior-advisors and hold a Council of Battle! Too long have the Calderans ruled from their mountaintop. It is time for the city-states of Thica to regain their freedom!"

"Treason," shouted a wyvern rider from the sky.

Three wyverns dropped to the ground. Made nervous by the large reptiles, the scorpions clicked their pincers and drummed their legs. The central rider wore a now-familiar black cape.

"Leta," said Thianna.

The head of the Keras Guard removed her helmet and dismounted. She walked to the assembled group.

"You will not throw off your yoke so easily, bull man," she said to the king. Asterion opened his mouth to reply, but she walked on to where the frost giant stood.

"I thought only to find your friend, to use as leverage against you," Leta explained. "But here I find the two of you together. We will return you both to the capital immediately, where this insurrection will be reported."

At the edge of Leta's vision, Desstra had begun to back away.

"Not so fast, little elf," the woman said. "I won't make the mistake of underestimating you again. Nor will I leave you alive to plot your revenge." She turned to one of her two soldiers. "Light her up," she said.

Desstra stilled as a fire lance was brought to bear on her. But before the soldier could touch the trigger, Thianna hurled something through the air.

The snowball wasn't much of a weapon in the Thican heat, but it still made for a marvelous distraction. The former knattleikr player tossed her projectile in a perfect pitch, straight through the helmet's right eye slit and into the woman's face. Blinded, and with an ice-induced headache, she toppled from her saddle.

Leta roared and drew her sword, racing toward Thianna.

The giantess met the blow with her own blade and trapped it. Slowly Thianna forced Leta's sword down.

"I am head of the Keras Guard," Leta said. "I have succeeded where all others have failed, and I will not be bested by you anymore."

"I am Thianna Frostborn," replied the Ymirian girl. "And I don't care what you think."

Thianna thrust her shoulder into Leta's sternum, knocking the woman back. As she fell, Desstra somersaulted into her path, tripping her legs. Leta stumbled into her own mount, which suddenly whipped its head up in a savage jerk. The Keras Guard captain was tossed through the air to crash into King Asterion's mount. Alarmed, the huge scorpion grasped the unfortunate soldier in its pincers. Her screams were loud but short-lived.

Thianna looked away. She saw that the soldier who had taken the snowball was immobilized by her friends, while the minotaurs had the only still-mounted Calderan surrounded. The woman took in the situation and wisely held up her hands in surrender.

Thianna turned to the wyvern.

"That was a pretty treasonous move you made there yourself, friend," she said.

The power of the horn fades as the time of the Great Hatching approaches, it replied in her mind. *Also, didn't she get on your nerves? She was really getting on mine.*

*   *   *

257

Thianna lay awake on the bed of straw. Minotaurs didn't seem to think bathtubs were a necessary component of guest quarters. At any rate, it wasn't the unfamiliar bedding that troubled her. She had other things on her mind.

The giantess stood, tiptoeing so as not to wake her companions. Desstra and Daphne each lay on their own straw pile. The dryad was snoring softly and didn't seem capable of being disturbed. Desstra had explained that the tree girl was diurnal. Apparently that didn't mean she came equipped with two urns like it sounded. It meant that like a flower she shut down when the sun went down.

Thianna paced about the room. They had spent most of the day in conference with the king and his warrior-advisors, along with representatives summoned from Dendronos who arrived via the Greenway. Both cities would begin battle preparations on the morrow, but the giantess hoped they wouldn't be necessary. If they could pull off what they had plotted, war might be avoided outright.

Karn had actually contributed the bulk of their plans. The Thrones and Bones expert was proving to be quite a strategist. She was proud of the way the Norrønur had spoken before a gathering of adults. He had come a long way from the irresponsible boy who didn't know better than to eat snow when he was lost in a frozen wilderness.

The Great Hatching would occur in two days. It was agreed that while the horn remained under Thican control, a ground-based assault would be futile. So a covert team would be sent into the city. A large force would be detected immediately, but Karn reasoned that just a few individuals entering through the Greenway could sneak into Caldera under cover of darkness. Thianna had been chosen to lead a small team on a mission to steal the horn. Naturally she had picked her companions, old and new. Asterion had objected at first, but adult minotaurs weren't known for being sneaky, and Thianna had a certain leverage when it came to the Horn of Osius and her ability to wield it. When it was safely in her control, the minotaur and tree folk forces could approach. But without air support, the hope was that the Calderans would surrender peaceably.

That was the hope, anyway. She was reminded of a Norrønian proverb that Karn had taught her. "The gods' end may be written in the runes, but not even they know the path to get there." Who knew how the plans would play out? Thianna didn't care much for fortune-telling anyway. She preferred to chart her own destiny. But tomorrow she'd be casting runes for more than just herself. The fate of an entire country was in her hands.

She sat down on a stool before a small dressing table. Fumbling absentmindedly in the dark, her hands found a comb on the table. She held it in her lap, thinking of the cousin who stood aligned against her.

"Can't sleep either?"

Thianna saw a slender figure in the dark that could only be Desstra.

"Don't sneak up on me like that," she said.

"Sorry," said the dark elf. "I suppose it's hard to put aside old habits."

Thianna grunted at this.

"Care to talk about it?" said Desstra.

"With *you*?" said Thianna.

For an answer, the smaller girl lifted the comb from Thianna's hands, then began to comb the giantess's hair. Thianna tried to pull away, but the elf laid a hand on her shoulder.

"Relax," she said. "I can see in the dark, remember?"

Thianna tried to sit still. There were aspects of Thican culture that she didn't mind. Combs, and bathing.

"I'm sorry," she said. "I'm still getting used to this combing thing. There weren't any girls my age when I grew up. Dad didn't really know how to comb hair. And my mentor Eggthoda wasn't exactly concerned with appearances either."

"So you could use a friendly ear?" prodded Desstra. "Come on, mine are longer than most. And it's been weeks since I last tried to kill you."

That drew a chuckle from the giantess.

In the dark, without being able to clearly see the elf's face, it was easier to unburden her mind. It was almost like talking to herself.

"I just wonder," said Thianna, "am I doing the right thing?" Desstra listened silently, working her way through the tangles in Thianna's locks.

"I mean," Thianna continued, "the way the Calderans run their own city, that's bad. And the way they rule the whole island-continent is worse. I know they've had it coming a long time. But is it right that I'm the one to topple them?"

"What do you mean?" said Desstra.

"They're *my* people. I left my mountaintop to find them. Not destroy them. I wanted to understand my mother's culture. And when I found it, I found it's horrid. How can I be proud of my human half when my human half comes from this?"

"Do you know what I think?" said the elf. "I think you need to broaden your definition of your mother's culture."

"What do you mean?"

"I thought that being a member of the Underhand was the best that life could be. When I didn't graduate, I thought life was over, with nothing for me. You and Karn showed me how limited that thinking was. The Underhand seems small and petty now."

"Like Thrudgelmir," said Thianna. "And all the giants who picked on me growing up."

"Right," said Desstra. Though she didn't know who Thrudgelmir was, she could imagine what growing up had been like for the littlest giant.

"Every since we came to Thica," said Desstra, "we've seen all these odd beings and creatures. People who are half goat, half human. Creatures that are half lion, half goat, half snake."

"That's three halves," laughed Thianna.

"Half bull, half man."

"You're wondering why there are no half-elves?"

"There are half-elves," said Desstra. "But don't stray off topic. Karn rode to Labyrinthia on a half rooster, half horse."

"So there's a lot of halves here," said the giantess. "What's your point?"

"My point is that you're a half giant."

"So?"

"So your cousin and the queens, they've made the mistake of thinking of themselves as Calderans first and Thicans second. But you fit in here better than they do, with all these mixed beings. You're a Thican first, and you're acting for all of Thica. That's something you can be proud of. And something your mother would be proud of too."

"I'm a Thican," said Thianna. "I'm a Ymirian. I'm a Thican." She caught the dark elf's wrist to stop her from combing her hair. "I've been terrible to you."

"'Terrible' is what you've been to your hair," said Desstra. "But if you're saying you'll finally accept my help, you're welcome."

"I guess that is what I'm saying," said Thianna. "Thanks. I just hope we can pull this off. And that when we do, all the city-states don't just tear the country apart."

"Actually," said Karn from the doorway to their chambers, "I have some ideas about how to handle that too. Someone I met on the way to Labyrinthia."

Thianna looked at her friend's face, shining in the light of the phosphorescent stone about his neck.

"Can't sleep either, Norrønboy?" she asked.

"Who sleeps before a battle?" he replied.

"Look at us," said Thianna. "Three barbarian kids from the frozen northlands, about to change the world."

"Again," said Karn.

"Who are you calling a barbarian, barbarian?" said Desstra.

Eventually the friends drifted back to bed, but later that evening Thianna woke once more in the night.

"Karn?" she said. But the Norrønur had gone back to his own quarters.

"Desstra?" she called. But this time the elf was asleep as well.

And Daphne still snored from her own bed.

The frost giant sat very still, listening in the dark. Something had woken her. But what?

On the edge of her awareness, so faint that it might be one of her own thoughts, she heard a voice.

Message received, it said. *We are coming.*

We? thought Thianna. Who is 'we'?

CHAPTER NINETEEN

The Best-Laid Plans . . .

In the northernmost section of the city of Caldera, in the helot district near a large amphitheater, a green glowing light suddenly limned the outline of a doorway in the trunk of a large elm.

More of the otherworldly light spilled into the surrounding glen as a door in the trunk opened. A seagull that had been resting in its branches squawked and flew away. Then Thianna Frostborn climbed from out of the Greenway, stepping aside to allow Karn Korlundsson, Desstra, Daphne, and Asterius to follow her out.

She glanced at the sky above.

"The dark'll favor us," she observed.

The larger moon was just a slender curve of light, while its smaller satellite was being eclipsed by her larger sister.

"Good thing Manna's moon is in its crescent phase," said Karn.

"Whose moon?" asked Daphne, stifling a yawn. The little dryad had bound her leaves to keep them from curling up.

"One of the Norrønir gods," explained Karn. "We say the larger moon is hers."

"Here we say it is Noe's realm," said the dryad. "And we call it Mene."

"Frost giants don't worship any gods," said Thianna. "But I'm grateful to whoever's moon it is that it's not full."

She turned to the elm tree.

"And to you too," she said. "Thank you."

"Good fortune to you, Thianna Frostborn," the hamadryad replied. "I wish you success. Noe is also the goddess of the hunt. May she guide you in your hunting tonight."

Taking their farewell of the hamadryad, the five companions left the grove of olive trees. Desstra both led the way and scouted ahead. They moved upslope through the helot district, approaching the first of the intercity walls. This time the elf was properly equipped. She had ropes and gear for scaling, so the team didn't need to travel either by the gate or by the watercourse.

The little elf quickly ascended the wall. Reaching the top, she paused as her hypersensitive ears alerted her to the coming of a patrol. A hand signal alerted her companions to wait. Then she melted into the shadows so that even her friends—who knew where to look—couldn't tell where she was. Watching from the shadows of a building below, Karn held his breath as a Calderan guard approached Desstra's hiding spot. A slender needle pricked the unfortunate woman on the neck, then the dark elf lowered the unconscious soldier gently to the walkway. She listened once more. Satisfied they were alone, she motioned for the rest of the team to proceed.

"Nicely done," said Thianna as she joined Desstra on the wall. Then the frost giant descended the rope to the ground. One by one, her companions followed, all except for Daphne. The dryad simply leapt into the air. She spread the leaves beneath her arms and whirled around and around like an overlarge elm seed falling from a branch.

"Also nicely done," said Thianna. Daphne smiled at the praise.

They were in the city's middle district, the home of the dactyl dwarves. Thianna spoke to the group.

"I need to pass a message here," she said.

Stepping from an alleyway, she startled a passing dwarf.

"Be healthy," she said, using the common Norrønian greeting.

"It's hard to be that way with you leaping out of the shadows and startling me," objected the dactyl. Then his eyes grew suspicious. "Say, you're a big one. You aren't that half giant everyone's so concerned with, are you?"

Thianna grinned and placed a finger to her lips.

"Shh," she said. "I need you to do something for me. Tell Herakles that if he wants to see real change, he can join us tomorrow."

"Herakles?" said the dactyl, feigning ignorance. "I've no idea who you mean. I don't know anyone named Herakles."

"Sure you do," said the frost giant. "Tell the Hammer-fist that I've arranged quite a party, and he's not going to want to miss it."

"Supposing I pretend I know what you're talking about," said the dwarf. "How will this Herakles know when it's time to act?"

"He'll know," said Thianna. "Believe me, he'll know. You all will."

The dactyl nodded curtly and hurried away. But, Thianna noticed with satisfaction, not in the direction he had been going.

The five companions climbed the second wall as smoothly as the first. Thianna paused to look at the view of the summit. Her eyes swept from the sky docks in the south across the central Twin Palaces to the Tower of Damnameneus in the north—the top of the mountain, the heart of the empire. Here, where every citizen doubled as a soldier, they would have to be extra-careful.

Moving through the streets, Desstra's ears again alerted them to danger. The elf slipped into the shadows, taking down a two-soldier patrol with two quick jabs of slender needles. They approached the Twin Palaces from the south, avoiding the broad avenue leading to the Court of Land and Sky, and aided by the convenient presence of a row of trees.

A soldier stood guard at the front gates to the court. When a snowball rolled to a halt at her feet, the soldier was understandably puzzled. Even more puzzling was the line of snowballs she saw leading around the corner. She followed them, confused by the freakish weather that had balls of ice falling from the sky. The fist of the frost giant was the most surprising thing, but she didn't have long to consider it before she was being lowered to the ground, dropping into unconsciousness.

Thianna pointed to Desstra, Asterius, and Daphne.

"You three, stay outside. Spread out, and let us know if you hear anyone coming."

Desstra nodded. Then Thianna and Karn snuck inside.

The Court of Land and Sky was deserted at night. As quietly as Thianna walked, she winced at every footfall on the polished marble floor. But nothing stirred in the shadows of the room.

She mounted the stairs. Naturally the Sky Queen's throne had been righted since she'd upended it. Thianna grinned to think she might be toppling a throne again, in a manner of speaking. The giantess placed her palm on the wall as she had done the last time she was here. As before there was a faint glow as the magic recognized the child of Talaria. And the doorway slid aside.

Thianna stepped into the small chamber. Sure enough, the Horn of Osius was on the altar at the far end. But Thianna wasn't alone in the hidden room. Sirena the Keras Keeper sat crosslegged on the ceremonial flat-topped marble block holding the horn in her lap.

Sirena grinned at the larger girl.

"Greetings, cousin," she said. Then she tapped her forehead with a finger. "Don't look so surprised to see me. I felt you coming when you were miles away."

Thianna burst from the secret chamber.

"Get out of here!" she yelled. "It's a trap."

Karn's hand dropped to his sword, but soldiers were already emerging from doors to either side of the room. Others raced down the balcony stairs or flowed from the front doors. Thianna started to draw her sword, but even she knew the situation was hopeless.

Then she saw Desstra, along with Asterius and Daphne, being marched into the room with a company of women. The entire team had been captured.

"Troll dung," the frost giant swore. She leapt from the dais, flying over the heads of several surprised foes. Landing alongside the wall, Thianna grabbed a tapestry and gave it a savage yank. She flung the wall hanging—the same one her cousin had ensnared her with!—over the nearest group of soldiers.

"See?" said Thianna to her cousin as Sirena emerged

from the chamber behind the throne. "You did manage to teach me something!"

As the women floundered beneath the heavy material, Thianna bounded across their struggling forms. Muffled cries of "Ouch!" and "Get off!" issued from beneath the tapestry as the enormous girl used lumps that could be heads or backs or shoulders for stepping stones.

Knocking two women aside who were foolish enough to try to block her path, the former knattleikr player barreled through a doorway, leaving the Court of Land and Sky behind. Thianna knew that if she could get away, she might return and free the others. But if she were captured there would be no way to warn her allies in Labyrinthia and Dendronos of the change in plans. Worse, the Calderans might be able to use her friends against her to force her to play the horn. Either way they were all doomed.

The frost giant found herself outdoors in the central courtyard of the Twin Palaces. There were buildings on three sides. She ran to the fourth, saw the daunting cliff face that dropped away to sharp rocks in the waters below. There was no way she could scale that, at least not quickly.

Turning from the precipice, Thianna's gaze fell on the centerpiece of the outdoor courtyard. An oversize Queen's Champion board.

Then a sea of soldiers issued from all three wings of the Twin Palaces.

"Sometimes," she said with a rueful smile, "the only way out is through."

The soldiers met her when she was roughly at the center of the checkered ground. She took the first three down with the force of her charge. Then booted feet crashed into her side.

Thianna swung and kicked. She noticed that the women didn't draw weapons, so Thianna didn't either. Hopefully this meant they were under orders to take her alive. If that were the case, she wouldn't make it easy for them.

The next woman to come at her paid for her bravery with a fist to the jaw. The one after went flying into the stands. Then they rushed at her en masse and at least a half-dozen Calderan soldiers grappled with Thianna. She fought to throw them off, but the numbers were too great. Like the worst knattleikr pileup ever, soon she was facedown on the game board struggling under a heap of armored women.

She resisted a moment longer, straining under their combined weight if only to show them she could, but it was no use. Then she saw that her captured companions had been dragged out into the courtyard as well. Thianna sank to the ground, gritting her teeth in frustration.

"Troll dung," she swore.

"Such language," said Queen Xalthea, striding onto the playing field. "Though it's precisely what I'd expect from an uncouth barbarian."

"Let me up, and I'll show you something else to expect of a barbarian," Thianna replied.

The Sky Queen laughed. It wasn't a friendly sound.

"That might be interesting," the queen said. "But it might be more so if I order these women to strike your head from your shoulders."

"You need me," said Thianna.

"Do I?" The queen wasn't addressing Thianna. Beside her, Sirena stepped forward and knelt to peer at the giantess's face. Thianna scowled as her cousin reached out to lay a hand on her forehead. Then her eyes opened in surprise.

I bet you're surprised to see me in here too, Sirena thought into Thianna's mind.

Then the Keras Keeper rose and faced the queen.

"Not anymore," Sirena said to the monarch.

"How?" asked the stunned frost giant.

"You've rubbed off on her," laughed the queen. "It seems her contact with your own mind, primitive though it is, has awakened her latent abilities."

Thianna grunted. She knew that her own exposure to Orm's thoughts while using the Horn of Osius had enhanced her telepathic abilities. It shouldn't have surprised her that Sirena's repeated contact with her, most of it while one or the other of them possessed the horn, had done the same. They shared the bloodline after all.

She put her face down, staring at the checkered marble floor of the Queen's Champion board. She had failed.

Thianna heard the sound of a sword being drawn from a sheath.

"I will do this one myself," said Xalthea. "I won't let you ruin us."

"Ruin you?" said Thianna. "You are ruining yourselves! You don't let the dactyls vote in your society, but it was a dactyl who designed your mirrors. You don't let men take part in running your city, but it was a man who forged your horn. You sit on your throne at the top of the hill and rule over a city where almost nobody is a citizen. It doesn't matter what you do to me. You're still not going to last. Sooner or later you're going to crumble. You better start thinking about another way to live if you want to stick around at all."

"We endure because we are the strongest," said the Sky Queen.

"There's more than one way to be strong," said Thianna.

Xalthea snorted derisively. But another queen spoke.

"That almost sounds like a challenge," said Melantha. "Truly you are Talaria's child." She walked over to Thianna and bent to meet her gaze. "There is still a way forward, one that doesn't end with your head leaving your shoulders. At least not in the next few moments."

"What are you saying?"

"There is one option open to you now. Only one. If you can grasp it . . ."

Thianna didn't understand.

273

But Karn did. He opened his mouth to tell her, but a sword poked him in the ribs.

"She has to make the challenge herself," the woman whispered. "Or it holds no weight."

He gritted his teeth in frustration, willing his friend to understand. He'd followed her so far. He wouldn't lose her now. Not when there was a chance. If only she would look his way. Kvir, the Norrøngard god of luck, was thousands of miles away. He couldn't be trusted to help now. But Karn's trust was in someone else. They'd been through too much, learned to rely on each other for everything. Thianna wouldn't face this challenge alone.

Sure enough, the frost giant looked his way. As their eyes met, Karn mouthed the words "Look down."

But Thianna didn't grasp his meaning. She stared at him in puzzlement. The soldier gripping Karn noticed and pulled him aside.

Thianna hung her head. She didn't understand what Karn meant. "Look down." Down where? Off the mountain? What option could there be? It was over. The two queens had won.

Two queens, she thought. Then suddenly she noticed the ground in front of her eyes. The solution, literally staring her in the face. The Queen's Champion board. The stage upon which political disputes were settled.

Thianna smiled, the biggest grin of the evening.

"I challenge you, Xalthea," she said.

"You challenge me?" the queen repeated, not under-standing.

"I challenge you to a live Queen's Champion game."

"Don't be absurd," said the Sky Queen. "You have no right to challenge me. Only citizens of Caldera can compete in the game."

"Actually," said Melantha, "Thianna has every right."

Thianna lifted her head to stare at the Land Queen.

"Her mother, Talaria, was never tried for her crimes," the Land Queen continued. "So Talaria's citizenship stands. As her only child, Thianna is entitled to all the rights of citizenship. In fact, Talaria still has a business operating in the helot district, if I'm not mistaken. You may even have thirteen years back income, child."

Thianna snorted at this. The people who were about to kill her might owe her money.

"This is preposterous," said Queen Xalthea, her cheeks burning angrily. "Even if I accepted her challenge, what Calderan citizen would stand with her? She cannot play in the game unless she can gather supporters for a full team."

Thianna's brief hope died in her. She knew none of the Calderans would dare oppose their queen, certainly not for a barbarian outsider bent on overturning their way of life.

"I will stand with her," said Asterius, tossing his horns in the air in defiance.

"Impossible," said the queen. "You're not a citizen."

"Actually, I am," said the minotaur. He turned to Queen Melantha. "You said so yourself."

"Did I?" asked the Land Queen, smiling slyly.

"You did," said a newcomer to the scene. All eyes turned to see Talos, the automaton, striding toward them. "Your exact words were 'You will all be honorary citizens of Caldera. In time you will appreciate this honor.' I believe that time has come. We appreciate the honor now. I too will stand with Thianna Frostborn."

"And I," said Daphne.

"And I," said Desstra.

"Me too," said Karn.

"Wait," objected Xalthea. "These last two children are certainly not citizens."

It was true. While Desstra and Karn had temporarily been housed in the hostage suites, no honorary status had been granted them. Thianna thought about this for a moment, then an idea occurred to her.

"Isn't it true that you allow the perioikoi to compete in the game?" said Thianna.

Queen Melantha smiled.

"We do," she said. "It is their one chance to participate in matters of Calderan government."

"Well," said the frost giant, "these two are my perioikoi."

"Preposterous," said Xalthea.

"No it isn't," replied the frost giant. "They go into bat-

276

tle with me. Karn is my strategic advisor, and this one"—
she pointed her chin at Desstra—"doubles as my advance
scout, spy, and medical support."

"Triples, not doubles," said Desstra. "That's three
things." But the dark elf was smiling.

"There you have it, Xalthea," said Melantha. "If that's
not the very definition of perioikoi I don't know what
is." The Sky Queen scowled at this, but before she spoke,
Melantha continued, "We accept Karn and Desstra as
viable competitors."

"You are still shy two players," Xalthea said. "You need
eight individuals to make up a full team."

"We'll play," said Jasius, appearing seemingly out of nowhere. Behind him was the dactyl king. Although she was
as surprised as anyone to see them, Thianna knew they
must have appeared from another of their secret doors.

"Who are you?" said Xalthea to the older dwarf.

"King Herakles Hammerfist," said the dactyl. "Pleased
to make your royal acquaintance."

"King who?" stammered the Sky Queen, her control
of the situation spiraling away from her.

"Never mind, we'll get around to formal introductions
later, I'm sure. Right now we're here to play." He turned
to Thianna and winked. "Told you we all look alike to
them."

Xalthea was at a loss for words, but not so her co-
monarch.

"Very well," said Queen Melantha. "The game will

commence at daybreak tomorrow. That way we can re-solve this matter before the Great Hatching." She addressed the frost giant. "I have your word as a Calderan that you will abide by the rules of the challenge? No hostilities or escape attempts until tomorrow's game?"

"I'll behave until tomorrow's game," said Thianna. "I give you my word as a Calderan, but also as a Ymirian!"

The Land Queen nodded. She turned to the soldiers still pinning Thianna to the ground.

"Let her up. Show all the contestants to quarters where they can properly rest and prepare for tomorrow's conflict." Then she strode to the Sky Queen. "I hope you can find seven supporters as easily as this 'barbarian' girl has," she said.

"She has one," said Sirena, stepping proudly to Xal-thea's side. Her aunt gazed at her in disappointment, her lips set in a grim line.

"Very well," said Melantha.

Sirena strode to Thianna as the soldiers released her, and the frost giant regained her feet. "You're going to wish you'd never left your mountain when we toss you off of this one."

"All we have to do is beat your side at a board game," Thianna said. "How hard can that be, right?"

"You big fool," her cousin replied. "Don't you know? This is a fight to the death."

CHAPTER TWENTY

Queen's Champion

Dawn did not arrive early in Caldera. The sun's rays had to climb the steep cliff walls of the actual caldera before falling into the courtyard of the Twin Palaces. For Thianna, the anticipation proved worse than any actual battle to come. Her stomach was in knots. It surprised her how nervous she felt. So much lay on her shoulders.

When they finally came for her, it was almost a relief.

She stepped blinking into the morning light. The courtyard was packed. Both the Land Queen's and Sky Queen's stands were full with their soldiers. There were no men, no nonhumans, no perioikoi or helots. Only the soldier-citizen women of Caldera were allowed to witness the game.

A special cushioned seating had been installed

midcenter of the Land Queen's section for Queen Melantha. Under most circumstances, she would have been on the field, not watching the game. Thianna waved as she was led onto the board. Melantha nodded slightly back at her in what might be encouragement. Still not a friend, but clearly not an enemy.

Thianna stopped in the Queen's starting square, with Karn in the Champion's square. To their left, Jasius, King Herakles, and Asterius. To their right, Desstra, Talos, and a very nervous Daphne. They had agreed on the order the night before during a strategy discussion. Ordinarily the queens would be very aware of their team's individual fighting capabilities. Unfortunately, with the exception of Sirena, Thianna had no idea how the other side's soldiers would perform. Nor did she have full knowledge of her own side's strengths and weaknesses—apart, of course, from Karn's and Desstra's considerable abilities.

Opposite them across the board, six soldiers were already standing at attention, each armed with a sword and the distinctive pelta shield. Sirena approached and took up her position as Champion. The trumpets blew and Queen Xalthea marched out of her palace accompanied by a small retinue. They followed her to the edge of the board, then took up places in the stands. The queen did not immediately take her position, however, but strode to Thianna.

"One last chance to back down," said Xalthea. "There is no sense in all of your friends dying as well. If you surrender now, I promise that I'll spare them. You will have accomplished that much."

Thianna thought about that. She turned to her team.

"Anyone want to back down?" she asked.

No one spoke. She felt a surge of pride.

"I guess we're going to play," she said.

"But surely you don't think you can beat me?" asked the queen.

"You're right," Thianna said. "I can't beat you."

"You admit it?"

"Sure," she said. "I can't beat you. But he can."

Stepping aside, she exchanged positions on the board with Karn.

"What are you doing?" said Xalthea.

"I'm switching places," said the giantess. "I'll be the Champion. Karn can play the Queen's position. Maybe we could call it a King's position."

"How about the Jarl's position?" Karn offered with pretend helpfulness. "I usually play Jarl's side in Thrones and Bones at home."

Xalthea ignored Karn.

"But you are the one who challenged me."

"I challenged you to a game of Queen's Champion. And brought my team. Now here we are. Are we going to play or not? I'm still playing. Only in a different position."

"You can't do that!" objected the Sky Queen.

"Why not?"

"The queen always plays the Queen," she said, then caught herself when she realized her mistake.

"There you have it," said Thianna. "I'm no queen. Just an uncouth barbarian from Ymiria. So it shouldn't matter which position I take, should it?"

"She has you there!" called Melantha. "Come on, let the girl play whichever position she wants."

"Fine," said Xalthea. "You can be your own Champion. It won't make any difference in the outcome. In fact, you'll go off the cliff even faster this way."

She turned and stormed back to her position on the board. Sirena straightened beside her, trying her best to look confident and proud. She glared at her cousin. Now each of them was playing the same position, but for opposite sides.

"For Caldera!" she called.

The six soldiers on the Sky Queen's side repeated this call. Thianna thought they seemed more stiff than confident. Their eyes betrayed their nervousness. She imagined that they may not have been given much choice in "volunteering" to stand with their queen. And if they were used to serving under Xalthea, then they'd have a pretty good idea of the value she placed on lives not her own. The giantess smiled. She looked at her own mismatched forces. No matter the outcome of the game, she knew which side she belonged on.

"Ready when you are!" she shouted.

"Let's get this charade over with," Xalthea replied.

Queen Melantha stood and addressed the assembled crowds.

"The game of Queen's Champion has long been used to settle political debates. Today Queen Xalthea is challenged by Thianna Frostborn over the matter of the Horn of Osius and the future of Caldera.

"Before we begin, a brief demonstration for those contestants who are new to our game." She nodded at Thianna's team. "When two opposing players meet on adjacent squares, battle ensues. The fight is to the death. Should either player step outside the confines of their position, they forfeit the match. When either death or forfeit occurs . . ."

Melantha nodded.

A square in the center of the board fell away.

"That's a trapdoor!" exclaimed Thianna.

"A one-way trip down the mountain," Desstra said. "Not a ride I'd like to take."

The square slid back into place.

"Any questions?" the queen asked.

"I think we get the point," said Thianna.

"Good," said the Land Queen. "Play will continue until one side surrenders or is entirely removed from play. Those remaining after a surrender will have their lives spared, although the challenger herself forfeits her life in defeat. As the defender, Queen Xalthea has the first move."

Trumpets blew. The game commenced.

Xalthea began by ordering Sirena two steps forward.

"Was that a good move?" asked King Herakles, in a somewhat too-loud whisper.

Thianna looked to Karn.

"It's a bold move," he replied. "It means she isn't afraid to risk her Champion, rather than keep Sirena back for her own protection. Also, it suggests that she doesn't think highly of our chances."

"She doesn't know us," said Thianna.

Karn was less assertive in his own move. He sent Desstra ahead only one space.

"That was a good move. Was that a good move?" asked Herakles again.

"Timid," said the Sky Queen with a sneer. She ordered another piece forward.

Karn sent Herakles forward only one space.

This puzzled Xalthea. Karn had effectively wasted two turns by not sending either piece forward its allowed two spaces.

"The boy doesn't know what he is doing, and so he is afraid to act," she said. "Your 'Queen' plays like a fool, Thianna," she called to the frost giant.

"How do you know what a fool plays like?" Desstra shouted at her. "Are you basing this on your own experience?"

Xalthea scowled. The little elf creature was annoying. But she was also puzzled by Karn's lack of aggressive strategy. She whispered to Sirena, "What is that northern boy playing at? Is he trying to draw us out? For what purpose?"

Sirena studied her opponents, who, for the most part, were still in an ordered line in the back row.

"I think he is afraid to lose any of his pieces," she said.

"But why?" said the queen. "His fellow barbarian, perhaps. But these others, they aren't his kin, or even from his country. Why should he care what happens to dryads and automatons and whatever that sickly girl is?"

"Maybe it is a weakness you can exploit," Sirena replied.

Weakness or no, Karn continued stepping pieces forward only one square. Meanwhile Desstra continued to taunt Queen Xalthea every time the latter spoke. If she was baiting the haughty monarch, it was working.

"You are speaking to a queen," Sirena hissed.

"Oh, don't worry. I'm very impressed," replied the elf. "In fact, I've never met such a small mind inside such a big head before."

The monarch scowled at this.

"Time to close your mouth," she said. Xalthea ordered Sirena forward and began to concentrate all her efforts on reaching and attacking Desstra.

The distance closed and Desstra found herself facing Thianna's cousin.

"Your mouth is as big as your ears," the Keras Keeper said. "Perhaps I'll slice them off before I close it."

"Remember when I asked your opinion?" the elf replied. "Me neither!"

Then both girls drew their weapons. Sirena held a sword and shield. Desstra still carried the hammer she had claimed in the dactyl caverns. The absence of a shield should have put the elf at a disadvantage, but her speed made up for it. She leapt in and around the other girl, dodging every blow. But when she somersaulted over Xalthea's Champion to land behind her, she was oddly slow in taking advantage of the position.

Watching them fight, Thianna judged that the elf was holding back, fighting only defensively. Having fought Desstra herself, she knew what Desstra was capable of. Then, while dodging a vicious thrust of Sirena's blade, Desstra seemingly misstepped. The former Underhand student stumbled backward, stepping off of her square onto the next one. To do so was to forfeit the fight.

The marble square beneath the elf fell away. Without a scream or even a shout, Desstra dropped through the hole.

There were cheers from the crowd, but they were drowned out by the voice of a frost giant.

"Desstra!" hollered Thianna, loud enough to silence the audience.

So quiet were they that everyone could hear the soft whir of gears as the floor of the square slid back into place.

"You have lost your first piece!" Xalthea called. "Do you surrender?"

"Desstra," called the frost giant again. But the elf was gone.

"Do you surrender?" the Sky Queen repeated adamantly.

"I'll surrender you," said Thianna, unsheathing her sword and starting to step forward.

"That doesn't even make sense," Sirena said.

"Don't step off your square," Karn cautioned his friend. "You'll forfeit your life if you do."

Thianna fumed.

"Send me forward," she said. "I want to pay the queen my respects."

Karn nodded. He sent the frost giant two spaces into the field.

As the game continued, it was impossible to avoid conflicts. King Herakles battled one of Xalthea's soldiers and won. Talos fought with another.

Then the worst happened. Karn had been shielding the timid dryad as best he could, but a seemingly clumsy play on his part left her exposed. A soldier moved to a vacant square and Xalthea called a challenge.

Daphne had no weapons of her own, so she had been given a short sword and small round shield. She hung behind the latter now, eyes shut in fear as the soldier battered her with her own sword. The little dryad fell back, landing outside her square.

"Oh dear," she said. "That was a mistake, wasn't it?" Then she dropped out of sight.

Thianna closed her eyes at their second loss.

"You're shedding supporters," the Sky Queen taunted.

"Still not surrendering," the giantess replied.

"I wouldn't accept it now if you did," Xalthea answered. "I will take you down one by one until none of you are left."

"Maybe you should come over here and say that!" Thianna roared.

But the Sky Queen made no move forward. Rather she sent Sirena across the field to match her cousin. Thianna glanced at Karn. An understanding passed between them, and he ordered her forward, closing the distance between Champions.

The two girls faced each other, each in her own square. Although Thianna was significantly taller than her relative, she knew from their earlier conflict that Sirena was a highly skilled warrior.

"You're on the wrong side," said Thianna.

"Go to the crows," Sirena replied.

Then blades were swinging. The sound of metal clashing on metal rang in the air.

Thianna fought hard, but her cousin gave no less effort to the battle. It was tricky, having to keep inside the confines of your own square. The giantess found it hampered her movement and nullified some of her size advantage. Not all of it, though.

"Give it up," she taunted. "Your reach is too short!"

"Long enough to reach your heart," Sirena shot back.

Thianna paused in her assault. Would her own cousin really strike to kill?

"You know," the giantess said, "as family reunions go, this one is kind of lame."

"Then let's get it over with," her cousin replied.

But as the fight continued, neither combatant proved able to gain an advantage over the other. Thianna felt the sweat trickling down her back, and even her strong arms were growing tired. The determination in Sirena's eyes never faltered, but frustration and doubt appeared there as well.

Around them, the audience held its breath as the two girls continued to battle.

"Get on with it!" Xalthea shouted at her Champion. "Finish her. The Great Hatching approaches."

"I'm trying to," Sirena replied through gritted teeth.

But beating the frost giant wasn't easy. The fight continued until the audience began to grow restless. There were jeers and calls to one side or the other to resolve the battle. Sirena felt a growing suspicion that Thianna was toying with her, dragging things out on purpose. She buckled down and fought harder, but still victory wouldn't come.

Then the giantess paused. She cocked her head as though listening for something. Then Thianna swung her sandaled foot upward and kicked the bottom of Sirena's shield. The pelta was driven into Sirena's own chin, stunning her, and she toppled backward.

The audience gasped as the Keras Keeper stumbled out-of-bounds. Sirena's eyes widened as the floor dropped away beneath her. Then she was falling. She screamed, not in fear but in frustration. The fight was over, and it was she who was going to the crows.

Thianna leapt and caught her cousin by the wrist. She held the smaller girl suspended over the yawning chasm, their eyes meeting. Then Thianna drew Sirena to safety on her own square.

Gasps and catcalls issued from the audience. Mercy was not a quality they appreciated in their warriors.

"Why?" asked her cousin. "The fight was yours."

Queen Xalthea had a similar question.

"Why did you arrest her fall?" the Sky Queen asked. "She was defeated and you won."

"It was never about winning," Thianna replied. "It was only about waiting."

"Waiting for what?" the queen asked.

Suddenly, shouts came from the Sky Queen's wing of the Twin Palaces. A soldier burst into the courtyard, alarm all over her face.

"Minotaurs!" she screamed. "An army from Labyrinthia is attacking the city at the south gate!"

Another soldier raced from the Land Queen's wing.

"Tree folk!" she yelled. "They are leaping off the caldera's rim and gliding on their leaves to land here upon our summit!"

A third soldier came from the Court of Land and Sky.

"Dactyls!" she hollered. "Pouring from the walls! Rising out of the floors! We are under attack."

"That," said Thianna with a smirk. "I was waiting for that."

CHAPTER TWENTY-ONE

The Battle for Caldera

"Burn them all!" shrieked Xalthea. "Rain fire on them from the skies."

Soldiers hurried from the stands to carry out the Sky Queen's orders. Thianna started to oppose them, but Karn caught her arm.

"Wait," he said.

Sure enough, the first of Xalthea's players to move from her position unwittingly activated the trapdoor mechanism. The woman fell screaming through the hole in the game board. The rules and penalties were still in effect.

"Thank you," whispered the giantess.

Across the board, Xalthea shouted orders. "Shut it off!" she roared. "Shut the gears off."

Then she drew her own sword and advanced on Thi-anna.

"This one is mine," said the queen. Around her Xal-thea's remaining soldiers closed in on Thianna's team. Then Asterius lowered his head and bellowed. The mi-notaur charged across the field, butting a soldier with his horns and tossing the woman high in the air.

"Now that was a good move," laughed Herakles Hammerfist, swinging both fist and hammer to batter another soldier. Beside him, his son Jasius did his part to live up to the family name.

As for the automaton, Talos's bronze skin was as ef-fective as any shield. Talos didn't worry about attacks and swung both arms like heavy metal clubs. As for Karn, he wielded Whitestorm expertly, the blade's dragon-bestowed magic an aid to his own growing ability.

Amid the fray, Thianna faced the Sky Queen in a mo-ment of stillness at the center of the board.

"I'll offer you the same deal you offered me," said the giantess. "Surrender now to save lives. We don't have to fight this war."

"Ignorant barbarian," Xalthea sneered. "War is the mother of all."

Then the Sky Queen swung her sword.

When Desstra had fallen through the trapdoor, she had been prepared. In fact, falling—and being the first to fall—had been her plan all along, part of the strategy that she and Karn had worked out the night before. That was why she had tried so hard to provoke the Sky Queen and why she had deliberately misstepped in her fight.

This meant that the former Underhand student was ready when she dropped through the floor. The silken thread that she had collected from the spider caverns had proved its usefulness once again.

Desstra had hung from the underside of the game board, dangling perilously alongside the cliff and over the jagged rocks below. She waited only until the dryad fell. The tricky part had been to catch Daphne when she dropped, though the tree girl arrested her fall by gliding slowly on her leaves.

Together they had made their way across the cliff face, coming up north of the Twin Palaces. From there, the two girls, elf and dryad, had made their way to the Tower of Damnameneus.

Once they had reached their goal, the explosive bat poop again made for an effective distraction, while the odd mushrooms Desstra had gathered sent the soldiers in the tower into a deep slumber.

Having neutralized the operators of the deadly parabolic mirror, they paused to survey the battle.

Daphne pointed to where dryads and drus were leaping off the caldera's rim to the north, gliding across the lake to arrive at the city summit. Desstra looked from there to spy dactyls clashing with soldiers all through their own district and even in the upper district as well. And on the south side of the helots' district, the girls saw minotaurs making their way into the city. The south gate had been no obstacle to warriors who rode giant scorpions.

But along the castle walls, Desstra's sharp eyes saw a new threat. The Calderan forces were rolling out enormous weapons of war.

"Are those cannons?" asked Daphne, pointing at the odd devices.

"I don't think so," replied the elf. "Not ordinary ones, anyway. They're too long and thin. They look almost like—"

Desstra's ears quivered as she recognized them.

"They're giant fire lances," she said. "They're going to spray Thican fire at the invaders."

Even as she spoke, the first of the cannons belched forth a jet of flame. Tree folk screamed as they ignited in the air. They folded their leaves to drop into the lake below, where hopefully the flames would be extinguished.

"We've got to do something," said Daphne. "Those are my people."

Desstra looked to the enormous parabolic mirror rising over them.

"You think you can give me a hand figuring out how this works?" said the elf.

The dryad looked at the death ray and smiled.

"Now this is one task where I won't shy from getting my hands dirty," she said.

"Whoever Damnameneus was, he certainly knew his stuff," said Desstra as she looked over the controls. The genius of the ancient mathematician and inventor was clearly evident. The entire mirror moved easily in a track, operated by a clever array of switches and buttons. Together the two girls threw the controls that would uncover the polished metal surface. It gleamed in the morning sun. Then they angled the beam at the city's walls.

As the ray of intense light passed across the fire cannons, the chemical components inside overheated and exploded. Soldiers dove from the walls to escape the bursting contraptions. Seeing what was coming for them, others abandoned their positions and fled before the ray even reached their posts.

Shouts came from the base of the tower.

"I think we've been discovered," said Daphne.

"You think so, do you?" replied Desstra, as soldiers climbed the winding stairs to reach the pair. But she was grinning. "Do you think you can operate this machine by yourself?" she asked.

"Nothing to it," replied the dryad.

"Good," said the elf. "You keep melting cannons. I'll hold them off."

She hefted the dwarven hammer and moved to stand at the top of the stairs. Then she paused and dropped a hand to a pocket. She pulled out her smoked quartz glasses and put them on.

"It's kind of bright up here," she explained.

"I know," said the dryad. "I've always loved the sunshine. And now I get to share it with all those nice soldiers and their weapons."

Giggling, the tree girl set to work exploding more cannons.

Thianna battled the Sky Queen across the board. Xalthea's earlier reluctance to fight had not been because of a lack of ability. The frost giant was already tired from her drawn-out battle with Sirena, and now her enemy was pressing her hard.

Their swords clashed again and again.

"Traitor," hissed the queen. "Your mother was a traitor to her city, to her country, to her kind."

"Don't talk about my mother," said Thianna.

Then the Sky Queen cast a look aside and made a quick gesture. Thianna wondered what she meant by it. Was it a signal of some kind?

Thianna guessed and leapt seconds before the ground at her feet gave way. The trapdoor beneath her yawned wide. Xalthea had ordered the gears activated. As Thianna landed, she felt the new square shift. She jumped again. Someone was operating the mechanism of the board manually, aiding the Sky Queen by dropping the ground away at her opponent's feet.

"That's cheating!" the giantess roared. Then she flung

herself aside, somersaulting from the square as it dropped away.

"Stand still and die," growled Xalthea.

"Excuse me if I don't," replied the frost giant.

They fought on, holes across the board yawning wide. Then the Sky Queen tossed her shield at the giantess. Thianna raised an arm to block it and Xalthea smashed into her. The smaller woman only drove the half giant back a pace, but it was enough. Thianna slipped. And fell.

She caught herself with one hand, dangling in the air. Below her Xalthea's discarded shield sailed on its long fall to the rocks.

The Sky Queen smiled down at the giantess.

"Now you die like all traitors."

She raised a foot, preparing to bring it down on Thianna's fingers.

Desstra was having a time of it defending the tower. She was finally beginning to appreciate the dwarven hammer, but she was also tiring. Then she noticed something in the sky. A shadow cast by something large. Very large.

"How are we coming?" she yelled to Daphne.

"Just melting the last of the cannons now," replied the dryad.

"Good," said Desstra. She tossed an incendiary down the stairs to buy her a moment's respite. "Because we need to abandon the tower."

She fixed the spider silk to the balcony railing, tossing the line over the edge. Then the elf was over the side, sliding down the webbing. Daphne leapt into the air, spreading leafy wings to glide with her to the ground.

"Won't the soldiers use the mirror now?" she asked the elf.

"Not if they're smart," Desstra called back. "They won't be sticking around at all if they see what's coming."

"Why? What's coming?" the tree girl asked.

Desstra smiled and pointed.

"That is."

Daphne looked where the elf indicated.

"Drakon," she said in awe, her voice catching in her throat in shock.

Then a flame like nothing the Thicans could ever produce struck the mirror of Damnameneus and transformed it into a lump of molten metal.

The great dragon Orm wheeled in the sky.

The first blast of his deadly breath had reduced the mirror to slag in seconds. Soldiers fled from the remains of the tower, yelling and screaming delightfully.

"I had forgotten how fun it could be," the Doom of Sardeth said, laughing, "to take an active interest in the affairs of the world. I really should travel more often."

"Remember, little brother," said his sister Orma, gliding in the air alongside him. "We're only here to fight the bad people. Not burn the place to the ground like you did the last time you attacked a city."

"Watch who you are calling 'little,'" Orm replied. But he chuckled. It was good to have his sibling back. And to think he owed her return to the world to the boy Karn and the half giant Thianna.

"I may not be the biggest, but I'm still firstborn," Orma reminded her brother.

"Firstborn but no longer eldest," he replied. "Not by many centuries."

Granted, Orma had been the first of the siblings to hatch, but through an accident of magic Orm was now over a millennium older than she was. And also considerably bigger.

If you want my opinion, you are both frighteningly large, said the wyvern in Orm's mind. The small reptile fluttered between the two enormous dragons like a moth between hawks. Long ago it had borne Talaria all the way to Ymiria, and recently it had carried Thianna's message to the Dragon Queen of Gordasha. But Orma had insisted on enlisting her brother's aid before invading Thica.

"We have company in the skies," observed Orma.

A squadron of wyvern riders were lifting into the air, heading for the dragons.

"We're agreed that these are 'bad people'?" the great dragon asked.

"The riders are," said Orma. "But the mounts have no

choice but to serve. Eat as few as you can. Try to scare the bulk of them away."

"Were you always such a killer of joy?" grumbled Orm, tucking his wings and going into a dive. But he laughed like a thunderstorm as the squadron maneuvered frantically to escape the enormous dragon.

"I knew getting out once in a while would be good for him," said Orma, beating her wings to join her "little brother."

The snowball struck Xalthea full in the face.

She stumbled, her foot failing to crush Thianna's fingers. The queen spit the snow from her mouth, anger boiling in her eyes.

"Impudent creature," she said. "You don't mock me! This is your moment of death."

"Then mocking is exactly what I do," said Thianna, who hurled another snowball.

Xalthea deflected this one with her arm, but she was no less angry. Then she raised her sword.

Karn crashed into the monarch, knocking her aside. She recovered quickly, thrusting her blade at the Norrønur who had spoiled her moment of triumph over the frost giant.

Karn caught Xalthea's attack on Whitestorm. He had a pelta shield and used it to batter at the queen.

Then Desstra appeared, striking with her dwarven hammer.

Thianna hoisted herself from out of the hole and joined her two companions.

"Bet you wish you had some friends now too, don't you?" she taunted the queen.

Faced with three determined attackers, Xalthea retreated. Her withdrawal took her to where the edge of the board met the edge of the cliff. But her path was blocked.

Queen Melantha stood waiting for her fellow monarch, sword in hand.

Xalthea smiled.

"Now the odds are more even," the Sky Queen said.

"You are mistaken," replied the Land Queen. "Now the odds are four to one."

Xalthea was stunned.

"You—you oppose me?"

"I should have opposed you long ago," said Melantha. "We are not the strength that Thica deserves." She glanced at Thianna. "And there is more than one way to be strong."

"Lies," said Xalthea, and she struck with her sword at her co-monarch.

"Watch out!" the giantess called, but it was too late. The blade found its target. But as Melantha collapsed, she clutched Xalthea tightly. Fear shone in the Sky Queen's eyes as she found herself yanked off her feet.

Thianna moved to catch them, either of them, as they fell, but it was hopeless. The two queens of Caldera tumbled over the cliff's edge, plunging to the rocks at the base of the mountain.

The frost giant looked to Karn and Desstra. Beyond them she saw that their other companions had triumphed over their opponents. But of one person there was no sign.

"Sirena," she said. Her cousin was gone and Thianna knew where she was headed. She would have to be stopped or all of this was for nothing.

The first cracks in the eggs were appearing. Thin lines growing and spreading in shell after shell. The noise of hundreds of infant wyverns chipping away from the inside of their prisons was like the incessant drumming of rain on a rooftop.

Sirena held the Horn of Osius. She could still fix things. When the young reptiles hatched, she would sound the notes that would enslave them to a life of servitude to Caldera. Her people would still rule the skies. This rebellion would be put down. Caldera would be strong again. They had suffered defeat before. They would suffer this. The city-states would be brought to heel again, the dactyls punished for their betrayal. It was all still possible. As long as they had mastery of the skies.

Shells began to burst around her. The air filled with

susurrations as infant wyverns crawled hissing into the light.

Sirena smiled. And blew the horn.

A hundred pairs of eyes fixed on her. She had their undivided attention. And she could feel each of their minds. Now, when their newborn minds were still empty of anything else and at their most receptive, it was time to lay down the commands that would last throughout the wyverns' lives. Now she would play the music of obedience and servitude and duty to Caldera.

Sirena could feel the walls of the wyverns' minds collapsing as she pushed her own will into them. They hissed in fear at the invasion of their thoughts. But she flooded them with herself and they could not resist.

Then unexpectedly something pushed back. It was another mind. A powerful one. Interfering with her own commands.

Sirena spun. Thianna Frostborn stood at the doorway to the hatchery. The frost giant tapped her own temple and grinned.

"Do you have to ruin everything?" Sirena spat.

"It's a gift, I know," replied her cousin.

"A gift?" the Keras Keeper replied. She drew her sword and began advancing up the stairs toward the larger girl. "Come here and let me give you another one."

Thianna readied her own weapon. Then Sirena was swinging for her. The frost giant's height should have given her the advantage, but combined with her position higher on the stairs she was almost too tall. She had to bend awkwardly to defend her legs, while her cousin's fury gave the smaller girl strength.

They danced amid the reptiles, which hissed and cried at the battle still playing out inside their minds. As sword clashed against sword, will clashed against will. Thianna and Sirena struggled for control of the Horn of Osius. Each of them could feel it, a power almost too terrible to contemplate that would belong only to the victor.

Karn smiled as Desstra joined him on the palace grounds.

"We've gotten them on the run here," he said.

"Tower's gone too," the elf replied.

"I noticed," Karn said. "But I admit I didn't expect dragon fire to be the cause."

"Yes," said Desstra, "nothing like having a dragon up-stage your performance."

"I think you did pretty well," said Karn.

"I think Thianna did pretty well," said Desstra. "I could hear her raging when I was dangling off the cliff. She almost convinced *me* I'd been killed."

Karn laughed. Making sure that Desstra had been the first one on their side to fall in Queen's Champion had been tricky, but their plan had worked beautifully. He pointed at the gate to the middle district.

"Let's see how things look from there," he said. "See where we can do the most good."

Daphne, Asterius, and Talos joined them as they made their way to the gate. King Herakles's forces held this section of the wall now, so they weren't challenged as they ran. They stood under the raised portcullis and gazed down at the city of Caldera. At the city's south gate, the scorpion riders had overwhelmed the hippalektryon cavalry. The dactyls had joined with scattered bands of helots who saw a chance at freedom. Together they had taken much of the middle and lower districts. And the forces of the tree folk controlled the northernmost sections of the island. Calderan forces were split amid the city, cut off from each other, and divided by the need to protect the city while dealing with the dragon threat from above. And without their queens, the soldiers appeared directionless and uncertain.

"I think we've won," said Karn.

"Wait," said Desstra, "what's going on there?"

Karn followed the elf's gaze. An enormous wave was rolling in off the coast. It broke up on the breakwaters at either end but as it was nearly perpendicular to the city, its midsection passed straight through, a gigantic wall of sea and foam that sent boats hurling out of their moorings to crash into buildings at the docks.

"Tidal wave?" asked Karn.

"Not this far from the ocean," said Talos. "That was not natural."

"Not natural?" Karn fought a growing sense of alarm.

"What do you mean, not natural? Those waves are huge. What in the world could be making waves that size?"

Something colossal rose from the waters beyond the battered docks. A giant dragonlike head.

"That's . . . that's even bigger than Orm," said Karn.

"Who?" asked Asterius.

"A Great Dragon," Desstra explained.

"I think this is a Greater Dragon," said Talos.

Then another head rose from the water.

"Two Great Dragons?" said the minotaur.

Another head rose. And another.

"I do not believe so," said the automaton.

"How many of these things are there?" wailed Daphne. Her leaves were trying to curl up over her face.

"Only one," said Talos as more heads rose from the water.

"One?" said Karn. "Aren't you seeing what we're seeing? There's dozens of them!"

"No," said Talos. "There are not."

The heads were all lifting from the water and moving toward the city. As they rose, their long scaled necks were exposed. The necks each connected to a single gargantuan body.

"Behold," said Talos. "The Mega Hydra."

CHAPTER TWENTY-TWO

Heading for Disaster

Thianna and Sirena battled amid the screeching newborn reptiles. They stepped in and among the wyverns, moving up and down the concentric steps of the hatchery.

"I've already fought you once today," said the giantess. "Haven't you had enough?"

"Never," replied her cousin. "But if all I can do is pay you back for what you've done . . ."

Suddenly Thianna's foot slipped on the discarded yolk sac of a newly hatched egg. Her legs went out from under her and she landed hard on her backside.

"Oh gross," she said, sitting in the sticky mess. "See? This is exactly the sort of occasion where wearing barbarian pants would be useful."

Sirena wasn't amused. She took the opportunity of her cousin's distraction to launch herself at the larger girl, knocking her back and attempting to pin her down.

Straddling the giantess, Sirena raised her blade in both hands. She brought it down.

Thianna caught her wrists.

Sirena strained to drive the sword into her cousin's throat. The big girl was strong. But the smaller girl was determined. The point of the blade lowered.

The door to the Hatchery banged open. Karn Korlundsson ran into the room. His face was white. Whiter than usual.

"Thianna, you've got to see this!"

"Can it wait?" replied his friend. "I'm sort of in the middle of something."

Karn leapt to where the two girls were still locked in a deadly conflict.

"Sirena," he said. "You need to come too. Something more important has come up. Your city is in terrible danger."

"I know," the Keras Keeper replied through gritted teeth. "I'm taking care of that danger now."

"Not from us," said Karn. "Something else is attacking. It's gargantuan—the biggest thing I've ever seen. You have to come now before it's too late."

Sirena looked from Karn to Thianna.

"We're *all* in danger," the boy said.

"We can finish this later," Thianna added.

Sirena hesitated, then nodded. She slipped off the larger girl.

"Show me," she said to the Norrønur, then the three of them ran from the room.

"Sweet Ymir's . . ."

Thianna's voice dropped off. The creature climbing out of the harbor and advancing up the hillside was like nothing she had ever seen before. Or even imagined.

"What in the wide, wide world of Qualth is that?" she said.

"It's called a Mega Hydra," said Karn.

"What *is* it?" the frost giant said.

"It's like a hydra," said Karn. "Only mega. Only don't ask me what a hydra is."

"An ancient monster," said Sirena. She looked every bit as stunned as her cousin. "A creature from the Dawn Age."

I warned you, said a voice in her mind. Sirena looked to the sky above. Thianna, who must have heard the voice too, did as well. The traitorous, battered wyvern flapped above their heads.

I warned you that strong blasts carry far, it said. *Now look what you have awoken.*

"This is my fault," said Sirena. She turned to Thianna. "I thought . . . I thought you were destroying my city. But I have. Help me."

"Against that?" said the frost giant. She was still having trouble coming to terms with the Mega Hydra's size.

"Please," her cousin said. "There will be nothing left of us if we don't do something." There was no pride in her voice now. Only pleading.

Thianna tore her eyes from the colossal monster to look between Karn and Sirena.

"Give me that," she said.

Sirena looked at the Horn of Osius in her left hand. Then she passed it to her cousin without objection.

Thianna raised the horn.

Instantly her mind was a jumble of sound. She felt little sensations, like swarms of insects buzzing at her ears. That was the wyverns. Two larger minds were clearly Orm and Orma. But dwarfing all of this was a cacophony of overlapping awarenesses, massive and angry.

She let loose a blast, forcing herself on the titanic creature. All the heads suddenly turned her way.

The frost giant was thrown backward. She flew across through the air like a rag doll and landed heavily in the dirt.

"Thianna!" shouted Karn, racing to his friend's side. "Are you all right?"

Thianna shook herself, wincing at the pain in her forehead.

"Too many . . . too many heads," she said. "I can't do more than irritate it."

Karn helped her to her feet. Below them the Mega

Hydra was clambering up the slope of the hill. It crushed homes under its bulk, smashed walls and buildings to splinters. People were running screaming from it, but its attention was fixed at the top of the hill.

As they watched, a group of wyvern riders approached, readying flame lances. But their deadly Thican fire was like a tiny candle flame sputtering against the impenetrable scales of the Mega Hydra. Then it turned one of its many heads and vomited a cloud of purple smoke. Wyverns folded their wings and dropped from the sky.

"It breathes clouds of poison gas," said Karn. "Why am I not surprised?"

"We're lost," said Sirena. Her voice was distant, defeated.

The Great Dragon Orm was surprised. It wasn't a sensation to which he was accustomed.

"Now that's something you don't see every day," he said.

His sister broke off her pursuit of a squadron of wyvern riders to see what had her sibling's attention.

"Oh dear," she said. "We have to do something."

"We?" replied the Great Dragon.

"It will destroy the city," said Orma.

"What if it does?" rumbled Orm. "I've destroyed cities too. Why should I have all the fun?"

"What happened to taking an active interest in the affairs of the world?" she asked.

"There is active, and then there is active," he replied.

"Fine, *little* brother," she said, emphasizing the word *little* because she knew that it would rattle him. "If you're afraid, you can stay back and watch how it's done."

Then Orma folded her wings and dove at the monster.

As the dragon approached, she unleashed a blast of flame at the Mega Hydra. The white-hot dragon fire roiled over one of the creature's heads. But when Orma banked aside, the head was unscathed.

Two more heads lunged at her and it was all she could do to dodge them and escape.

Then a third head seized her tail in its teeth, yanking her from the air. She roared. Twisting, she brought her jaws down on its neck. With a satisfying crunch she bit through its vertebrae and tore the head off. The severed head fell crashing to the ground and the neck spasmed, flinging gore across the city.

"That will teach you to grab a dragon by the tail," Orma proclaimed. She beat her wings to rise into the air, out of reach of the Mega Hydra. But as she watched, the severed neck ceased to thrash and straightened. Something appeared to be pushing out of the stump. Two somethings.

Orma watched in amazement as two new heads emerged from the neck. The neck itself divided down its length, so that each head had its own connection to the beast's torso.

"It regenerates!" she said. "How does one defeat an opponent that grows more terrible as you strike it?"

Orma was stunned. She'd missed out on the millennia-plus of life that her brother had experienced, but she was still a dragon with several centuries of age. She wasn't used to foes she couldn't defeat or devour. But she wouldn't give up. She would fling herself against the Mega Hydra until it finished her.

"I wish Acmon were here," she said, thinking of her friend and fellow Gordashan monarch. "It would be good to see him once more before the end."

Then Orma saw that her brother was descending to the summit of the hill.

Orm was none too careful where he landed. He took out a row of trees in front of the Twin Palaces, but thankfully no buildings or people. His eyes fixed on the frost giant and the Norrønur, his agents in the world.

"You have the hateful thing," he asked Thianna, meaning the Horn of Osius.

"I do," the giantess replied. She locked eyes with the dragon. Beside her, she could sense her cousin wilting at the presence of the Doom of Sardeth. But she was proud that Karn straightened and stood alongside her.

"Good," said the dragon. "Give it to me now and I will carry you out of here."

Thianna squared her shoulders. She knew that an

offer to be carried by so proud a being as Orm was no small thing. But she wasn't ready to leave.

"I'm not done with it yet. And I'm not done here."

Orm growled. It was a deep rumbling sound that began somewhere in his belly and traveled up his long throat to emerge from between his spear-sized teeth.

"Give it to me and I will destroy it. Withhold it and melt with it."

"You'll get it when I am done with it," said Thianna. "As much as Karn and I have been through on your quest, you owe us."

"I owe you?" said the dragon. He repeated the words again, as if he couldn't believe them. "I. Owe. You? I owe nothing. You breathe now at my sufferance. I want the hateful thing destroyed."

"Wait," said Karn. "We do too. Believe me, we do. But the city—the Hydra—"

"I cannot fight that," said Orm. "Even if it were my fight."

"It's true," said Orma, landing beside her brother. She was smaller than he, but also more careful where she put down. "I cut off one of its heads and it grew two more. There is no defeating a monster like that."

"Fire," said Sirena. "The old legends say it's vulnerable to fire."

"It resists fire," said Orma. "Even my breath had no effect."

"Outside it's impervious, yes," said Sirena. "But inside

315

it's vulnerable. If you burn the stump after you strike off a head, it can't sprout any more."

"But there are too many heads right now," said Orma. "Only Orm and I are large enough to bite through the necks, but it has too many chances to attack us if we get that close."

Thianna looked to Karn.

"You're the strategy expert," she said.

"We distract it," the Norrønur replied. "Give it something to divide all of its attention."

Thianna smiled.

"I can be annoying when I want to be," she said.

"Can you really save my city?' Sirena asked. "Can you save Caldera?"

The giantess nodded.

"It's going to take all of us," she said. "All of us. Working together." She gazed up at the two dragons. "What do you say, Orm and Orma? The plan depends on the two of you."

"Well, brother," said Orma. "You may slink back to your ruins if you like, but I am going to help these children save this city. Come now, who wants to live forever?"

"I do," grumbled the Great Dragon. "Still, perhaps this plan could work." He turned his gaze on Thianna and Karn. "If I let her tackle the monster alone," he said, "I would never hear the end of it."

"Good," said Thianna. "Now I'm going to call the

wyverns. And we need to find King Herakles. And, Sirena, this is going to cost you."

"Cost me?"

"Their freedom. We're giving everyone their freedom. The city-states. The wyverns. Perioikoi. Helots. It will be a new Caldera on the other side of this day. But it's the only way there will be any Caldera at all."

"What can I do?" said Sirena, meaning "What choice do I have?" But Thianna didn't take it that way.

"Ride with me," she said. "We'll do this together, cousin and cousin." Then she called to the battered reptile, still hovering in the air above, "How's the wing?"

Much stronger, the wyvern replied. *It seems flying thousands of miles as your courier is better for the muscles than spending thirteen years locked away in the dark.*

"Imagine that," said Thianna. "Think you can carry two?"

Karn and Talos ran through the middle districts of the city. The automaton had tapped him on the shoulder, asking him to follow. Talos wouldn't say why, only that Karn's presence was required for his plan to work.

"You're sure you know where you are going?" the Norrønur asked.

"I will not dignify that with a response," the Talosian replied.

The automaton stopped before a row of statues. They stood on plinths in a square.

"It is time," he said. "I invoke our ancient obligation."

"Who are you talking to?" asked Karn.

His companion did not reply. But an answer was not long in coming.

One by one the statues stepped off their pedestals.

As they moved, cracks appeared in the marble-colored pigment that had been applied to their bodies. Bronze metal showed underneath the faux-stone paint.

"These aren't statues," Karn said in wonder. "They're all Talosians. You had spies in the city."

"This is why I could not leave with you. I am the only one that can wake them." The automaton gestured between the boy and his fellow Talosians. "Karn Korlundsson," Talos said, "may I introduce you to Talos One Hundred Twenty-three, Talos Four Hundred Seventy-six, Talos Eight Hundred Twenty-two, Talos Nine Hundred Thirty-four, and Talos Nine Hundred Ninety-nine." The automaton addressed the Talosians: "Wake the others in the city. We have much to accomplish."

"Others?" said Karn. "How many of you are there?"

"Caldera is full of statues," said the Talosian.

The Mega Hydra had reached the middle district of the city now. Desstra watched as it smashed through the inner walls, crushing stone towers under its massive torso. She turned to Daphne.

"It's a good thing fire doesn't work on this thing's hide," she said.

"Why?" asked the dryad.

"Because now I don't have to slap myself for melting all the cannons." She handed one of her improvised explosives to the tree girl.

"Ready?" she asked.

"No," said Daphne. "But then I never am." She managed a nervous smile.

The two girls lobbed explosives at the colossal monster. It was the signal for the distractions to begin.

Dactyls poured out of doorways and trapdoors. They struck at the creature's feet with hammers and mallets. Tree folk leapt from the higher city walls to glide as near to the Mega Hydra as they dared, dropping rocks onto the monster.

Desstra gazed higher, where a wyvern carried two passengers.

Sirena clung to her cousin's broad back. Having spent so long wanting to battle the larger girl, it was strange to be so close to her now. But the disaster they faced was Sirena's doing, and it was Thianna who would save them.

The giantess surprised her by passing her the horn.

"You want *me* to use this?" she asked.

"Yes," said the giantess. "You need to touch it to work it. I don't. So you take it. But I'll be using it with you."

"How?"

"Both of our minds. Like when you searched for me. Like when we battled. But don't fight me, Sirena. We do this together."

"Together?"

"Two cousins. Saving the city."

"Two cousins," Sirena repeated.

Here we go, said the wyvern.

"Here we go," the girls repeated.

Sirena closed her eyes. She felt Thianna's mind alongside hers. Instinctively she wanted to lash out, to fight. But that wouldn't work. They had to be united. To put enough shared will into the horn to stand up to the monster. Tentatively, she let her thoughts reach out to her cousin.

Sirena swayed in the grip of a vision. She saw Thianna, not as she was now but younger. She was playing a ball game against giants twice her size. They bullied her terribly, smashing her face into the ground, but Thianna fought her way to her feet, spitting blood and snow in anger. Refusing to give up. Then Sirena saw a glimpse of the sunset over the snows of Ymiria. It was every bit as beautiful as her cousin claimed. More scenes from Thianna's memories raced by. There was Karn, battling alongside his enormous friend in country after country.

Their bond lent a different kind of strength than any Sirena knew. She saw Thianna's nobility, her heroism, her bravery. These were qualities she herself was supposed to embody as a Calderan, all present in a barbarian girl. Sirena wanted to hate so badly, but she couldn't, not from the inside. Reluctantly, like tossing ashes into the sea, Sirena let hate go.

Their minds snapped together.

Now, thought Thianna. Let's give this Mega Hydra the worst headache of its life. Or would that be *headsache*?

Whatever works, thought Sirena. To the crows with it.

The wyvern wove and dodged between the monster's heads. Smaller than a dragon and nearly as fast, it could wheel and bank in the air in much tighter maneuvers. It carried Thianna and Sirena on a twisting path, while the cousins struck at its mind in blast after blast of the horn.

In their wake, Orm and Orma dove at the beast. But while most of the Mega Hydra's heads were focused on the horn, enough remained alert to block the dragons' attempts to fly in close.

"It's not working," said Desstra, from where she watched on the wall. "It's not enough."

"What do we do?" asked Daphne.

The elf looked at the creature. What could they do, here on the ground?

"So many heads," she said. But then she had a thought.

"So many heads. But only one body. If only I had an effective way to poison it."

"Look," called Daphne. "It's Asterius."

The minotaur rode atop a giant scorpion. Behind him they saw Talos the automaton. Several more minotaurs rode in their wake. They swarmed right up the walls to join the elf and dryad on the walkway.

"Either of you two need a ride?" the bull boy called.

"We both do," said Desstra. "Though you may not like where we're going."

"Where is that?" asked Asterius.

"I'll tell you in a moment," said the elf. "But first you tell me, just how much poison do your scorpions' stingers pack?"

Asterius grinned.

"Quite a lot," he said.

"Good," said Desstra. "Because a lot is just what we need."

The Mega Hydra's mind was old, ancient, and angry. Thianna could feel its irritation that so many small creatures dared challenge it. Even Orm and Orma were only minor aggregations in its view. The only thing it really hated was the horn. The horn and anyone using it.

Her stomach rolled as the wyvern dove suddenly. A noxious purple cloud rolled above them. So far they were dodging the creature's deadly breath. The winds off the

322

sea prevented the poison gas from hanging for long in the air, but one direct hit would finish them.

Then one head struck. The wyvern's tail was caught in the vise of its jaw. As it struggled, another head bit savagely into a wing. The two heads tugged, stretching the shrieking wyvern and threatening to tear it apart like a wishbone. Thianna tumbled from the wyvern's back, Sirena beside her.

The frost giant caught onto a wing with one hand. She grabbed her cousin with the other. They dangled in the air as a third head rose before them. The Mega Hydra drew breath, readying a blast of poison that would finish them all, girls and reptile.

Then suddenly it yelped. Both heads clasping the wyvern let go. The girls dropped, but the wyvern rolled to the side to carry Thianna and Sirena into position atop its back.

Secure? it asked.

"Yes," said Thianna.

Good.

"But now I'm really mad."

Even better.

Below them Thianna saw an incredible fight. Led by the minotaur boy and Desstra, giant scorpions had swarmed up the torso of the Mega Hydra. They were now stinging it mercilessly, their wicked tails rising and plunging into the monster's back. Though its scales were impenetrable, the scorpions were able to thrust their stingers between them, delivering injection after injection of venom. Half the Mega Hydra's heads turned their way.

"It's now or never!" shouted Thianna. "Let's make this one count."

Together she and Sirena poured all of their combined will into blasting the monster's mind.

It roared from every mouth at once.

Then it screamed.

Orm and Orma were tearing savagely at its necks, severing one after the other. As each dragon bit through the neck of a Hydra head, the other would let loose a blast of flame. The dragon fire, hotter than any other flame in the known world, cauterized the stumps before they could regrow.

Head after head began to fall. Sickened with venom, the creature swayed on its feet. And Thianna and Sirena whirled around and around it, harrying it with blast after blast of the horn.

Below, dactyls still smashed at its toes with their hammers. Dryads and drus tossed vines to snare its legs. And what looked like an army of marble statues, led by Karn and Talos, hurled projectiles at its many faces. Above, wyverns with their riders shot blasts of Thican fire, which, if they didn't wound, certainly added to the monster's confusion.

When it was down to less than half its heads, it suddenly turned and began to lurch down the hill toward the harbor.

"It's fleeing!" shouted Thianna in joy. "Pour it on!"

The Mega Hydra half ran, half stumbled down the slope. Reaching the docks, it crashed into the water. As Orm and Orma laughed the terrible laugh of Great Dragons, and Thianna laughed the laugh of frost giants, its few remaining heads dove beneath the waves.

A huge wake marked the monster's path as it swam in the direction of the ocean. Then the waters stilled. And whether it had submerged or died, none could say. But one way or another the Mega Hydra was gone. They had won.

CHAPTER TWENTY-THREE

From a Thorn, a Rose . . .

Thianna Frostborn stood before the Twin Palaces. The grounds immediately in front of her were full of reptiles. Hundreds of baby wyverns squawked and cavorted on the grass. They were ringed by their elders, adult wyverns watching the frost giant with cold anticipation to see what she would do.

Beyond them the various forces that had until recently struggled with each other waited to see as well. Minotaurs, tree folk, Talosians, Calderan soldiers, perioikoi, helots—all waited uncertainly. Only a little while ago they had been at each other's throats. Now they weren't certain what their new relationship would be. But the presence of two very large dragons to either side of the palace kept everyone on their best behavior as only dragons can.

Sirena handed the horn to Thianna.

"I don't know what this means for Caldera," she said. "Only that the horn is yours to do with as you see fit. You earned it in ways I never could."

Thianna nodded at her cousin. The former Keras Keeper surely thought this was the end of her city. But endings could be new beginnings.

Thianna raised the Horn of Osius to her lips and began a song. Only the reptiles present could hear it, but everyone stood silent.

As she played, she unwove the magic of the horn, like pulling apart a tapestry and seeing it unravel. She felt the terrible desire to force one's will on another being, and she rejected it.

Thianna played a song of freedom. And in her mind, she thought to the wyverns: You are released! You are let go! Never to be compelled, never to be ridden again!

Around her the wyverns began to hiss. It was soft at first, then gained in volume. The hissing rose and fell with her invisible music. They were singing. And unlike the music of the horn, everyone could hear. It was beautiful.

Thianna felt the knots of obedience in the reptiles' minds dissolve away.

"You're free," she said.

A shadow fell across Thianna.

"Is it fair to assume that you are done now?" rumbled a deep voice. The Great Dragon Orm loomed over her, twitched his wings in irritation.

"I'm done," said Thianna.

"Then give it here."

Thianna drew back her arm, preparing to toss the horn like she'd toss a knattleikr ball. Orm leaned forward in anticipation. Then she spun and tossed the horn the other way, to where Orm's sister waited.

Orma opened her mouth and blew a concentrated blast of flame. When it stopped, the horn was gone.

"What have you done?" roared Orm.

"You've already eaten one," said Thianna.

"Its power fades as I digest it," he replied.

"You wanted it destroyed, it's destroyed," said the frost giant. "You don't need power over the wyverns any more than the Sky Queen did. Now nobody gets it, and you don't have to worry about anyone using it on you ever again. On either of you."

Orm turned to Orma.

"You aided her in this. You and the girl dared trick the Doom of Sardeth?"

"Doom of Sardeth?" snorted Orma. "That was a long time ago. Now that I'm back, we can straighten you out. You're not just the Doom of Sardeth anymore. You're the Defender of Caldera."

"Nonsense," said the Great Dragon.

"You saved a city, brother," his sister replied. "Everyone here owes you their life. Maybe this could be the turning over of a new leaf for you."

"Hmm . . . ," rumbled the dragon. "It has been a few centuries since I've added new titles to my name."

"Hard to do when you stay shut up in a ruin."

"Orm, the Great Dragon, Largest of Linnorms, Doom of Sardeth . . . Defender of Caldera." He smiled, showing off all his wicked teeth. "I like the taste of that on the tongue. But do you suppose we could add Bane of Mega Hydras?"

"I don't see why not," said Thianna.

"Very well," said Orm. "Then I suppose I won't roast you alive today. I promised you answers if you undertook my quest. Are you satisfied that you have been paid?"

"In full," said Thianna. She knew that was the only answer the dragon would accept, the only answer it was safe to give.

"That is good," said Orm. "Thianna Frostborn, Karn Korlundsson, I release you from my service." Beside him, his sister made a coughing noise in her long throat. Orm scowled at her, but he added, "And I, the Defender of Caldera, offer you my gratitude."

"Nicely done, brother," Orma said.

Beside her, Karn bowed. And Thianna wisely did too.

Orm rose into the air.

"Now I will return to Sardeth. You may call it a ruins, but it's my ruins. And I have much to think about. Perhaps it is time to take a more active interest in the world. Perhaps I have done enough this century. But I intend to sleep on it for now."

With that Orm beat his wings and began his long journey westward.

Orma took to the air after him.

"I better get back to Gordasha, and Acmon," she said. "I've got a city to rule, after all. Karn, what are your plans? You would be an honored guest in my realm for as long as you like."

"Thank you," he said. He looked at his friend. "I need to get home soon, but I don't think we're quite done here."

Orma nodded her large head.

"When you are ready, make your way to Gordasha. You've certainly earned a ride home if you want it."

"Thank you," said Karn, who recognized the honor being done him.

Then the Dragon Queen of Gordasha joined her brother in the skies.

"What do we do now?" asked Sirena. "The city is a mess. The queens are gone. There's a path of ruin carved right through Caldera like a slice cut out of a pie."

"You'll rebuild," said Thianna.

"I don't know how to build," said her cousin.

"So you'll learn. The dactyls can help."

"So can the helots," added Karn. "Though if I were you I would grant them both citizenship immediately."

"And a seat at the table," said King Herakles, joining them.

"I'm not in a position to grant anyone anything," said Sirena.

"No?" said Thianna. "I seem to recall you were being groomed to be queen once upon a time. Caldera doesn't need a Keras Keeper anymore, and there is a job opening. It will be a different city from the one you expected to rule over, and it will only be a city, not an empire. You told me that night in the tower that I had to do the right thing for all of you. Now it's your turn to do the right thing for your people." Thianna waved her hand to take in the lower districts. "All your people."

"But how will we protect ourselves? How will Thica survive? The city-states will go back to warring among themselves and then we'll fall prey to other nations all over again."

"I might have an answer for that," said Karn. When Thianna gave him a surprised look, he continued. "I visited the Sanctuary of Empyria recently. There's a certain sphinx there, not to mention an army of kobalos, who would love to see the Empyric Games reinstated."

"The games?" repeated Sirena, considering the idea.

"You already use game play in your politics," said Karn. "This would be a lot more fun, and less deadly, than live Queen's Champion. And it was used to forestall warfare in the past. No reason it can't be again."

"I like the idea," said King Herakles. "What do you say,

Your Majesty? We could make it our second joint decree, after freeing the helots and granting everyone citizenship who wants it."

"I'm not sure," said Sirena. "Could it work?"

"Of course it could," said the king. "We can talk it over across some spanakopita. And I can show you Caldera Under Caldera."

"What under what?"

"He'll fill you in," said Thianna.

Sirena stared at her cousin.

"We are not friends, Thianna," she said. "You were the cause of all my troubles. But also their solutions. We are no longer enemies, but I am not sure what we are."

"That's okay," said Thianna. "I know what we are. We're family."

Thianna sat in the warm bathing pool and resisted the urge to use her frost magic to chill the water. She didn't think her friends, new and old, would care for a change in temperature. They had turned the huge square-shaped pool into an impromptu swimming pond. Karn was on one side of her and Desstra on the other. Beside the Norrønur, Asterius the minotaur was enjoying blowing bubbles through the water with his snout. Beside the elf, Daphne's foliage was looking particularly green as she soaked in the tub. They had arranged for a stool to be placed in the pool as well so that Jasius the dwarf didn't need to bounce on tiptoes to stay above water.

"Your mom's apartments," said Karn, smiling. "Now yours?"

"If I want them," said Thianna.

"You aren't sticking around, then?" asked her friend, a hopeful note in his voice.

"I need to, for a while," she said. "I want to learn more about my mother's people." She glanced around the room. "About my mother. But don't worry, I don't think palace living is really my style. Bathing is nice, though." She splashed Karn, who splashed her back.

When the resulting splash fight had died down, she spoke again. "What about you, Norrønboy? Ready to get back to farm life?"

"Almost," Karn said. "When I'm sure you're really all right here. I can take a hippalektryon to the Fortress of Atros and catch a boat to Gordasha from there."

"What about you, then, Long Ears?" Thianna asked Desstra.

"I can't go back to Norrøngard," replied the elf. "Maybe I'll stick around."

"Still think I need a bodyguard?" asked the giantess.

"Maybe not," said Desstra. "But maybe you still need a friend."

Thianna smiled. "I can always use another of those," she said.

Karn was glad to see his two friends getting along. It had taken long enough.

The frost giant looked around at the group. "I'd say everything turned out for the best."

"From a rose, a thorn, and from a thorn, a rose," said Daphne. "That's what we say in Dendronos."

Karn smiled. Then he rose from the pool and walked to where Talos was seated at a table, studying a Queen's Champion board.

"Care for a game, Karn Korlundsson?" the automaton asked.

"I wouldn't mind," said Karn. He took a seat opposite the metal person and began to arrange the pieces for his side. "But answer one thing first. I never understood why you joined us on the board. And that's not all. When I played the hostage princes and princesses, I won too many times for a game with so much chance."

Talos studied Karn for a moment.

"Do you still have the die I gave you?"

For answer, Karn reached into his clothing and placed the die upon the table.

Talos picked it up, indicating one of the pips carved in its surface. As Karn watched, a slender needle slid from one of the automaton's fingers. Talos pressed on the pip with the needle, which punctured easily.

"Wax?" said Karn.

Talos nodded. Tilting the die, he shook a small lead weight out of it.

"It was rigged?" said Karn. "You cheated on my be-half?"

"I judged that your victory was important."

"Why?"

Then the automaton reached a bronze finger to tap Karn's ring. Karn looked first at the silver emblem of the Order of the Oak, then at the Talosian.

"You're—" he began.

Talos held a warning finger to metal lips.

"We all are. Their allies of old," the automaton said. "An ancient obligation. Now fulfilled."

Karn was amazed. In fact, he was so surprised that he almost lost the game.

That evening, Thianna took the time to freeze the enor-mous bathing pool properly, then covered it with a tap-estry she had borrowed from the wall. She stretched out on the huge block of ice, enjoying a bed large enough to accommodate her for the first time in months. Staring up at the tiled mosaics on the ceiling, she felt closer to her mother than she had in years. And she felt good.

Then she felt something else. A familiar tug at her mind. She rolled over and crawled off the ice. There was a balcony in an adjoining room with a view over the cliffs.

Stepping into the cool night, she was not surprised to see the wyvern hovering outside her quarters. Talaria's wyvern. Thianna stared at the reptile that had carried her mother all those years ago. She only existed because of its courage.

Talaria was the first to sympathize with our kind, it said, obviously reading her thoughts. *She was brave. Noble. Quite an exceptional girl. As humans go, of course.*

"As humans go."

Her daughter shares those characteristics.

"Thank you," she said aloud.

No thanks is needed, it said in her mind. *Not from you anyway.*

"I only finished what she started," said Thianna. "She wanted the wyverns to be free."

Wyverns, said the reptile. *Wyverns is what the humans called us. It is not our name. It is not what we call ourselves.*

"What do you call yourselves?"

Suddenly the air was full of reptiles as hundreds of the newly freed creatures rose up from the cliffs below to hover in the air. All the adults and all their newborn children. The beat of their collective wings blew like a small wind in her face.

We are in your debt, Talaria's reptile said. *For now, and for all time. You have given us back the skies. And the Skyborn thank you.*

"The Skyborn," repeated Thianna. It was a beautiful name.

Then the Skyborn turned as one and flew away from Caldera, never to return.

As Thianna watched them go, she wondered if her ability to communicate mind to mind with reptiles would fade now that the horn was destroyed. Or would it always be a part of her? It didn't matter either way. She was Thianna Frostborn, daughter of the giant Magnilmir and the human Talaria, child of Ymiria and Thica. She was whole now, and she had the whole of the world to explore.

GLOSSARY

Arachne (uh-RAK-nee): Once upon a time, a woman dared compare her beauty to that of the goddess Casteria. For her vanity, the goddess turned her into a monster, the first of her kind. These days, the arachne are a race of half-human, half-spider people. In females, a human torso rises up from a giant spider's body, with eight beady spider eyes in place of two human ones, a thirst for warm blood, and a bad reputation where it comes to visitors. The males, large spiders without any human characteristics, are just as vicious as the females but less interested in making conversation with their food.

Asterion (ass-TEER-ee-on): The king of the minotaurs (see minotaur) rules from the city of Labyrinthia. He chafes under the yoke of the Calderans but knows that the time is not yet right for rebellion.

Asterius (ass-TEER-ee-us): The young son of the king of Labyrinthia, Asterius would rather see his father fight and lose than bow the hoof to the queens of Caldera. He's champing at the bit for a chance to prove himself and can be stubborn as a bull, but watch saying cattle metaphors around him if you don't want to catch the wrong side of a horn.

Caldera (kahl-DAIR-uh): The capital city of Thica ever since 920 AG, when the Thican Empire was reformed by Timandra II. Caldera is an island, the cinder cone of a dormant volcano in the center of an actual caldera. The city is composed of citizens, all of whom are soldiers and female, freedmen called perioikoi, and state-owned serfs known as helots. The perioikoi and the helots far outnumber the citizens, but somehow the leaders of Caldera aren't the least bit nervous about this.

chimera (kye-MEER-uh): A creature with a lion body and three heads: one lion, one goat, and one serpent. The goat's head breathes fire. The other two only have a nasty bite. Still, as far as the chimera's prey is concerned, three heads aren't better than one.

Cratus (KRAH-toos): God of the forge and metals, Cratus the Smith is revered by the dactyl dwarves and all Thican blacksmiths. His brothers and sisters tried to kill him when he was born because of his deformities, but the dactyl dwarves hid him underground until he was strong enough to protect himself. These days he has better relations with his siblings.

Damnameneus (dahm-nahmeh-NAY-oos): A famous mathematician, engineer, and inventor who lived more than 1,500 years ago, Damnameneus was a dactyl dwarf who is credited with dozens of inventions. During his lifetime, he built the famous Claw of Damnameneus—an enormous crane with a hook that could lift ships out of the water and capsize them—for the city of Zapyrna. He also oversaw the construction of the first of the giant parabolic mirrors that protect the Thican coastline. A restless overachiever, he designed far more than he could build. Among his unfinished designs were plans for a submersible vehicle and several more war machines.

Daphne (DAFF-nee): Seedling of the Council of Elders, princess of the forest kingdom of Dendronos, Daphne is a young dryad. Though not the bravest tree in the woods, she has hidden talents waiting for the chance to flower.

Dendronos (den-DROH-nohs): A city in northern Thica, Dendronos is grown from out of the forest by citizens who sing the trees into their desired shapes. The people of Dendronos are called Dendronosi. But they don't object to being called tree folk. Visitors to their city, however, are advised to leave their axes at home.

Drakon (DRAK-on): The Thican word for dragon. But what's in a name? A dragon by any other name is just as fierce.

dryad (DRY-ad): A female tree person.

drus (droos): A male tree person.

empusa (em-PYOO-suh): A female vampirelike creature with living flames atop her head in place of hair. Their flames burn higher and hotter as they become angry, but you don't want to stick around for that.

Empyric Games (em-PEER-ik): Athletic festivals traditionally held at the Sanctuary of Empyria that served as both a way to honor the Twelve Empyreans and a means to channel the aggression of rival city-states away from war and into athletic competitions. The last Empyric Games were staged in 799 EE as Timandra the Magnificent's conquest of Thica rendered them unnecessary.

hamadryad (ham-uh-DRY-ad): Unlike other tree folk, hamadryads are stationary. They appear as actual trees with faces on their trunks. The oldest and wisest hamadryads of Dendronos serve as the town elders, making political decisions for their more mobile kin. They are very happy in this role and think walking is overrated.

helot (HELL-uht): Slaves more comparable to serfs who have the right to marry, practice religious rites, own personal property, and retain fifty percent of their labor. However, helots are required to receive a set number of beatings per year regardless of wrongdoing to remind them of their slave status. Being too physically fit is punishable by death, but being out of shape is also punishable (though less severely). Once a year the Calderans declare ritual war on the helots, allowing any citizen to kill them with impunity.

Herakles Hammerfist (HAIR-uh-kleez): The secret king of the dactyl dwarves of Caldera Under Caldera, Herakles is fond of his subjects, his kingdom, his dinner, and his namesake fists that are so very good at thumping people.

hippalektryon (hip-uh-LEK-tree-on): A hybrid animal that is half horse and half rooster. Hippalektryons have the forelegs and head of a horse but the wings and hindquarters of a rooster. Their plumage is always yellow but their coats vary in color. Hippalektryons are among the fastest mounts in the world, but be sure to keep plenty of hay and chicken feed around or you'll be going nowhere fast.

Ithonea (ee-thoh-NAY-uh): A port city on the western coast of Thica, Ithonea is a city of twisting narrow streets winding up a hillside. It is broken into districts by ancient Gordion fortifications and has a population that is predominantly human and satyr. Ithoneans can be traditionalists, though, so visitors are advised to dress like the locals and avoid overly barbarian fashions.

Jasius (JAY-see-oos): A young dactyl dwarf in the city of Caldera, Jasius is embarrassed that his beard still hasn't come in. Despite this he's ready to make his mark on the world.

Keras Keeper (KAIR-iss): A hereditary position, the title refers to the Calderan female whose heritage enables her to master the magic of the Horn of Osius. *Keras* is the Thican word for horn. While it's a great honor to be Keras Keeper, it's not an honor one can safely refuse.

kobalo (koh-BALL-oh): A little creature native to Thica but similar to the goblins found in parts of Katernia. The kobalos are impudent, mischievous, and thieving, but they enjoy games and are excellent cooks.

Labyrinthia (lah-BRIN-thee-uh): A city of minotaurs. The streets of Labyrinthia are laid out like a maze marked by tall inner walls. Houses are built into these walls, hanging aboveground so the bull men and kine women can run through the streets on festival days. The city is surrounded by a large circular wall with four gates at each of the cardinal points. Visitors are encouraged to tour the impressive Palace of the Double Ax, but try to avoid the head-butting contests.

Leta (LAY-tuh): Formerly a soldier under the command of Sydia, Leta was the sole surviving Calderan from the Battle of Dragon's Dance. Shamed at her failure to retrieve the Horn of Osius, she aided Karn and

Thianna in their quest to find a second horn, only to snatch it away from them at the end of their quest. For her triumph, she's since been promoted to head of the Keras Guard, but she'd love a chance to eliminate a certain half giant, Norrønur, and dark elf if given the opportunity.

Mega Hydra (MEG-uh HIGH-druh): A hydra is a multiheaded sea serpent found in the waters surrounding Thica. A Mega Hydra is like a normal hydra, only mega.

Melantha (muh-LAN-thuh): One of the two co-monarchs who rule the Thican Empire, Melantha is Land Queen. Her forces ride the hippalektryons whose incredible speed give the city of Caldera supreme mastery of the land. Somewhat milder-tempered than her fellow monarch, Melantha rarely contradicts the Sky Queen directly, though she has been known to soften Xalthea's edicts here and there.

minotaur (MIN-uh-tohr): A half-human, half-animal creature, minotaurs have the body of a human and the head and tail of a bull. They are proud, stubborn, fond of mazes, but somewhat skeptical about pancakes, which they see as a waste of good wheat.

Noe (NOH-ay): The Thican goddess of the hunt, childbirth, archery, the moons, and animals. In some stories, she is the mother of the empusas. There is a temple to Noe at the summit of Caldera.

pelta (PELL-tuh): A distinctive crescent-shaped half shield that marks Calderan soldiers. The Calderans have a saying, "either with your shield or on it," which means they are expected to carry the pelta home from battle in triumph or be carried home upon the pelta in death. A barrel of laughs, those Calderans.

perioikoi (PEER-ee-uh-koy): Free noncitizens who serve as a military reserve, skilled craftsmen, and agents of foreign trade. The majority of perioikoi are dactyl dwarves and are employed to craft and repair weapons and armor. The Calderans take them for granted and may not realize just how many perioikoi there are underfoot.

phoreion (FOR-ee-own): A sort of curtained litter or palanquin that is carried, usually on poles by people but occasionally on ropes by wyvern.

Pogos (POH-gohs): A little boy in Ithonea who just might grow up to wear pants. What a rebel!

Sanctuary of Empyria (em-PEER-ee-uh): Once home to the Empyric Games, the sanctuary is now a ruin of its former self. Few travelers visit the sanctuary these days, and it's truly a riddle why so few that do return.

satyr (SAY-tur): A race of beings native to Thica with the body of humans but the ears, tail, horns, and legs of a goat. Satyrs are fun at parties, but be careful that they don't eat the serving utensils along with the food.

Sestia (SESS-tee ah): The goddess of war, martial strategy, and combat. There is a temple to Sestia at the summit of Caldera.

Sirena (sigh-REE-nuh): The cousin of both the Land Queen and the former Keras Keeper, Sirena was on the fast track to be Queen Melantha's heir when she was drafted to be Keras Keeper instead. She's fiercely proud of her city and her heritage but harbors a deep resentment for a certain half frost giant for messing up her career path.

spanakopita (spah-nah-KAH-pee-tah): A traditional Thican dish, spanakopita is a rich savory pie filled with spinach, feta cheese, onions, and other ingredients. Authorities differ on whether the dwarves of Caldera or the kobalos of the Sanctuary of Empyria make the better spanakopita, but one could get quite plump and happy during a taste test.

sphinx (sfingks): A creature with the body of a lion and the head of a human, sphinxes have a fondness for games and riddles. Unlike their cousins across the Sparkle Sea in Neteru, Thican sphinxes are wingless. They might not fly, but they have plenty of other ways to amuse themselves.

Talos (TAY-loss): Talos-10,051 is an automaton, an artificial person crafted of bronze. It is one of a race of such who dwell in the city of Mereon. The first of the Talosians was constructed by the god Cratus the Smith to be his companion. There are never more than three hundred Talosians in the world at any one time. As they are all called Talos, that's probably enough.

Teshub (TESH-oob): God of sky and storm but not one of the Twelve Empyreans, Teshub is worshiped by the minotaurs and no one else in Thica. Thunder is said to be the sound of his hoofs as he races across the sky. Whether this is so or not, debating the point with a minotaur would be a most foolish thing to do.

Thica (THEE-kuh): Thica is an enormous island-continent off the eastern coast of the larger continent of Katernia. Originally a vast land of independent city-states, it was united by Timandra the Magnificent during the Era of Empires then conquered by the Gordion Empire. After the fall of the Gordion Empire, Thica was exploited by raiding neighbors for a time, until Timandra II formed the Second Thican Empire in 920 AG.

Twelve Empyreans (em-PEER-ee-unz): The chief Thican gods and goddesses. They aren't the only gods of Thica, but they are the most important ones. Just ask them.

Xalthea (ZAL-thee-uh): One of the two co-monarchs who rule the Thican Empire, Xalthea is Sky Queen. Her forces ride the wyverns that give the city of Caldera supreme mastery of the air. She assumed the throne when she defeated her own mother at a live game of Queen's Champion, and there's nothing she won't do to make sure she never loses it.

THE RULES OF QUEEN'S CHAMPION™

A GAME OF CLASSICAL THICA

The game of Queen's Champion dates all the way back to the Era of Empires, at a time when Thica was a series of independent city-states that occasionally warred with each other. At that time, it was called King's Champion. The name was changed after the rise of Timandra the Magnificent and the establishment of the first Thican Empire.

Queen's Champion is played by two players on a board of eight-by-eight squares and represents a conflict between two armies.

A popular game in many cities across the island-continent, in the city of Caldera it is played on a life-sized board with living contestants, a rather deadly expression of the traditional pastime.

OBJECT OF THE GAME

The object of the game is to defeat the opponent's Queen, or, failing that, to eliminate all of the Queen's forces from play.

Starting the Game

Each player begins the game with their forces arranged in a row along opposing sides of the board. The playing pieces include one Queen, one Champion, and six Soldiers. These begin play placed from left to right: Soldier, Soldier, Soldier, Queen, Champion, Soldier, Soldier, Soldier.

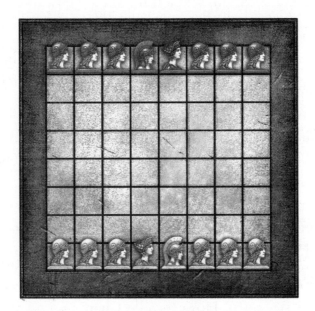

Turn order is determined randomly or by roll of a die. Pieces may move two spaces forward as they leave the line. Afterward all pieces move one space at a time in any direction, although a player may not return to a space they have just vacated. This prevents the same move from being repeated over and over.

Challenges

When a piece lands in a square orthogonally adjacent to an opposing piece (not diagonally), it may challenge. Note that challenge is not mandatory. When a challenge is declared, the two pieces engage in combat.

One six-sided die is rolled by each piece (see the Champion exception).

The challenging player gets to add +1 to their roll.

The highest number wins.

The defeated player is removed from play. The winning player then occupies the square of the defeated player.

In the event of a tie, both pieces remain in play. Either player may choose to challenge again on their next turn or ignore their opponent and make another move.

The Champion

The Champion is a special piece that may roll two six-sided dice and choose the higher result (to reflect their greater strength). However, the Champion gains no +1 bonus for attacking.

Queen's Prerogative

If the Queen comes under attack, before the dice are rolled the player may exercise the Queen's Prerogative.

The Champion may substitute for the Queen and the two pieces exchange their positions. If the Champion has been removed from play, the Queen plays like any other piece.

Winning the Game

The game ends when the Queen is defeated or when all other playing pieces other than the Queen are defeated and she stands alone.

Optional Setup

In some places in Thica, particularly the cities of Naparta and Dodotara, this alternative setup is used for play:

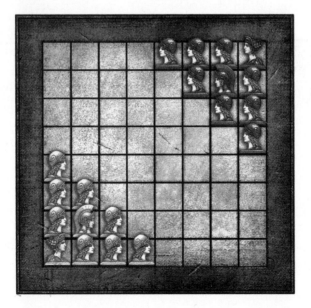

THICAN TIMELINE

DA: The Dawn Age
EE: Era of Empires
AG: After Gordion

- ? to 4000 DA: Gods and monsters roam the world.

- 3367 EE: The Bronze Age, when Early Thican cultures start to emerge. On the mainland of Katernia, a Light Elf empire rules much of the known world.

- 1967 EE: The great Dragon King civilization is founded when Osius of Talsathia forges the three horns (and many other legendary artifacts).

- 1912 EE to 1565 EE: The War of the Dragon King vs. the Light Elves.

- 1565 EE: The destruction of Talsathia (later immortalized by the great poetess Hemesa). Many Talsathian refugees—particularly dactyl dwarves—immigrate to Thica.

- 1517 EE to 1217 EE: Development of the first Thican alphabet, taught to humans by dactyl dwarves. (The Talsathians used a system of runes and numbers, unlike the Thican alphabet.)

❖ 1243 EE: The First Empyric Games are staged.

❖ 1220 EE: On the continent of Katernia, the city of Gordion is founded by Gordius and Gordilla.

❖ 1217 EE: Thicans establish a colony on the island of Jalta and at Setrai (present-day Syrium).

❖ 1217 EE to 1167 EE: Hemesa writes *The Talsathiad* at the behest of the goddess Helenyx. The cycle of epic poems is written in hexameter and consists of twelve books to honor the Twelve Empyreans.

❖ 1197 to 1177 EE: The First Lassathonian War; the Calderans conquer southern Thica.

❖ 1138 EE: Ambracia is founded by dactyl dwarves in a period of Thican colonial expansion.

❖ 1088 EE: Megreon's code of law is introduced.

❖ 1067 EE: Thican coin currency is introduced.

❖ 967 EE to 90 EE: The Thican Classical Period. The game of King's Champion is thought to date from this time.

❖ 972 EE: Chrolos introduces democracy in Pymonia.

❖ 957 EE: Start of the Thican/Ljósálfarans Wars. Jalta falls under Ljósálfarans rule.

❖ 942 EE: The Thicans defeat the Ljósálfarans at Setrai

(Syrium). Jalta is abandoned but remains independent.

- 935 EE: Adaeus writes his first tragedy.

- 928 EE to 913 EE: The Pymonian Wars begins between Caldera and Pymonia.

- 916 EE to 899 EE: Construction of the Akronaos in Pymonia (*akros* means summit; *naos* means temple).

- 908 EE: Lanera writes her first tragedy.

- 897 EE: Outbreak of plague in Pymonia.

- 898 EE: Second of the Pymonian Wars between Caldera and Pymonia.

- 866 EE: The philosopher Leonasus is executed.

- 853 EE: Leonasus's protégé Metarchus founds the Association.

- 823 EE: Timandra the Magnificent is born. (It is at this time that the god Krobus is said to have been supplanted by his queen, Casteria.)

- 800 EE: Timandra the Magnificent defeats the Gordions and is ceded the right to march on Neteru. The Horn of Osius factors in tales of her exploits.

- 799 EE: The Last Empyric Games are staged. Timandra the Magnificent conquers Neteru.

- 798 EE: Timandra the Magnificent founds the city of Timandria in Neteru.

- 795 EE: Timandra the Magnificent invades Naga Rajya but is convinced to return to Thica after her army mutinies and refuses to march farther east. However, the Naga rulers are frightened of the Horn of Osius and so, despite their defeat of Thican forces, decide not to expand their influence to the west.

- 790 EE: Timandra the Magnificent dies. Around this time the game of King's Champion comes to be called Queen's Champion. However, the Horn of Osius is lost, signifying an end of Thican dominance.

- 779 EE: Timandra's former general Althara seizes control of Neteru, declaring it an independent power.

- 739 EE: The Thican colony of Ambracia surrenders to the Gordion Empire and soon all the remaining Thican colonies of southern Nomerosa follow suit. (Setrai is renamed Syrium.)

- 691 EE: An earthquake destroys the Kolossos of Empyria. This same year Creos is menaced by a hydra.

- 681 EE: War machines designed by Thican mathematician and dactyl dwarf Damnameneus save the city of Zapyrna from a Gordion naval attack. The Claw of Damnameneus is instrumental in this victory. But this is the first time the Gordion Empire has threatened continental Thica.

- 679 EE: The first of the giant parabolic mirrors, designed by Damnameneus, are created along the eastern coastline to protect against Naga Rajya invasion. Unfortunately, the Naga have no designs on Thica. The coming Gordion war might have gone differently had they built the mirrors upon the west coast.

- 667 to 663 EE: The first Gordion victory over Thica. Queen Arosa V loses to the Gordion Empire.

- 638 EE: The Third Gordion/Thican War begins.

- 634 EE: At the end of the Third Gordion/Thican War the Gordions divide western Thica into four republics.

- 620 EE: Hostilities resume between Gordion and Thica.

- 616 EE: Gordion troops destroy the city of Pythira. Subsequently the Gordion general Otrarius captures the city of Pymonia. Thica becomes a province of Gordion.

- 613 EE: The Great Chain stretching from Gordasha to the Fortress of Atros across the Thican Straits is forged by dactyl dwarves out of orichalcum.

- 606 EE: Slaves revolt in Ithonea, resulting in the crucifixion of 4,500 slaves.

- 604 EE: Second slave revolt in Ithonea.

- 571 EE: Third slave revolt in Ithonea.

- 568 EE: Gordion troops massacre Ithonean rebels.

- 389 EE: Acmon the Anvil, a Gordion conscript from Thica, discovers one of the three Horns of Osius. He and the dragon Orma lead a rebellion against the Gordion Empire in Ambracia.

- 386 EE: Acmon and Orma are turned to stone by the Gordion Empire. The great dragon Orm flees to Sardeth on the border of Norrøngard.

- 200 EE: Turmanic tribes from Herzeria raid the Thican cities.

- 198 EE: Turmanic tribes raid the Thican cities for a second time but are defeated by Gordion emperor Ogdius II.

- 174 EE: The Rosnians overrun Thica.

- 3 AG: Official end of the Gordion Empire. The collapse of trade routes will have a negative impact, and the withdrawal of Gordion forces will leave Thica vulnerable to other powers.

- 69 AG: A seemingly global climate event causes crop failures and famine in Thica.

- 143 AG to 400 AG: Thica is attacked both by old enemies (Turmanic tribes, Rosnians) as well as by new ones, appearing for the first time in Thican history (chief among them, the Cormeerians).

- 380 AG: Thica becomes Thican again after long period of foreign invasion.

- 630 AG: Significant growth and prosperity.

- 632 AG: The start of antagonisms between Thicans and the Sacred Gordion Supremacy Crusaders. During this period, large-scale construction begins on the ancient Damnameneus parabolic mirrors around the entire Thican coast.

- 881 AG: The Obsidian Fever ravages western Katernia. An estimated one-third of the population is thought to have perished within the first year. Thica's western and northern coasts are hit the hardest, while its southern and eastern coasts are least affected. This has the unfortunate outcome of strengthening Caldera's relative power among the city-states.

- 920 AG: The Thican Straits fall fully under the rule of the Sacred Gordion Supremacy, but non-Thicans are expelled from Thica. The Great Chain between

Gordasha and the Fortress of Atros is covered by treaty. However, as the chain is raised and lowered on the Gordashan side, there is little for the fortress to do but leave it alone. Timandra II rises to power in Caldera. A period of Thican isolationism begins. Thican ambassadors are recalled from continental Katernia. Another Horn of Osius is rediscovered and is instrumental in the establishment of a single unified Thican Empire. The Calderans set out to conquer Creos, Dodotara, Eronos, Harmos, Ithonea, Labyrinthia, Lassathonia, Naparta, Pymonia, Starissa, and Zapyrna. The last of the parabolic mirrors of Damnameneus is completed.

❖ 952 AG: A rebellion at Labyrinthia is severely put down.

❖ 968 AG: Xalthea becomes Sky Queen after defeating the previous queen, her own mother, in a deadly game of Queen's Champion.

❖ 972 AG: Talaria steals the Horn of Osius and flees Thica.

❖ 985 AG: The events of the novel *Frostborn*.

❖ 986 AG: The events of the novels *Nightborn* and *Skyborn*.

KING HERAKLES HAMMERFIST'S
BEST SPANAKOPITA EVER RECIPE
As prepared in Caldera Under Caldera

2 pounds of fresh spinach, chopped small
1 teaspoon of salt (or maybe 2)
1 pound of crumbly goat cheese, crumble crumble
1 small onion, chopped in little bits
4 eggs, beaten but not bruised
Salt and pepper, or pepper and salt
2 teaspoons of olive oil (or more)
15 sheets of phyllo dough
1/2 pound of butter, melted over hot magma
    (simple fire works too)
1 pound of uncut diamonds (optional)

Begin by washing your spinach thoroughly in an underground spring or washing basin. Then invoke your ancestors' blessings with a loud war cry and chop that vegetable very fine with your sharpest ax. Next, sprinkle it with a spoon of salt. Now walk away and allow it to stand for a quarter of an hour while you do kingly things elsewhere. Next, return to your spinach and squeeze it in your mighty fists until it has well and truly surrendered and given up all of its moisture. Place this defeated spinach in a bowl. Again invoke your ancestors' blessings as you add chopped onions, goat cheese, olive oil, salt and pepper. Mix this while showing off the muscles of your arms. Careful not to catch your beard as you stir! (That's messy.)

Now grease a ten-inch by fifteen-inch pan. Lay nine of the phyllo dough sheets across the pan, and then pour the spinach filling atop it. Next, call one of your many servants to do the boring bit. Have them lay out six phyllo dough sheets, one at a time, brushing each with copious helpings of melted butter as they do. Threaten them with your mighty fists if they tear a sheet! Now push them aside—this is *your* pie—and pinch down the edges to seal in the filling!

Place the pan in a cool cavern or other area where it can chill until firm. Now take your sharpest ax and cut through the top layers to mark out triangular pieces. Take your uncut diamonds and push one gemstone into the middle of each triangle.* Now place the pan on a lava-heated stone (or in an oven) and cook at 350 degrees Fahrenheit until golden brown (usually three-quarters of an hour or more). Let cool to room temperature for five to ten minutes.

This is the king's way to enjoy spanakopita!

*Optional for humans and others with soft teeth

ACKNOWLEDGMENTS

Thanks as ever to my tremendous beta readers: Justin Anders, Judith Anderson, Logan Ertel, J. F. Lewis, Janet Lewis, James M. L. Parker, and Cindi Stehr, as well as my wife and son.

For help with my geology, specifically working out the feasibility of freshwater springs occurring on a cinder cone rising out of a saltwater lake in a caldera, I am indebted to Janet Freeman-Daily, Rich Howard, Sean Patrick Kelley, Geoffrey A. Landis, Chip Nyman, Kimberly Unger, and most especially James Howard.

Thanks again to Trond-Atle Farestveit for continued help with my Norrønian pronunciation. And to RPG Gamer Dad and his family for lifting my spirits with their boundless enthusiasm and Karn cosplay during the cold winter throughout which I wrote the first draft of this manuscript. Thanks to John Picacio for talking me off the ledge by pointing out the mountain yet to be climbed.

Thanks to my agent, Barry Goldblatt of Barry Goldblatt Literary. Thanks to my editor at Crown Books for Young Readers, Phoebe Yeh, and to Random House Children's Books publisher Barbara Marcus. Thanks to Cassie McGinty, associate publicist; Alison Kolani, director of copyediting; Isabel Warren-Lynch, executive art director; and Ken Crossland, senior designer. Thanks to

Julianna N. Wilson, my audiobook producer at Penguin Random House Audio's Listening Library, my audiobook director Christina Rooney, and my fabulous narrator, Fabio Tassone. Thanks to Dominique Cimina, director of publicity and corporate communication, and to Kim Lauber, director of marketing, Sonia Nash Gupta, Nicholas Elliot, and everyone who worked on the promotional trading cards and the incredible ThronesandBones.com site.

For many nights play-testing multiple versions of the rules of Queen's Champion, I am enormously indebted to my patient and wonderful wife.

ABOUT THE AUTHOR

Lou Anders drew on his adventures traveling to Greece in his twenties to write *Skyborn,* combining these experiences with his love of adventure fiction and games (both tabletop and role playing). While he has yet to ride a hippalektryon, creating his own board games for *Frostborn, Nightborn,* and now *Skyborn* is one of his favorite indulgences. Anders has won a Hugo Award for editing and a Chesley Award for art direction, and was named a Thurber House Writer-in-Residence. He has published over 500 articles and stories on science fiction and fantasy television and literature, and regularly attends writing conventions around the country. He resides with his family in Birmingham, Alabama. You can visit Anders online at louanders.com and ThronesandBones.com, on Facebook, on Tumblr, and on Twitter at @Louanders.